Sky of Death . . .

As the plane zipped in front of Blake, his hand went instinctively to the trigger of his carbine before he realized it was Franklin DeWitt—a Fokker locked on his tail. As Blake pursued his friend's attacker, another German plane came at him with guns blazing.

Should I dive to shake my own attacker, Blake thought to himself, or try to save Franklin?

Then the citation flashed across his mind:

> *"Ignoring an enemy aircraft on his own tail, Aviation Sergeant Blake Langley Hunter heroically went to the rescue of his fellow pilot, the late Sergeant Franklin DeWitt."*

With but a split-second to spare, he banked his plane, leveled it and slipped into position behind the Fokker in pursuit of DeWitt. Blake fired, thinking as he did so that he could easily hit Franklin.

Then he heard the sound of bullets slashing into his Nieuport—the other German had come around and had him right in his sights. Again the thought of the decoration raced through his mind—but there was a difference. It looked as if they would have to add two words to the end of his citation:

"Awarded posthumously."

The FREEDOM FIGHTER *Series*

TOMAHAWKS AND LONG RIFLES

MUSKETS OF '76

THE KING'S CANNON

GUNS AT TWILIGHT

BULLETS ON THE BORDER

STORM IN THE SOUTH

THE TURNING OF THE TIDE

THE FRONTIER WAR

SHELLFIRE ON THE BAY

VOLUNTEERS FOR GLORY

Volunteers
for
Glory

Jonathan Scofield

A DELL/BRYANS BOOK

Published by
Dell Publishing Co., Inc.
1 Dag Hammarskjold Plaza
New York, New York 10017

Dell ® TM 681510, Dell Publishing Co., Inc.

ISBN: 0-440-09405-4

Printed in the United States of America

First printing—December 1981

Volunteers
for
Glory

THE BOMB ARCED over the heads of the crowd lining the street, missed the open motor car, and rolled along the rough pavement of Sarajevo's main thoroughfare. A woman screamed.

"Look out," a man shouted, his cry in Serbo-Croatian. He was a farmer, Milos Dusan, his boots caked with mud and manure. June had been an unusually rainy month, and he had not moved his sheep and goats to the high mountain plateau that he used for summer pasture. Thus it was that he stood with hundreds of townspeople and farmers who had come to see the man who might one day be their emperor.

Actually, politics mattered little to the farmer. He did not care whether the Hapsburgs of Austria-Hungary ruled his province of Bosnia or not. Not that he was unaware of the turmoil surrounding and frequently poking its bloody fist into his homeland across the Adriatic sea from Italy. His eldest son, bored with farm work, had joined the Black Hands and died in his first act of terrorism. The Black Hands were assassins bent on forcing the emperor to free the province to join Serbia in the east.

Dusan had heard all the arguments from his son: All the people who spoke his language should be together, working to build a greater Serbia. A Serbia which needed Bosnia if it was ever to be free of the "pig politics" of the Hapsburgs, who closed the landlocked nation's access to the sea on the slightest whim.

So far the sporadic revolt had taken the strong body of Dusan's eldest son from him and returned him nothing.

Since he had seen his boy build just such a bomb as the one rolling across the pavement, he was the first to cry out a warning.

"A bomb!" he yelled.

A woman screamed, then another, and men bulled their way backward, determined to put bodies—anyone's body—between them and the explosive. A mounted police officer made a gallant effort to snatch up the weapon. Then, quicker than the concussion itself, he was gone. The explosion roared in the two-story canyon of brick and stone buildings, each pressed tightly against the other to conserve space. In an agricultural area, land left around a building was a regrettable waste. Only the aristocrats and rich merchants could afford homes or castles or mansions surrounded by yards or virgin woodlands where poachers were driven off or shot.

The explosion rebounded between the walls, and

with random impartial fury, thrust missiles of steel and concrete into the crowd. One woman's face was bathed in crimson, the broad peasant features obscured by the rush of her blood. A child of seven cried and pressed a hand to both eyes. A policeman was on his back, partially hidden by the smoke, his horse lying on its side, hoofs kicking as if to fight off its pain.

Panic sprayed the area along with the bomb fragments. Those nearest the street, who had been so pleased with their excellent viewing position, reeled back, pushing others through a haberdasher's window display and an adjoining bakery. One man found himself sitting up in a display of fresh, gooey pastries, spattered with blood. The broken glass had dropped like a cleaver, slicing through his trousers and into his legs.

The black two-seat motor car with the folded canvas top jumped ahead. As the driver heard the cries, he worked the gas feed. Behind him the Archduke Frances Ferdinand ducked forward, escaping the explosion that shook the automobile. Mounted guards charged into the street, scattering the people in a frantic search for the bomber.

In the startled crowd, Gavrilo Princip, a young Serbian student, was first delighted by the bomb, then disappointed when he saw the plume of the archduke's helmet rise above the rear seat of the escaping motor car. The boy bounced into the street, his hands inside his jacket, his fingers clutched around the revolver tucked in his waistband.

"The fools," he cursed. He had told the other members of the revolutionary cult to leave the killing to him, but they wanted the glory for themselves. The bomb was to have been used only if his pistol failed.

With the police cordoning off the street behind the aristocrat's car, Gavrilo could not get off a shot. He did not dare show his weapon. He faded into the milling crowd, trying to see if any of his fellow rebels were being taken captive. One familiar face appeared in the group of suspects the royal guards were beating into submission.

"Gavrilo!" his comrade called, pleading for help.

His friends were cowards. They wanted him to come after them, to shoot in a suicidal attempt to free them. He paid no heed and moved away with the throng flowing down the main street. Discouraged, and yet determined, he made his way through the city on foot, approaching the public buildings where he knew the archduke had gone to confer with the officials of the province.

A crowd had gathered here too, and it was buzzing with reports of the assassination attempt. Guards lined the pillared front of the building, their rifles with bayonets attached forming a picket against further threat.

"No use waiting," Gavrilo heard people saying around him.

"Not after the bombing."

"He will come out again," insisted an old hunched woman in a black shapeless dress, black stockings, and worn black shoes. "Aristocrats are never cowards."

The spirits of the waiting killer soared. Perhaps there was still a chance. With luck, the archduke would feel obligated to make his second appearance on schedule. It was a tenet of royalty: never let the masses know you fear them.

Still hopeful, the boy crossed the square to an outdoor cafe and sat under the awning. Over the next hours he sipped slowly at his coffee, ordering cup after cup as he studied the activity across the square. Around the public building, guards were searching people, handling the spectators roughly, arresting a few on one pretext or another. None of the guards bothered Gavrilo, though, and he was still at the café when the great bronze-covered doors opened and the provincial officials formed a corridor to the waiting car.

Most wore formal suits with tails and white gloves. A few assumed the more traditional dress of the area. The archduke's driver in his white jacket and beaked cap waited patiently with the engine running.

"Now," Gavrilo said to himself. He rose, put a coin on the table to pay for all the coffee he had drunk during the long afternoon, and started across the square. As he walked, his hands at his sides to avoid attracting attention, he sensed for the first time the meaning of power.

He was more powerful than any of the men on the steps, regardless of their age and position, regardless of their regal attire. They were nothing compared to him. He would strike down an archduke, strike a blow for the unification of the Serbian people. Thousands would rise to his defense; they would revere him.

Gavrilo Princip, father of greater Serbia.

The people were applauding before he reached the other side of the square. A few were cheering . . . Already they were cheering him, Gavrilo Princip.

They were pretending to honor the archduke as he appeared in the open bronze doors, the parallel lines of brass buttons sparkling against his light gray, double-breasted uniform jacket. His left hand was on his ceremonial sword; his right saluted the honor guard that stood beyond the automobile. Beside him, in white, was his wife, her face shaded by the broad-brimmed hat decorated with dark ostrich feathers.

Then they were in the car, and Gavrilo could hear people marveling at the royal couple's bravery.

The car rolled in the direction of the railroad station along a thinner line of sidewalk spectators. Mounted guards trailed front and rear.

As the moment approached, Gavrilo's saliva dried to the consistency of glue. The car was less than fifty yards away. His hands began to perspire. Forty yards left to separate him from history. His thin mouth quivered. He had not expected the reaction. The planning, the anticipation, were more pleasurable than the act itself.

Thirty yards. Twenty-five.

He positioned himself in the second row of onlookers. A man cursed him for pushing him aside.

Twenty yards. The boy ran a finger around the inside of his collar. The finger came away wet.

Ten yards. His hand reached for the gun and missed the handle. Everybody must have seen his fumbling. They must comprehend what he was about to do, despite the hypnotic presence of royalty. Commoners adored royalty. The regal superiority reminded farmers and shopkeepers that there was more to life than drudgery.

Five yards and Gavrilo pulled the pistol. The front sight caught on the inside of his trousers where the belt held them tight against his waist.

He couldn't extract it.

He felt the threat of tears behind his eyelids. To

fail for such an insignificant reason . . . Impossible.

He brushed aside the left side of his jacket, freed the pistol and stepped forward into a vacant stretch between the spectators and the motor car.

"Gun!" a voice yelled.

"Stop him!"

"Assassin!"

The cries were in Serbo-Croatian, his own language. Hands clawed at him like small, blunted hayforks. His own people were trying to abort his mission. Maniacs! Didn't they understand? He was Princip, the great hero.

He jerked loose, placed one foot on the running board of the car and hung on with his left hand. He raised the pistol. For an instant he stared into the eyes of his intended victim. The heir to the throne showed no fear. There was contempt and there was a frightening threat, but no fear.

The piercing eyes seemed to sentence the boy to the eternal pains of hell.

Gavrilo's reasoning had done a complete reversal. He fired out of fear. The gun lurched in his palm. The crack was louder than he had ever heard from a pistol, and he had fired repeatedly during arduous training for his mission. He loved weapons. They gave him power.

It seemed as if the shot could be heard for miles, hundreds of miles, thousands of miles, all around the world. The shock was so great he fired a second time and then a third. He saw blood sully the archduke's uniform, and he was terrified at the punishment the man might mete out for soiling the royal cloth. He saw blood on the duchess's white dress. She sat too close to his intended victim. He had not meant to shoot her. She had been pointlessly sacrificed when she threw herself in front of her husband in a vain attempt to save him.

Gavrilo would have liked to apologize. He had not meant to hurt her.

The archduke was still staring at him when a hundred hands tore the boy from the running board. The assassin was denied the satisfaction of seeing his target pitch forward. Too many men were beating at him, twisting the gun from his hand, kicking at his head.

The fools . . . Didn't they understand what he had just done for them? Didn't they appreciate the blow he had struck for Serbia, for all the people with common languages who were forced by age-old conquests to live as foreigners in their own lands?

They were punishing him, punishing the hero. It was all so wrong.

"Union or Death!" He spat out the Black Hand's rallying cry.

No one heard him, in their frenzy of kicking and beating.

The guards galloped in with swinging clubs, beating off the people who were brutalizing the assassin. Then several of the armed men dismounted and caught Gavrilo, one at each arm and leg. They dragged and carried him toward an enclosed truck.

People spat on him, threw whatever objects were at hand, reviled him.

"Union or Death," he yelled again.

Why didn't they appreciate the blow he had struck, a blow that would wrench the provinces of Bosnia and Hercegovina from the oppression of the Austro-Hungarian rulers who lived far to the north? Who else had done so much? For years Serbian terrorists had been agitating for the union of the people with a mutual language, but he, Gavrilo Princip, had killed an archduke. Who else would have given himself in order to accomplish so much?

"Let the crowd have him," suggested one of the guards as they hurried him along. "Let them beat him to death."

"Save the firing squad a dozen bullets," another agreed.

Firing squad. For the first time Gavrilo saw himself tied to a pole in a prison yard, a blindfold across his eyes, waiting for bullets to tear his body apart. His triumphant smile drooped and faded.

My God, he thought. He would never know if the Black Hand had won.

2

W AR, WAR, WAR. That's all anyone talks about
anymore," a petulant Brooke Madigan complained. "They'll spoil the mood of the party."

Of average height with a youthful compromise of
slenderness and womanly endowments, the dark-
haired girl sat wedged between her parents in the
chauffeured motor car. They had driven slowly along
the Champs-Elysées, then turned south across the
Seine on their way to the embassy.

"See!" She pointed at the Eiffel Tower. Floods il-
luminated the Paris trademark halfway up and more
lights glowed at the very top. "Surely they would
turn off the lights on the tower if there were going
to be a war."

She had the dark eyes and deep rose complexion
of her mother, whose half-Indian and half-white fea-

tures had combined for a look that was more exotically aristocratic than recognizably Indian. At seventeen, nearly eighteen, Brooke's body and her mind drifted between maturity and adolescence. Her face had the expectant glow of youth; she flushed prettily at the sight of an intriguing boy, smiled or pouted with equal alacrity. The bone structure was good, the kind that with maturity would bring beauty to a face that was still a child's one moment, a woman's the next.

She was attractive enough now so that even the most jaded of men were arrested by her appearance, first by her facial characteristics and then by a lithe body that not even the primmest of gowns could disguise. After a year away from her home and family in America, there was still no veneer of ego or self-satisfaction over her cheerful insouciance. But studying at the Sorbonne had given her the self-assurance she needed to stand up to her parents.

They had come over to the continent to bring her home, the threat of war having made them fearful for their only child.

"There will be war in Europe soon enough," her industrialist father said with conviction.

He was a dear and generous man, in his daughter's eyes. Tall and distinguished with just the right touch of gray in his hair, W. Lane Madigan had not grown rich being soft on competitors, but he rarely said no to his daughter. She would stay in Paris another year, against his better judgment. That he knew. She was too like her mother.

"You should read the newspapers, Brooke darling," her mother chastised.

"All I ever see are French newspapers."

"You speak it fluently enough."

"Reading is harder. I read in French all day; I wouldn't want to spend my evenings struggling through a newspaper."

"Well, if you did, you'd know Austria-Hungary intends to declare war on Serbia any day now."

Brooke was adamant. "Oh, they've been saying that for a month. Besides, what did you do when there was a war, Mother darling?" The last was said with a teasing lightness. "You said I took after you rather than Father."

Joanna Vaughan Madigan reminisced inwardly. She was now a matron and a figure in international society, thanks to her husband, but she had not always been so locked into the docile femininity of her present image—not that she was truly docile, even now. She had not just talked about woman's rights or marched with the suffragettes. Born in Indian country and orphaned early, she emerged into adulthood as a true adventuress, seducing her way onto the regular staff of William Randolph Hearst's *New York Journal*. With spunk and determination she had covered the Spanish American War as a journalist. Only the violent death of her twin brother and the appearance of Lane Madigan in her life had stilled the wild Indian spirit that lay submerged under the placid surface of her present life.

Occasionally she wished for the excitement of the stormy seas that she had survived until she married Lane, and she could not insist her daughter return home quite yet. As nearly as she could tell Brooke had done nothing except study hard and make good marks so far. Give the child another year, Joanna Madigan decided.

"And what does a little war between the Hapsburgs and those backward Serbs have to do with Paris anyway?" Brooke persisted.

Her father answered after the car stopped alongside the formally uniformed marine standing guard at the embassy gate. Lane Madigan rolled down the window and greeted the young private, who laid his white-gloved hands on the door and peered in perfunctorily, then delayed a moment when he saw the girl in the center, half-illuminated by the outside lights.

"May we proceed?" Madigan asked with a hint of censure for the delay.

"Yes, of course, Mr. Madigan. The party's already started." The marine saluted with exaggerated snap.

"It's not just Austria, Hungary and Serbia who'll be fighting," Madigan said as the car rolled along the curved driveway to the front of the pillared embassy.

"The French want back Alsace-Lorraine which Germany took in 1871. Italy wants Trieste. Estonia, Finland, Latvia, Lithuania and Poland want to be free from Russia. Germany wants more colonies. Great Britain wants—"

"Enough, Father, enough," Brooke pleaded. "It's all nonsense."

Another marine opened the door and the Madigans were admitted to the embassy. For the girl it was a scene to remember. Women in fabulous gowns and men in the uniforms of a dozen nations swayed and circled to the music of an orchestra playing from a platform between the two curved staircases leading to a balcony above.

Thousands of facets in a broad chandelier shot prisms of silent fireworks over the assemblage.

Brooke thrilled to the sight of the whirling skirts of the women, but the brightly uniformed men were the peacocks of the affair. Their brass buttons, dangling medals, and brilliant braid seemed to catch the light, making the women's beautiful gowns no more than mere accessories. There was a magic in the prospect of war; the colors more vivid, as if everyone had dressed particularly well this evening to celebrate the coming excitement.

The men were more gallant than usual. A few wore gleaming swords and they were bowing with a flare that she had never noticed before. But most of the guests were older; they always were at these affairs. Young daughters of diplomats, government officials and high-ranking military officers attended, but rarely a boy her own age.

"Is he here?" she heard her father saying to the ambassador, the host.

The bearded man next to the ambassador said "yes" without altering the professional smile that he wore.

The ambassador nodded too, and Brooke could see who they meant: Rene Viviani, the French premier. The statesman stood a few steps up the staircase to the right of the orchestra, holding at bay a group of men in civilian clothes.

"Excuse me, Joanna," her father said. He escaped the reception line and crossed to the crowd around the staircase.

"Where's Father going?" Brooke asked. She had never known her father to dispense with any of the social niceties before.

"Business, dear," her mother answered.

"Business?"

Joanna patted her daughter on the shoulder and moved her farther along the line, whispering in her ear as they paused between diplomats and their wives. "War is big business; we'll make a fortune selling arms to the French if they get into this Serbian mess."

"But we're already rich."

Brooke's bewilderment at the necessity of accumulating further wealth went unenlightened as she recognized the familiar faces ahead of her.

The Hunters.

Brooke never did understand the role played in American diplomacy by the patriarch of the Hunter clan, but she knew he had served presidents at home and abroad since her mother was a girl. He must be in his fifties, she calculated, although he retained a certain youthful grace about him. He was not nearly as handsome as her own father, and his wife was almost dowdy. Yet they were nice and Brooke welcomed a familiar face as her mother extended a gloved hand to be taken and gently held.

With the curiosity that had made her an excellent newspaper correspondent years before, Joanna Madigan leaned close enough to whisper a question.

"Is there any news on the war, Bill?"

Hunter nodded. "The Hapsburgs may declare war on Serbia at any moment. It will be in the morning papers."

"Good lord! I hope it doesn't spread."

"It has," Hunter replied. "Russia is ordering a general mobilization. The kaiser will probably declare war in a day or two."

"On whom?" Brooke asked innocently.

Her mother moved her past the end of the receiving line, answering her question as they headed for empty chairs near the orchestra. Chairs were always subtly reserved for the Madigans whenever they attended a ball.

"The Russians," Joanna was saying, "and then the French no doubt. Probably Britain, too. They're part of the Triple Entente."

"But I thought the war was between Austria and Serbia. I don't understand."

"That's because you don't read the newspapers, darling. Germany is allied with Austro-Hungary. They're the central powers. I imagine the Turks will be in it soon, too. The Balkans are such a mess."

"It's all so confusing," Brooke said. "Will we be getting involved?"

"Heavens, no," Joanna reassured her daughter. "President Wilson promised no foreign entanglements. But don't you think you should return home with your father and me, darling? Wars can be nasty experiences."

"Certainly no one's going to attack Paris. It's far too lovely." Brooke spotted another familiar face at the edge of the men standing about the premier. "Allison," she called.

Allison Hunter was older, seven years Brooke's senior, but she was fun and daring. A real vamp, as audiences were calling Theda Bara since her most recent film. Or *femme fatale,* according to the few girls at the Sorbonne who knew her. She was blonde and there was talk she used peroxide on her hair. Brooke did not want to believe that, although occasionally the roots were darker than usual.

But then women were always catty about one of

their own who held such appeal for men. Since she had arrived in the embassy in Paris with her parents, Allison had been seen with every eligible American male available and innumerable Frenchmen with tenuous links to the aristocracy. Her blue eyes always danced with spirit, and flashed like diamonds for a man who was tall enough to tower above her own five feet eight inches.

"Brooke dear," Allison said, "how nice to see you!"

Allison was amazing. She could conduct a conversation while flirting outrageously. At the moment her attention was on Brooke's own father. The glint of interest in the Hunter girl's eyes was as obvious as orchids among snapdragons. She was such a hussy. Not that Brooke didn't consider her father attractive, but the idea of a girl in her twenties giving him a second thought was amusing. But then that was Allison Hunter. Never did she do the expected.

Of course, Lane Madigan was rich, Brooke reasoned.

And susceptible, she noticed. Her father had lost interest in the political discussion of the men and was holding his cigar away from his lips as if dazzled by Allison's attention.

When she had her current quarry hooked, Allison abruptly changed the direction of her charms.

"I don't believe you've met my brother, have you, Brooke?"

"No, I . . ."

Brooke followed her friend's gaze to the top of the stairs. What she saw was a tall, lean, dark-haired young man probably no more than three years her senior. His hair was as black as her own and wavy. His teeth were particularly straight and bright. His eyes were hazel in the light of the ballroom. They moved in quick, curious jerks as if he could not take in the life around him fast enough.

He was long-limbed and powerfully built, six feet at least and close to a hundred and ninety pounds. His body looked taut and hard.

Tonight he wore the prescribed tuxedo with black tie, a uniform that varied little from that of the other civilians, but Brooke was instantly aware that every woman in the room saw a difference in him. There was a certain self-confident vitality and a native curiosity that sparked their interest.

"Blake stayed behind to learn to drive flying machines, of all things," Allison Hunter said of her brother. "He's always into something new. Polo— nearly killed himself last year driving against that Barney Oldfield down in Daytona. Blake just now came up from Monaco where he flew in the Schneider Trophy race."

Flying machines! The words caught Brooke's imagination and immediately she had to know the man who stood surveying the room from the balcony.

She had always wanted to fly. Not to run the machine herself, of course, although there were women doing such things. But she wanted to soar up high in the air and look down on the foolish world below. She wanted to see the other side of the clouds. From above.

The possibility of a new thrill diminished the boredom that had been creeping up on her in these last few months. She had been ready to leave Paris and explore the rest of Europe when she finished her studies at the Sorbonne, but the silly talk of war had closed border after border to the cautious traveler.

She had been toying with the idea of agreeing to return home with her parents on the next ship from Le Havre. The appearance of Blake Langley Hunter changed all that.

"Blake," Allison said loud enough for her brother to hear from the top of the stairs. "Do come down and meet a friend of mine." She leaned close and whispered to Brooke. "He graduated from the University of Virginia by the skin of his teeth. My brother Duncan graduated *summa cum laude.*"

"Oh? And where is he?"

"Duncan? Still in Monaco. He'll be coming up to Paris soon, but he's married."

"Oh."

"Blake is the one the girls go gaga about. Especially since he learned to fly. Once he flew up the East River in New York, under all four bridges."

His smile was at once gracious and condescending, a combination that Brooke found confusing.

He greeted Brooke in flawed French, a dialect one picked up from living in the country rather than from a classroom. He had probably learned it while living with his parents when they served in France before.

"English is quite all right," Allison told him. "Brooke is an American, too."

When he was introduced, he was charming and yet a bit aloof, still a bit too confident. It was as if he found her attractive, but expected nothing to come of the meeting. Why? she wondered. It intrigued her.

"Madigan?" he said, placing the name. "Your mother was Joanna Vaughan of the *Journal,* wasn't she? The woman journalist."

"She is," Brooke replied, losing the fine hone of her

composure. "I mean she was the journalist. She's married now . . . well, of course, she's married. I mean, I'm her daughter and—"

He came to her rescue.

"I met your parents in the boat over from the States. We're related, I believe."

"Oh, imagine meeting halfway around the world," Brooke managed to say.

"Do you mind if I smoke?" he asked.

"Heavens, no."

He produced a gold cigarette case and matching lighter. Offered one, she declined, and he thoughtfully exhaled to the side, away from her face.

He was so debonair, she thought, but before the conversation progressed further, a commotion erupted around the French premier. A man in the uniform of a general had apparently crashed the party and made his way straight across the dance floor to the French leader's entourage.

He spoke a few words, and the hall was transformed as decisively as though a bomb had been tossed in the midst of the elegantly dressed guests.

The band stopped playing. The dancers parted, and the hall emptied of French officers, diplomats, and guests. They trailed the premier who strode across the floor through the column of bodies that separated before him.

"Jesus parting the sea," Allison remarked irreverently.

The silence that had fallen over the remaining guests was shattered with the closing of the front entry behind the last and lowest-ranking French officer. Immediately there was a babble of unanswered questions.

Brooke confronted her father as her mother and the Hunters rushed toward him.

"What happened, Father?"

Lane Madigan, who had been standing next to the premier, answered for more than his own family. His voice carried to the men around him, then spread across the waiting hall.

"The Hapsburgs declared war on Serbia. They claim the Serbs fostered the assassination in Bosnia."

"And the premier ruins a party for that?" Brooke remarked innocently. "How rude these French are."

Her father spoke directly to William Hunter and the ambassador himself. "Russia is ordering general mobilization."

"Good lord," the elder Hunter responded. "That will bring Kaiser Bill into it."

"And the French, I should imagine," the ambassador said solemnly.

Brooke interrupted. "Kaiser who?"

Blake answered her as the ambassador and his aides began rushing up the stairs to the offices and living quarters above.

"Friedrich Wilhelm Viktor Albert, Kaiser William the second. Emperor of Germany and king of Prussia."

"The silly man who struts around with a spike on the top of his helmet and a fur-collared cape tossed over his shoulders," Allison added.

Brooke recalled the few pictures she had seen of the strutting, scowling man who thought he could frighten the world with a look.

"You'd better plan to come home with us after all, darling," her mother was saying. "The French National Assembly will be declaring war any day, I'm certain."

"Then it won't be just a parade," Allison remarked.

"Parade?" Brooke asked.

"I was going over to Blake's flat in the morning—he's sharing it with another American boy—to see the troops marching off for the border. It should be quite a show," Allison said excitedly. "All those men . . . Wherever could a girl see so many men in their brilliant red and blue uniforms? I wouldn't miss it for the world."

"Joanna," Lane Madigan interrupted. "I think you and Brooke should go back to the hotel. I'll be along later."

"But, Father," Brooke protested, "it's early. The party has just started. And I've just met—" She stopped herself precisely at the point she had meant to. And the handsome Blake Langley Hunter's attention had been drawn away from the serious talk of the men.

"Perhaps you'd like to see the troops march off to war, Miss Madigan," he suggested.

"Yes, it sounds exciting."

"Brooke, no," her mother interjected. "We may be packing."

"I could send my car around for your daughter, Mrs. Madigan. I hired a steamer and a driver when I arrived in Le Havre."

"That's very generous of you, but I'm sure Mr. Madigan will be anxious to get back to the United States before transportation becomes difficult."

"I shouldn't think you'd be going anywhere tomorrow. Practically every train in Paris will be moving the troops east. You could drive to the port, of course, but I imagine the roads will be impossibly jammed for a day or two with lorries moving men and supplies. I'm sure we're quite safe here in Paris."

"May I?" Brooke asked.

Joanna Madigan sighed. "All right, dear. But you will be along too, won't you, Allison?"

"Certainly."

"Mother, do you really think that's necessary?"

"Yes, I'll be there," Allison smiled.

"Your daughter will be quite safe, Mrs. Madigan," Blake reassured her. "My roommate is a DeWitt. I'm sure you knew his father Lowell. He was with Commodore Schley at Santiago."

The party had dissipated and Brooke walked with her mother to the waiting car. A glance back told her what she expected.

Blake Langley Hunter stood following her with his eyes, glancing away only after their gazes met.

War, Brooke thought pleasantly . . . Perhaps it wouldn't spoil her stay in Paris after all.

3

FRANKLIN DEWITT sat on the sidewalk with a typewriter on his lap, moving his lips as he punched
the keys.

"The morning sun was warm, the sky cloudless, a
breeze sweeping down the chasm between the buildings. Men, women, and children in all manner of
dress crowded the curb, waiting expectantly, in a
holiday spirit. A boy dashed into the empty street,
peered to the south, and was drawn back by an impatient mother." Franklin thought of his younger
brother, Everett, who was not much older than this
boy, but was already caught up in dreams of going
to war—just like his big brother, and his father before him.

Blond like his naval officer father, Franklin DeWitt
was of medium height and slightly stocky in build.

Like his body, his hands were broad and powerful, and they made the typewriter appear diminutive, a machine too small for his hands. He had set it on the sidewalk, a position which required him to make a quarter turn and sit at an awkward angle. Nevertheless the keys slapped so rapidly against the paper that frequently two or three reached the imprinting position simultaneously. They had to be pulled apart so he could continue capturing the moods and scenes of Paris for his novel.

Paris was the right place for Franklin. In this city of artists there was nothing remarkable about a good-looking young writer—like Franklin, with just enough hook to his nose to make him look interesting—whetting his skills on the street. Occasionally a child would distract him by snatching at the paper and asking him what he was doing. The children he accepted. Sometimes a woman paused, hopefully perhaps, but he ignored them.

He ignored too the Frenchmen who muttered *Américain* in a tone that expressed their dislike for the eccentric foreigners who formed colonies in Paris. They wrote books that were seldom finished and painted paintings that were so bad they went unnoticed on street-side displays until the discouraged artists pulled them off the market. The French especially disliked symbols of American affluence such as the expensive motor car that pulled to a stop in front of the blue-eyed writer. He lifted a hand in recognition.

"Franklin," Blake Hunter said from the open car while the two women with him were helped out by the chauffeur.

Franklin rose, hooking a protective foot around his typewriter.

The first girl he knew—Blake's knockout sister Allison—but the second was new, distinctly younger and more to his liking. Not that he did not find the sophisticated Allison attractive. He did. But she was two years older than his twenty-two and seemed to equate her age with superiority. He had met her in gatherings of Americans in the Bohemian enclave where he lived. Usually she paid him little attention. There were always more interesting if not more attractive men to keep her busy. But today, since he was the only male available, she gave him the full treatment.

"Franklin, you're writing," she gushed. "Here in the crowd. About the coming war, I suppose."

His smile was tacit agreement.

"How exciting."

He was looking past her to the smaller girl, aware of a tingling sensation akin to the time he had first managed to get his hands on the breasts of a girl.

Allison noted his interest and introduced her friend.

"This is Brooke Madigan. I don't believe you two have met. Brooke is at the Sorbonne. Franklin came to Paris to write a novel."

"How marvelous!" the new girl exclaimed.

"Well, hardly," Frank said ruefully. "I'm having difficulty getting the first chapter written."

"Oh, but you will," the girl said enthusiastically.

Her assurance endeared her to Franklin DeWitt. He had been bursting with the urge to write when he sailed from home to "escape distractions" and surround himself with the artistic mood of Paris. That had been months ago. Today he was starting the novel for the fifteenth time, and with the excitement of the impending war and a lovely girl's confidence, he felt renewed dedication. He had the talent; it just had to be freed from whatever part of the mind that imprisons great literature. He was writing about himself, about his inner thoughts and the insights he had ready to expose, putting it all in the form of a novel.

"Sitting on the curb when we could see just as well from our apartment window?" Blake remarked. He taunted his new roommate in a good-natured way, yet he had managed knowingly or unknowingly to reclassify Franklin's sidewalk writing from artistic eccentricity to quaintness.

Hunter had ordered the car driven away and was about to take the two girls to his four-room flat on the second floor when a trumpet blared from down the street.

"They're coming," Allison said eagerly.

Excited children ran into the street. They yelled and pointed. Parents came out to retrieve them. All along the paved walk adults shoved and pushed for a better view. A few cheered.

Then an automobile flanked by several men on horseback rode into view.

"General Foch," Franklin said. Several people in the crowd recognized one of the nation's top military commanders.

Behind him came flags, a military band, and columns of troops with their rifles on their shoulders, marching shoulder to shoulder, filling the street. The tramp, tramp, tramp of their boots in perfect cadence roused a curious feeling inside Franklin DeWitt, a feeling he had not known existed within him. He yearned to be with the troops, a part of the massive whole. It was an almost primitive instinct.

Despite the robust build which might have made him an athlete, words had always been his forte. He had been drawn to literature and words when his contemporaries struggled to memorize the alphabet. As an early reader, he had read of wars, imagined the camaraderie of men bound together by a common enemy. But despite his father's military background—indeed, the military was a DeWitt tradition —he had never had any wish for more exposure to wars and armies than he had found in books.

With the exception of his books and Blake Hunter, he had never had a "best friend," never belonged to a gang. Although hardly unsociable, his relationships never lasted or became more than casual, nothing like the bond the men in the street must have felt as they marched toward war together.

"They're beautiful," Allison said enthusiastically. She ran into the street and kissed a handsome young officer. The crowd was not pleased until all along the column French women began to do the same.

The difference was her nationality. For the most part, the French managed to hide any fondness they might have harbored for foreigners. Franklin had found them insular except when you got to know them as individuals.

While the columns passed, the young writer watched in frustration. To protect his typewriter, he had to hold the heavy thing in his arms when he really wanted to be writing his impressions as they occurred.

It was worth writing about, the thousands upon

thousands of regular army troops marching in red
woolen sweat trousers, dark blue greatcoats, and red
woolen *kepis*, a military cap with a visor and a round
flat top sloping toward the front. Their heels drummed
the street in a rigid beat. The men's expressions were
serious in spite of the repeated cheers and applause
from the viewers.

Behind the infantry came the cavalry, steel breast-
plates gleaming in the morning sun. Their copper
helmets were topped with horsehair plumes and their
boots polished to a glasslike shine.

Along the walks, young men lifted their straw boat-
ers. "We'll be there with you soon," they called.

At the end came the artillery, caissons and horse-
drawn 75s, the fast-firing guns that the military boast-
ed about as the war approached at a quickened tempo.

"That's what you should do," Brooke Madigan said
to Franklin. It was the first she had spoken to him
directly and he turned and smiled down at her en-
couragingly. "You ought to join the military," she
said. "You'd really get material for your book."

"He's writing about a teen-aged boy growing into
maturity," Blake remarked.

"No, I've been thinking of a war novel," Franklin
corrected him.

"That's something you'd have to experience, isn't
it?" Blake countered. "Imagination is all well and
good, but the best novels come from personal experiences. I don't see how you could write about the
war unless you had participated."

Franklin felt deflated. Without meaning to, his
friend was questioning his ability to create the book
that occupied his entire being. What's more, the
novice writer felt embarrassed in front of the girl.

It did sound as if he were going to cheat in his writing, but it wasn't true. He had already thought of the experience angle.

"I'm joining up," he said flatly.

"The army?" Brooke said incredulously.

Allison was surprised, too. "The French army? But you'd lose your American citizenship."

"I've checked into that," Franklin replied. "If I join the *Légion étrangère,* I won't be swearing allegiance to France. The contract requires only that I promise to serve with faithfulness and honor. That's what your father told me."

"But the French foreign legion!" Blake's tone mirrored distaste. "It's notorious as a refuge for criminals, soldiers of fortune, all the outcasts of society."

"And adventurers. A writer could gain valuable experiences fighting alongside such men."

"You? With the scum of the Paris street? You can't, Franklin. I won't allow it."

"Blake, need I remind you that you're not my father?"

"Heaven knows you need one."

"I'm joining today if I can." Frank's decision was both expedient and impulsive, and meant to impress the lovely Brooke. Having been given voice, what had only moments before been an unexplored thought was now a commitment.

"You're serious about this then," Blake said, eying his friend.

"Yes. Hundreds of other aliens in France are signing up, too. That madman, the kaiser, will have the world in flames if someone doesn't stop him. I might as well do my part."

"You're very brave," Brooke Madigan said effusively. "May I see you in your uniform?"

"Of course."

"I wish I were a man!"

"A war is hardly a place for a pretty girl."

"Tell that to my mother. She served as a correspondent during the war over in Cuba. She was practically in the thick of things."

"You can always join the nursing corps," Allison suggested.

"I have no training."

"I'm certain they'll find a place for you to help. A nurse's aide or serving in the rest camps. That would get you close to the excitement."

Brooke was interested. "I might just do that. *After* mother and father return home and aren't here to stop me. But I think it's so exciting, Mr. DeWitt. You going off to war, and writing a book."

"Franklin, please. But will you forget me if I leave? Will you write?"

"Oh yes, Franklin. And I'll send you things. I can knit sweaters and gloves. I'm so proud of you. I've considered writing myself. Mother taught me a few tricks and I've done well in my writing classes—in both French and English."

DeWitt clutched at the common interest. "Perhaps you could write a novel, Miss Madigan."

"Call me Brooke if you expect me to use your given name."

"Of course." Was he reading too much into it or was she suggesting they see each other again? His knowledge of women was limited to cheap tramps that college boys went with when they did not have nerve to date an equal.

Blake Hunter had shared the limelight long enough. "I'd join you, Frank old boy, but I'll be going in as a flyer."

"You? Go to war?" his sister questioned.

"Yes. I already know how to pilot an aircraft, so I imagine the French will be glad to get me. Far more dangerous than the infantry or cavalry, of course, but if we do the job here, perhaps you girls and the folks back home will be saved the misery of war." He played the hero well before the fact, Franklin noted wryly.

"A flyer?" Brooke unknowingly voiced the opinion of generals and ranking politicians. "What on earth would they need airplanes for in the war? I'm certain they're great sport but surely they'd frighten the horses and they're so dangerously fast."

"They were used in the Balkan War and in Mexico for observation purposes, I believe," Franklin said. "They might be better than balloons. Imagine flying over the enemy troops, seeing precisely what they're preparing to do. And no one could stop you. They might shoot down a balloon, but certainly no marksman could hit an aircraft going ninety miles per hour."

"I predict they will be used in place of artillery eventually," Blake added.

"In heaven's name how?" His sister was dubious.

Hunter lost some of his confidence. "Well, I suppose you could carry the shells somehow on the aircraft and drop them on the enemy wherever you saw them."

"You're pulling my leg," Brooke giggled.

"No, seriously, I think it has been tried. I know

the French have some aircraft for observation purposes in the army already so I imagine they could very well use my skill."

"The French aren't accepting foreigners into the *Service de l'Aviation* directly," Frank pointed out. "They had too many Frenchmen applying to become pilots. But I was told if I joined the legion, I'd have a chance of transferring to the airplanes later."

"Well, I can hardly be expected to serve as a *poilu,*" Blake commented. "Not with my background."

"But you're going to try, Franklin?" Brooke asked.

"Yes. I'll take my chances on the ground and put in for transfer as soon as it's permitted. The experience should be broad and I'm certain I'll find my way into an escadrille eventually."

"Blake," Allison challenged, "isn't it worth the risk of a few weeks on the ground to get a chance to fly?"

Hunter scowled, but he was aware of Brooke Madigan's fascination with his roommate's plans.

"If that's what it takes to fly for freedom, then of course I'll join the legion first. But I suppose with father's help, I should be able to get a transfer soon. There's no sense in some poor untrained chap risking his life learning to fly when I already know how."

"Then you'll sign up with me tomorrow?" Frank said, his face lighting with pleasure.

Blake hesitated. "Well, yes. Sure."

The last of the troops had moved past and their footsteps faded.

The crowd was dispersing and an enthralled Brooke Madigan listened to conversation filled with war and glory and duty as the foursome strolled toward a sidewalk cafe.

Franklin DeWitt was more aware of the girl than of tomorrow's commitment. He wanted her to see him in his new uniform.

4

THE WAR STARTED gloriously for the two Americans. With forty-one of their countrymen they were sworn in, an elaborate ceremony with propaganda overtones, in the courtyard of the Hôtel des Invalides. Allison Hunter and Brooke were in the crowd watching while French officials praised the volunteers, who hailed from several different nations.

There were patriotic speeches and diatribes against the Huns who had bypassed the French "impenetrable defenses" two days after the countries officially declared war on each other. Cleverly, if not ethically, the Germans had avoided a straight-on attack against their common border. The attackers had invaded neutral Belgium, overrun it quickly, and were heading south toward Paris and east toward the English Channel.

Threatened with an invasion, Great Britain had come into the fight, readying its defenses and preparing an expeditionary force to fight on the continent.

The war was spreading like grease dropped in a hot skillet, tossing up dark clouds and leaving the burned remains of the defenders. It stretched all the way to Japan, which snatched up German colonies in Asia and the South Pacific.

In Africa the two colonial powers sought to take territory from Germany and shipped black troops north to save the northlands.

In Paris, the French attempted to maintain the appearance that they were a protected and secure nation, ignoring the obvious signs to the contrary.

There were lengthy speeches praising the men who had agreed to help fight the barbarians, and around the courtyard were army officers, diplomats in silk hats, and proud wives and lovers of the enlistees who were still in civilian clothes.

Above was the golden dome that contained the remains of Napoleon Bonaparte.

When the ceremonies were over the new legionnaires were allowed time for farewells.

Both Franklin DeWitt and Blake Hunter went to Brooke Madigan to say good-bye. Allison was with her.

"A beautiful ceremony," Brooke remarked. "Especially where they praised 'your selfless act in contributing your courage and blood to the history of France.' I'm so proud of you, Franklin. I know you will want a chance to write down your thoughts before you leave."

DeWitt pulled a pad and pencil from his pocket.

"I'm taking my typewriter, writing in longhand when I must, but I think this will be a great first chapter, don't you?"

"Yes. And Blake," she said, "I do hope you get into the air branch. I know you'd be a wonderful flyer."

"I'll get in," Blake said confidently.

"I heard from Duncan this morning," Allison interrupted. "A letter. He says he's coming to Paris immediately."

Blake was puzzled. "What in God's name for?"

"Duncan is our brother," Allison said for DeWitt and Brooke. "He'll join the French if Blake does."

"That's insane." Blake was incredulous. "He has a wife and children."

"You know Duncan, always doing the noble thing."

"That must run in the family." Brooke looked at Blake with approval.

Blake's momentary disapproval eased. Perhaps it would not matter whether his older brother joined him. It would take nothing away from Blake's own gesture.

Franklin DeWitt tugged at his sleeve. "Time to move out."

An artist's palette of emotions were daubed across Blake Hunter's vision. The bright blue of pride, the brilliant red of fear. Why had he gotten into this thing anyway? he questioned himself.

Then he saw only the soft pink of Brooke Madigan's lips and he took advantage of the situation. He drew her unexpectedly toward him and kissed her ardently, making the gesture as dramatic as possible. She was too surprised to resist, and when he drew away from her she was wide-eyed with bewilderment.

"Forgive me," he said, "but I might not be coming back, and there are things I should have said to you before . . ."

"To me?" Brooke blushed.

Blake smiled in response, his eyes resting on her before he turned to Allison.

"Farewell," Blake said, giving his sister a peck on the cheek and trotting off toward the lorries that waited for the legionnaires outside the compound.

Brooke waved. "Good-bye, Blake . . . I'll be seeing you again."

"Write," Allison called. "We'll come visit you when you have leave."

From the exit, Blake hesitated once more, waving, realizing DeWitt was not directly behind him. The fledgling writer was having difficulty saying goodbye. Then both Allison and Brooke kissed him on the cheek and he took off after the others.

There was no need, Blake thought. No need for Brooke to kiss Franklin, not even a small peck on the cheek. It would confuse poor DeWitt. Blake could already sense that his friend was smitten by the Madigan girl. He didn't need any encouragement. He'd just get hurt.

"Let's go," he said, helping his friend into the rear of the tarp-covered lorry. Most of the voices in the truck were speaking English, but there was a scattering of other languages too.

The truck had no sooner begun to move than Blake felt the let-down. The glory was over. People along the streets paid no attention. The city had filled with military vehicles and with civilian cars and lorries confiscated in an attempt to bolster the line to the east and north.

Inside the lorry the men introduced themselves, a few giving only nicknames, thus maintaining the anonymity the legion had offered for years.

Most smoked or chewed tobacco. With a canvas draped across the back and tied down, the confined quarters quickly became stifling and odorous in the summer sun. When the lorry jerked to a halt, Franklin tried to untie the canvas and lift a flap for some air, but a *poilu* cursed him from outside.

It was a frustrating time. They spent the day locked in the semi-darkness of the truck, moving occasionally after sitting for long periods as the long line of similar vehicles crawled to the railway yards. A Swede urinated in the corner of the flatbed, while others peed through the space between the upper tarp and the rear canvas.

Blake's bladder felt close to the bursting point before he stood at the opening, extended his penis through the slit and waited for the urine to release itself. It had barely begun to spray when the truck moved and he fell and wet himself, much to the amusement of the onlookers.

He had made a mistake in enlisting; he realized that now.

But he would have to make the best of it. There had to be glamour somewhere in this war he had joined. . . .

Hours later the new recruits, still in their civilian clothes, were ordered from the truck to join thousands of other men walking across coal and cinder covered rail beds to small wooden freight cars.

"Where are we going?" Blake asked a French sergeant.

"Rouen."

"Where's that?"

"Move," the sergeant ordered.

"When do we eat?" another man asked.

The sergeant laughed. "Get in," he said.

They obeyed, pushing each other, jostling to claim places along the wall where you could sit with your back comfortably braced. Additional troops were ordered aboard.

"Hey," Blake shouted, "there's enough of us in this car already."

Still more crowded in, until fifty were packed in cars that could comfortably carry thirty-five to forty. From the stench of manure, they had obviously been most recently used for transporting animals.

Again they waited, through the long afternoon, while other cars were loaded. Their rumpled clothing reeked of perspiration.

Blankets were tossed in, one for each man, along with a one-liter canteen and a large tin of bully beef.

"Form teams of four men each," a wizened sergeant ordered in French before slamming the door. "Open only one can for each team every day."

Then they were shut in. Blake Hunter felt claustrophobic.

"There isn't room for all of us to sit down at the same time," he protested, "and lying down is out of the question. What do they think they're doing to us?"

One man's reaction was more violent. With several others he pushed his way to the door and began pounding on it.

"Let us out, you damned frogs," he shouted. "We can't breathe. Let us out!"

Panic and anger squeezed the men in tighter.

The mood was not helped by the diversity of the men and their backgrounds. Even Americans were foreigners to each other. While many were idealistic college students or recent graduates, there was also a professional gambler from New Orleans, a Baptist preacher, a second-rate boxer, several blacks, and rugged, foul-talking youths boasting they were members of the Gopher Gang in New York. There were Swedes, Norwegians, Poles, Belgians and Brazilians.

Their reasons for joining were as mixed as their backgrounds. None had joined for the thirty cents per month they were to be paid. Whatever their reasons, a cross section sliced from a hunk of humanity was packed into the confines of the cattle car.

Franklin tried to make notes while he stood along the side of the car. One of the New York street gang members bumped his arm, repeatedly, deliberately.

"Would you mind?" Franklin asked politely.

"Watcha writin'?" the hood taunted. His face was greasy and marred by pustules, new and old. "A dirty story, about fuckin'?"

"I'm writing a novel."

"Books. We don't need no books. Give me da pen."

"What?"

"Give me da goddamned pen. You deaf?"

The Gopher snatched the pen from DeWitt and held it aloft. "Hey you guys, who'll give me a butt for this?"

Franklin reached to retrieve his property and a row ensued. Although no blows were exchanged— there wasn't room—there was some shoving and elbowing. The preacher started pounding on the door. Everyone yelled.

The growing ruckus threatened what semblance of order remained in the cattle car.

Gauging the growing animosity as the car jerked and the train started to roll ahead, Blake Hunter saw a chance to rescue his friend and exercise command. Subduing his own fear, he shouted out, "Shut up, all of you."

The shock of his battering-ram voice got attention, although it took a moment to translate his order into some of the languages spoken by the non-Americans.

"You there, parson! Stop pounding the door. And you . . ." He poked a finger into the gang member's chest. "Return the pen."

The New Yorker was taken aback, his courage waning when he saw that his friends were several layers of men away.

Franklin retrieved the pen.

When the voice of authority brought calm to the car, Hunter pressed his luck. "The place stinks; it's a hellhole," he said loud enough to be heard throughout the car. "It's stuffy and going to get stuffier." The only air came in through vents in the roof. They were open part way and sucked in as much smoke and ash as fresh air. "None of you are going to suffocate. The French have been transporting their own troops in these very same cars. They know what they're about. So calm yourselves. Take turns sitting, and hold down the complaining or you will deal with me."

"You?" The lean, ugly gambler from New Orleans laughed. Stubble covered his face and chin, but not the knife scar across his upper left cheekbone. "A fancy dude like you going to give orders?" He edged closer to Blake. "Only you ain't so fancy now, what with the stink from your fancy clothes."

"I said you'd deal with me," Blake repeated, losing none of his aplomb.

One of the Gopher Gang from New York smirked. "Who do you think you are? An officer?"

"Heavyweight boxing champion in my first year at the University of Virginia. I should not like to break any jaws, but I will if necessary. So settle down."

"Oh, the university. Did you hear that men? He's a college boy."

Franklin DeWitt eased closer to his friend.

A knife glinted in the gang member's hand. Others of his group tried to move through the car.

With the edge of his hand, DeWitt chopped the Gopher hard across the wrist. The knife clattered to the floor and a fist thudded hard against the gang member's torso. He doubled over, his hands clutching his gut as he began to vomit.

Franklin started to grin at his friend's finesse with his fist. Then he realized that Blake had not moved.

The fist that had ended the quarrel and established Blake Hunter's authority in a single blow belonged to the second-rate boxer with the broken nose, the misshapen ears and the bald head. He was as ugly as he was tough.

He turned to Blake with a sheepish grin. "Mulligan," he said, introducing himself. "You get into more trouble, you call Mulligan. Okay?"

"Okay." Blake grinned.

Mulligan spoke louder. "The rest you mugs, don' mess wid da kid no more. If he smart 'nough to write, maybe he write 'bout us. Eh, kid?"

Franklin nodded.

A few men groused and then quieted. Each was left with his thoughts. For an hour the mood was sullen and silent.

Finally from the center of the car a western drawl rose above the bumping and thumping of the car as it rocked along the rough track bed.

"S-h-e-e-i-t! Reminds me of the Balkan War of ought-twelve when I was fighting the Turks. Hotter'n hell, and I was just a cowpoke with buffalo shit still on my boots. Got in on the end, I did. Figured I done my part settlin' the mess and what does the 'poms' do but put me in a cell no bigger'n this car. In with a bunch of stubborn Bulgarians couldn't speak a word of English."

Craning his neck and straining to hear, Blake remembered the man who had ridden in the same truck with him. Bulldog Teeter, he called himself, although presumably he had used a different given name for the records.

A heavy-framed man with a forehead that ran six inches back between swatches of wild sandy hair, his gaunt face was weathered enough for that of a forty-year-old man although he was probably ten years younger. He was wearing cowboy boots, his dungarees bloused in on one side and hanging over the rim of the leather boot on the other. His shirt was faded blue, too, and he wore a battered western hat that he tipped over his face when he wanted to cut off the world.

He claimed he had stayed behind when the western circus act he was with had fled Marseilles just before the declaration of hostilities had begun to sweep Europe. Blake had heard him tell the story to another man during the enlistment ceremonies. "Figured I might's well dig in my spurs against them krauts as long as I was here abouts," he had said. "Ain't 'nough Indians left to fight back home. Shootin' one of them is like killin' a buffalo; you're wipin' out your own game. But now them krauts, there's more 'n 'nough to go 'round."

"You see much fighting in Bulgaria, Teeter?" a New York boy asked from the far end of the car.

"Fightin'? I seen enough blood to turn the Mississip' red for nigh on a month. Flied me a plane for them Ottoman Turks before I took up rodeoin' and circus stuff to keep me in chewin' tobacco."

Skeptical, Blake Hunter asked, "Where did you learn to fly?"

"Where a man's supposed to learn. Up in the fuckin' sky, a course."

The men laughed. They obviously didn't believe him.

"Don't you boys be laughin' now before you heared the whole story. There I was, up in a two-seater—this sultan offers me a fortune in gold to fly spottin' missions—so there I was, riding up front with this dago pilot, lookin' for them Bulgarians when some sneakin' bandito takes a pot shot at us from the ground. We wasn't flyin' more than fifty feet up."

"Fifty feet?"

"Cain't see nuthin' from above the clouds, boy. Anyways, I'll be damned if that one bullet didn't go right up the dago's balls and out his head. He dies on me right there and then, damned wop anyway."

"Hey," an olive-complected man growled from the side. "You watch your mouth, cowboy. The Italians are going to end up on our side in this war."

"No offense meant," Teeter apologized. "That's what that wop pilot called himself, a fuckin' dago. Damned good man until he done got hisself killed for nothin'."

"You telling us you never flew before and you survived that?" another voice asked above the clacking of the steel wheels on the rails.

"Tellin' you? I ain't tellin' you nothin'. I'm here. That tells you the whole damned story. I never been in one of them aeroplanes before . . . driven cars, a course. Raced them, matter of fact."

"Back to the story about how you learned to fly," Frank DeWitt insisted. He had his pad and pen ready and was trying to take notes.

"Well, like I said, there we was at fifty feet, goin' a hundred if we was movin' at all, and this son-of-a-bitch dies on me. Lucky he slumps backward, takin' the stick with him, and up we go, standing on our tail. We're at four thousand feet before I can climb up and get his hands off the controls."

"Then what?"

"I loosened his safety belt, that's what I did. Got back in my own seat. Rolled that plane over a couple of times until he come tumblin' out."

"You just dumped him?"

"No choice, boy. Them bodies is wiggly things when they's still fresh, and he kept bumpin' against the controls. Hard 'nough to learn flyin' without havin' him sendin' us off in all directions."

"But you landed her safely?" Blake sneered.

"Not 'til I mastered the contraption. Then I set her down on the water off Constantinople, swum into town, and held up a bank so's I could get money to buy me a ticket to France. Ain't flied since, but it wouldn't take nothin' to learn again. Easier'n ridin' a longhorn, I'll tell you that for true."

Teeter continued, his voice filling any gaps in the conversations and covering the gripes of the men who were suffering in the heat and bumping against each other and the walls of the malodorous railway car.

Hours later when the train finally stopped and they poured out to fight over the single spigot available for refilling their canteens, rumors swept the length of the town's rail yards.

The French *Grand Quartier Général* strategy had been put to the test. They had mustered three quarters of a million men in the eastern corner of the nation and plunged straight ahead for the Rhine.

"Machine guns cut them Frenchies down like a horse's tail flickin' away flies," Teeter capped the rumor, never bothering to give his source. "Only them flies don't get up to come back for another bite at the horse's ass. Three hundred thousand dead, wounded, or prisoners of war, I heared."

The men gave little credence to the rumors of an early defeat in the north until they were released from the cattle cars two days later at Rouen, their destination—four of their number already dead because they had not followed the sergeant's advice. They had each opened their own can of rations, saving what they didn't eat from one meal to the next. Before they finished the cans, they were eating rotten meat. They had become casualties of war before they had learned to drill.

In Rouen, the rumors took on substance.

The town teemed with wounded British and French

troops, refugees, fleeing south, reservists attempting to form up into units and service outfits that were providing the bare essentials to as many units as they could.

For the volunteers, there was another ominous sign. Stragglers from the Belgian army.

"Them krauts was smart, not 'tacking the French head-on like gentlemen," Teeter observed. "They snuck around through Belgium and now they got a free run at Paris from the north."

"Yes, and Belgium was neutral," Frank added.

Teeter laughed. "You learn somethin' fightin' Injuns, boy. You ain't neutral 'less the other side says you is. And Belgium ain't neutral no more. Kaiser Bill figured that for 'em."

Blake Langley Hunter stared around him as the group, still in their civilian clothes, marched through the village. Trucks loaded with dead bodies were headed off into the country. Other trucks with fresh troops were moving north.

In an aid tent, he saw men with bloody bandages on their heads. A quadruple amputee, his limbless torso lying on a cot, not even covered by a sheet, was screaming, begging to die.

The volunteers stared at him as they were marched to a shed where they spread straw and bedded down for the night.

In the morning they were issued uniforms and Blake succumbed to intense, albeit brief, despair.

What the hell was he doing here? he wondered. This was not his war. Where was the glory, the excitement in this? The town was practically deserted by the civilians. A few old men and women in black remained, hawking potatoes and beets, still caked in dirt, that they sold to the hungry soldiers at whatever price they could get. The only younger women he had seen were nurses.

There were a few exhausted women in costumes that reminded him of the Salvation Army in the States. Expressionless and as disinterested in men as reclusive nuns, they dispensed coffee and stale bread.

Then he looked over at his friend, Frank, who had his shoulders against the unpainted wall of the shed and was bracing his pad against his raised knees as he wrote.

"Loan me that pen and paper for a minute, will you, old chap?" Blake asked.

"Going to write Brooke?" Frank asked.

Blake winked as if his friend had guessed correctly. He moved to a corner where he had a little privacy, starting his letter with the address of the U.S. Embassy in Paris.

Dear Father:

It appears my talents are going to be wasted in the infantry. Any farm lad can carry a rifle. So I'm going to break my vow never to ask you to use your influence. I think I owe it to France to request your intervention. Please, expedite my transfer to the *Service Aéronautique*. There I will not be required to take weeks of training. I can be in combat almost immediately. With my knowledge of flying, I shall serve France and ultimately our own country better by using my abilities to the utmost, regardless of the terrible dangers of the air service.

Your devoted son,
Blake

5

Rumors, not the highly censored news, struck fear at the soul of Paris. Cafés emptied. Tourists— Brooke Madigan's parents among them—fled the country. Food supplies became scarce as the military commandeered all the means of transportation.

The Madigans had left, vehemently protesting their daughter's decision to stay behind, but except by using force they had no way of changing her mind. Her only concession was moving in with Allison Hunter at the American Embassy.

From there she watched troops marching to the railroad station and heard the streets rumbling with wheels of caissons and trucks. The beauty seemed to be draining from Paris, like blood from a hidden wound, and Brooke had stood at the window, near tears, wondering like everyone else what was happening. Although the French high command offered no explanation, the truth was slowly emerging. Germans were battling their way through Belgium and wheeling in around the French lines, heading south toward Paris.

Allison's voice jerked her out of her maudlin reverie. She was running up the stairs calling Brooke's name. "Brooke, Brooke, for heaven's sake, where are you? We're going to war!"

Brooke swung around from the window and watched her wild friend burst into the room they shared.

"Hurry, pack, just enough for overnight." Allison dived into the walk-in closet and emerged with a suitcase which she threw open on the bed. "Hurry, or we'll miss the fun."

"What on earth are you talking about?"

"The war, silly. The French are rushing men to the north; they're using every means of transport they can get, hundreds of taxicabs." She was opening drawers, scooping out clothes, and tossing them into the suitcase. Brooke found her own suitcase. As she listened, she packed. If they were going to flee Paris, there were many items she would not abandon. "Can you imagine, an army going to war in taxicabs? And we're going to drive troops, too. Imagine, us. Driving into a battle, a real life-and-death battle."

Brooke stopped what she was doing. "We're going to drive taxicabs?"

"No, no, no." Allison was in the bathroom grabbing up her toilet articles to carry them to the suitcase. "I've volunteered Blake's car—he left it for me since he had rented it by the month—and the chauffeur has been inducted and they need people who can drive the troops north and bring the vehicles back, and I've volunteered. For you, too. Father's car, it's here at the embassy. He'll simply die, of course, using an embassy car to transport troops when we're supposed to be neutral, but that's why it has to be you. You're not embassy staff. Do you see?"

"Not at all."

"I'll explain on the way . . . well, in the car . . . I don't know. Just hurry. My car is on the street and they'll be loading in three or four soldiers any minute."

"Allison, this is insane! Your father and mother won't allow it."

Allison snapped her suitcase shut, touched her fingers to her lips and threw a kiss of exuberance to the window. "Ooh la la, that's the beautiful part. All the French cabinet ministers and their deputies have fled Paris. Father and mother have gone with them to Bordeaux to serve as American liaison or something. They're not here to stop us. They think we're headed for Marseilles where we'll be safe. But we'll think up some fantastic story, I love making up stories. We were escaping Paris, running for our very lives."

Brooke wasn't fast enough for Allison's taste, and Allison finished packing for her, tossed her a coat, and steered her to the door.

"Oh, Allison, I can't."

"Don't be a 'fraidy cat. The government isn't going to let all those taxicab drivers get hurt. And if anybody asks, you're a nurse."

They were on the stairs, heading toward the exit.

The foyer that had so recently served as a ballroom was clogged with Americans, seeking help in their rush from Paris.

"I had to say we were nurses or they wouldn't let women drive. You do drive, don't you?"

"A little."

"Good. Just follow me."

"No, Allison, I can't do this. My mother would die."

"Your mother? The former war correspondent? And think of all those men. Paris is becoming a nunnery. The front line's where the boys are. Maybe you'll see Blake. That's worth a trip in itself, isn't it?"

"They can't be in the battle yet. They're still in training."

"Well, they will be soon and we'll find them. I have a diplomatic passport. It opens all kinds of doors. And you'll be seeing Blake in his uniform again. Tell me that's not more fun than sitting here in the old folks' home they call Paris."

"Perhaps we'll see Frank, too," Brooke remarked.

"Who? That DeWitt boy with his silly writing?"

"It's not silly."

"How do you know? You've never read anything he wrote."

"I received a letter this morning."

"From Frank?"

"Yes."

"I thought you were sweet on Blake."

"It was just a letter."

They reached the exit where an American marine politely opened the door to the Hunter car. Brooke slid into the driver's seat, struggled with the controls briefly before moving from the embassy in jerks and starts, carrying Allison a half block to her brother's car.

The street was jammed. Taxicabs, trucks and horse-drawn carts loaded with troops and their gear were moving in a steady stream north, using all available lanes. In minutes, Frenchmen, chattering so fast Brooke could not understand them, were putting their gear in the square trunk or tying it to the running boards. They squeezed in beside her and into the rear seat, their rifles held between their legs.

A sergeant along the curb motioned her into the flow of traffic, and she joined the writhing snake of vehicles that moved slowly from the city into the country. Military and civilian police all along the route saw to it that each driver closed up the distance behind the vehicle ahead.

The fact that Allison's car was just ahead was Brooke Madigan's only comfort as the men in the car with her broke out bottles of wine and cognac. They drank themselves into shouting, laughing, singing jags, and they said awful things about her in French, assuming she didn't speak their language. But she forgave them.

They were frightened. Big strong men with rifles between their knees. And although they were as frightened as she, they weren't allowed to show it.

She hid her fear too. Mustering every bit of control she had, she clutched the wheel, concentrated on the driving, and didn't flinch when she heard the first thunder rumble through the cloudless afternoon sky. The men fell silent and she realized the truth. It wasn't thunder; it was artillery.

The war was within hearing distance.

She wanted to turn back. Probably the men did,

too. But there was Allison's car ahead, a taxi behind her, other vehicles occupying the second lane. The only people going south had to limp along on foot through the ditches between the road and the trees. On one side were the walking wounded. Every mile or so she saw men who had given up, sitting in exhausted defeat, or lying on their backs, contemplating the sky.

Brooke saw three men facedown, apparently unable to go farther. Their wounds must have been more serious than the doctors at the front had thought.

Or . . .

Or they were men the doctors along the line knew didn't stand a chance.

On the other side of the road were the refugees fleeing the rolling wave of fire that must be coming up behind them. Old men, women and children. All carrying pieces of luggage or things tied in blankets. Some pushed baby carriages loaded with their belongings. Old men served as horses to pull two-wheeled carts loaded with furniture and family treasures.

All the refugees were leaning forward as if a strong wind was making their flight more difficult, as though they had not already been tormented enough.

Maybe there weren't enough doctors. Maybe the Germans could wound more men than the doctors could mend and patch.

It was an ugly new world she had entered. Brooke was annoyed that her life had been disrupted. Who was it who had turned the road through the hedgerows into a mire of horror? Only something evil would defile this lovely countryside.

As she drove on, her passengers quieted. They could see the smoke of the battle in the distance, could distinguish the individual bursts of the shells—more frightening than the general rumble of war because each explosion made the listener think. What if he had been crouched where that shell had landed, or that one, or the one that roared like a man-eating beast caged in an echo chamber. . .?

By nightfall the column stopped and the men were called out.

They went reluctantly, their officers cursing them to form into proper ranks. And here the smell of war was added to the sight of bursting shells flaming in the darkness and the crackle of rifle and machine gun fire.

Still behind the wheel of the car, Brooke was stunned by the sudden horror that had splashed across her watercolor life. The round of parties she had known in Paris, studying the art of the old masters, reading poetry that spoke of daffodils and newly mown hay . . . it suddenly had no reality for her. *This* was real. Death and pain.

War had sobered her with the speed with which it could extinguish a life. Her mind absorbed the myriad of new sights, sounds and odors that had yanked her from youthful carelessness.

In a dazed state, she was not aware when her friend appeared and opened the car door.

"We'll be going home now," Allison said. "A circuitous route, they tell me, awful roads, but don't be afraid. Just follow the lights ahead."

"I want to stay," Brooke said, still staring at the sights around her.

"You want to what?"

Brooke could not explain. Perhaps Franklin would soon be out there where the bombs were bursting. So would Blake. She couldn't return to the safety of Paris. She wanted to stay near as she could to him . . . them . . . she wasn't sure which one was the magnet that kept her here.

"We could be nurse's aides or cooks. Surely they could use us somewhere."

"I suppose. I mean they haven't time to chase people off who want to help. But that's crazier than what I talked you into earlier."

"Go home without me, Allison," Brooke said, hearing her words as if they were spoken from far, far away—soft and muffled, intelligible only when you listened carefully. And how could anyone do that with the roar ahead?

"Well, we can't stay here, but a few miles east there's a place they call a staging area," Allison was saying. "They told us about it in case we got lost. We'll drive there and then decide."

"I've already decided," Brook said decisively. "I want to stay near the front. Do what I can."

"All right," Allison laughed. "All right. I'm game for anything."

She ran to her car and climbed in as a Frenchman screamed obscenities her way for holding up the column. With the motor running again, she headed east, continuing in that direction when the rest of the voided caravan had turned south for Paris.

Behind her Brooke Madigan drove cautiously over potholed roads, her attention constantly drawn toward the battle. It seemed to be getting closer.

She was terrified yet resolved.

It must have been what her mother felt in Cuba, what men felt in every war.

Terror . . . titillating, exciting terror.

6

WITH THE SOUND OF BUGLE calls, the legionnaires
awoke scratching, their bodies covered with
red welts left by hungry lice. They were called
from their huts and directed to the makeshift quartermaster warehouse converted from a barn. It was
there the problem of language first caused confusion.
Most of the American enlistees spoke French quite
well, especially the college-educated boys. Many of
them had a reverence for Paris and everything French.
They considered Paris the cultural center of the
world; everywhere else, including home, was insular and uncultured. They had written home so much
about how life in France had altered them, implying
that it had made them intellectually superior, that
their glowing words about their adopted homeland

had painted them into a corner. Enlisting to save their beloved France was a must.

There were other Americans, however, including Mulligan, the second-rate prizefighter, and the Gopher Gang, who knew only a few words of French. They followed the others or asked for translations while they struggled to learn. No one knew or could learn how or why they had come to Europe in the first place. The braggart, Bulldog Teeter, who quickly picked up the nickname of "Cowboy," spoke a passable combination of several languages, all apparently learned in the streets or the back country and all flavored with a languid southern drawl.

At the quartermaster's, each drew a heavy blue greatcoat, coarse white duck fatigue uniforms, a red *kepi*, laced field shoes, wool shirts, a blue sash nine feet long, a second blanket and long underwear.

They were issued a Model 1868 Lebel, a ninepound bolt-action rifle that held eight 8mm bullets. With a long thin bayonet attached, the weapon became an unwieldy six feet in length. A scabbard for the bayonet and two large leather cartridge boxes went with the rifle.

"Hey," Blake Hunter objected as he accepted the issue of clothing. "What about socks?"

The French supply clerk laughed and tossed him small squares of cheap muslin.

"Next you'll be wanting a necktie," the clerk ribbed him.

Hunter thought his French had been misunderstood, but in the barracks later, Frank showed him how the muslin could be positioned on the foot, the pieces overlapping, and held in place while the hobnailed shoes were slipped on.

"How disgustingly primitive," Blake sniffed.

His friend took the makeshift socks less seriously. "On the contrary. This way, one size fits all."

More supplies were piled on them later. Mess gear, twenty pieces of hardtack, and two cans of "monkey meat" for a grand total of one hundred and twenty pounds they were expected to carry on their backs.

Once outfitted, they began training. They were assigned to officers who were nothing less than martinets, thinking more in terms of discipline than actual fighting ability. For hours they practiced close-order drill before advancing to the rifle range where they were grudgingly given a few rounds with which to punch holes in targets at three hundred yards.

Bayonet drill was cheaper, and they spent days driving at bales of hay, the corporals concentrating on the volume of the gutteral grunt they gave when they pierced the straw body of the imaginary enemy.

Blake quickly became a student-corporal, amid rumors he had bribed a sergeant for the exalted position from which he lorded his authority over the lesser trainees.

"He gets four cents a day instead of one like the rest of us," Frank grumbled in the barracks after a particularly grueling day in the rain.

"He ain't worth it," one of the Gopher Gang snorted.

On the field maneuvers Frank moved up, too, from nothing to *éclaireur de marche,* one of the two scouts who went ahead of the seventeen-man squad to draw fire first so the enemy would be forced to give warning before the entire body became exposed.

With each day, the men were more convinced that

war itself was preferable to the boredom of training and endless marches.

Frank was the first to go before the *sous lieutenant* and claim he was ready and fit for front-line duty. Blake followed when DeWitt was denied his request for action, but he fared no better.

It was Teeter, returning from a gambling session in an adjacent barracks, who brought rumors that promised respite from the grueling boredom.

"There's a savvy Yank over there who says them krauts is within twenty miles of Paris, and the Frenchies can't get men trained fast enough to hold the line. So the regiment's sendin' a battalion of us tanglefoots to the front. Five hundred regulars and five hundred of us with previous fightin' experience."

"Are you going?" Frank asked.

"You can bet your balls on it. I ain't wearin' out my feet trainin' when I could be on the line shootin'."

"Then so am I," Frank said. He had been sitting on the straw mat of his bed, and he rose with determination.

"But you have no military experience," Blake Hunter objected.

"Two years with the Salvation Army," Frank joked.

Teeter roared, "Hot shit! If that don't beat all. Two years with the Salvation Army!"

"It'll never work." Blake had jumped up and trailed DeWitt through the exit.

"Worth a try," his friend responded as they stepped into the line where several hundred men were signing up for the battalion moving north.

"Name?" the sergeant at a card table asked in French.

"Franklin DeWitt, U.S. citizen."

"Previous experience?"

"Two years, U.S. Army, salvation group."

The sergeant blinked, scribbled the name and spoke as he wrote. "Get your gear. Form up in one hour. Next."

Frank grinned. "Do me a favor, Blake, and write Brooke Madigan for me. Tell her I'm going into action. Tell her . . . tell her I think I love her. I'll write when I have a chance."

Blake Hunter grinned uncertainly. Love? Was he kidding? No, Frank wasn't the type to joke about something like that. Love . . . which Blake had never really felt, for all his success with women. And another thing . . . Franklin was going into battle first. The weaker of the two was going into action. What would the girls think?

"Next," the sergeant said again.

"Frank, this is insane. You'll ruin your chance at the air branch. They're not going to pull you off the front line."

"I think you're wrong."

"Next." The Frenchman was impatient. So were the men behind the two Americans.

"Damn," Blake sighed.

"Name?" the sergeant asked.

"Blake Langley Hunter," he said, his mind torn in two different directions. "Previous military experience, reserve officer training corps service, one year."

"Get your gear. Form up in an hour. Next."

"Great!" Frank exclaimed. "We're going together." He ran toward the barracks, Blake Hunter following more slowly, cursing his decision. But he couldn't let Frank go alone—the would-be writer needed him, he told himself, needed his strength.

Then his spirits rose. He would write to Brooke Madigan—omitting Frank's message, of course. He'd write Allison and his parents, too. His friends back home.

Blake Langley Hunter was doing it again, something exciting, dramatic, shocking.

He sprinted to the barracks, gathered his gear and joined Teeter and DeWitt as they fell into formation.

A thousand strong, they marched off, the regimental flag fluttering in the noonday sun. They sang as they marched for the trains.

> *Nous sommes soldats de la Légion,*
> *La Légion étrangère;*
> *N'ayant pas de patrie,*
> *La France est notre mère!*

Again they were in the crowded cattle cars, moving north to Mailly-le-Camp, the staging ground behind the front lines. It stretched for thousands of acres over rolling hills where sparse patches of scrub pines were the only vegetation.

Disembarking, the volunteers inched closer to the battle. Here the station windows were shattered and the siding pocked with shrapnel scars. There were jagged holes in other buildings and roofs caved in. A pile of charcoaled wood was all that remained of several houses.

Amid the rubble, like tombstones in a graveyard, trees stood stark and denuded or jabbed blackened, erose stumps toward the sky.

Quarters were even more primitive than before and their bodies crawled with "Monsieur Toto." Stripped to the waist, they sat like monkeys, picking the lice off each others' backs. Within days they began the fifty-mile march to the current front, their leg and neck muscles cramping, their feet blistered and raw. To drop out was to confront an officer on horseback, a gun in his hand, ready to kill if a man failed to rejoin his squad. On the last night, they flopped in an eighteenth-century Benedictine abbey.

Deep in the cellar bottles of wine were discovered, and the night was a cacophony of shell bursts a thousand yards away, drunken singing, insane laughter, and squabbles that came close to duels. In the morning they moved again to a point where they could clearly hear the popping of rifles as well as the thump of artillery. They slogged through mud that stuck like glue, mud that sucked their shoes off, mud that smelled of death and excrement. Still closer to the battle, in a position from which they could see the geysers of dirt and rubble tossed skyward by intermittent shellings, they waited for darkness.

When the sun set, they moved through a cemetery of trees. Passing them in the other direction were slumped black shadows, unspeaking, like black wraiths scudding across the moon. Then the legionnaires were at the main line itself, and Blake Hunter, a man who was as punctilious as he was pampered, for all the excitement he had tried to put in his life, slipped into a shallow rifle pit, his long rifle pointing into the darkness, not knowing what to expect or what to do.

"Blake, that you?" DeWitt asked from the next pit over.

"Yes."

"Keep your voices down," a sergeant ordered.

But Bulldog Teeter spoke from a few yards to the left. "Bulldog over here. The sons-of-bitches before us sure as hell didn't leave doodly shit for cover, did they? I'd feel safer circlin' three wagons against a thousand redskins than seeing the sun come up with me in this pisshole."

"Mulligan over here," the prizefighter said from beyond Teeter. "Them Gophers is just past me. Huddled together like fighters in a clinch. Don't think they feel so tough anymore."

"There's a crude ditch running off to my left. Must connect us, Blake," Franklin added.

Hunter scratched at the lice eating at his skin, and called softly to the sergeant: Would it be okay to scout a few yards to his front before dawn? he asked.

The sergeant grunted and Blake crawled cautiously over the packed mud that formed a low parapet in front of his rifle pit.

"Hunter, be careful." Franklin DeWitt whispered.

"Man got to be loco as a rabid coyote to go out there tonight," Teeter remarked.

But Hunter laughed and crawled a few yards forward. Cautiously he swept his hand ahead of him, pausing frequently to listen. He heard a rustle to his front and froze. The sound came again, closer, and he moved his rifle to his shoulder, trying to follow the sound with the barrel.

Then the sound stopped and he waited in the silence, his heart pounding in his chest.

Suddenly the sound seemed right on top of him and he lunged at it, driving the bayonet into the dirt. Whatever it was scampered off; a rat, a fox, he had no idea what it was. But it wasn't a man.

He had reacted like the rookie he was, and when

he heard the men calling from behind him, he was overwhelmed with embarrassment.

"Blake, you all right? Blake?"

He didn't answer. He lay where he was, staring at the clouds. The slightest motion and he might attract the attention of the Germans somewhere in the darkness.

He lay there for hours before he slowly worked his way back.

"Hold your fire, men," he said as he approached his friends. "It's me, Hunter."

Sliding into his slit trench, he pressed himself against the forward wall and drew his shoulders in as if he were trying to assume the fetal position. His hands were shaking. He was cold and miserable and his teeth chattered.

"Blake?" DeWitt's voice was only inches away and Hunter opened his eyes to see his friend creeping into his pit from along the ditch that connected them. "You all right?"

Blake laughed. "Hell, yes. I'm great."

"We heard a noise, then silence. I thought—"

"I got myself a hun," Blake lied.

"Killed him?" DeWitt was awed.

"Not likely," Blake said. "He was coming up behind me, thinking he had me. Must have been on patrol."

"But there was no shot."

"Bayonet," Blake told him. "I wasn't going to draw the wrath of hell by taking a shot there in the dark. Bayonet's not such a sure thing as a bullet, but I also had to consider what would happen if I missed. I might have hit one of my own men, shooting toward our lines. So I took off the bayonet and jammed the dirty kraut."

"But we didn't hear no yelp," Teeter said, crawling closer. "Generally you knife a man an' he'll beller like a bear cub with a thorn in his paw."

"Smart bastard, I'd say. He knew he'd get it again if he called out. Rolled away soon as I jabbed him. I couldn't find him to finish the job, but unless I miss my guess, he's out of the war for a while."

"You're the first of us to get a kraut," DeWitt marveled.

"Well, enough of that. You boys get some sleep. I'll keep my ears open, so don't you worry."

"Bulldog Teeter worry?" Teeter croaked. "Buffalo shit. I can remember nights back in the badlands, Injuns skunk-drunk on that rotgut whiskey them agents sold the poor sons-of-bitches. Crazy out of their minds, crawling around the leavings of my camp fire, trying to cut my throat so's they could get my guns and sell them for more firewater. Slept like a baby, I did. Crawled off a few yards, snuggled up in my bed roll like it was Mabel Norman sacked in with me. Every time those red bastards got close enough, I come half awake, made a rattlin' sound like a snake and send them Injuns skitterin' away faster'n a scorpion durin' matin' season."

"Oh, come on now, Teeter. You can't expect us to believe all that," Blake said skeptically.

"Don't give a horse fart if'n you believe me or not, dude. You just watch my dust, come mornin'. I won't be just stickin' pins in those sons-of-bitches that started this war. I'll be blastin' their balls off like they was balloons in a carnival dart game."

"Okay, Teeter, show us in the morning," Blake suggested. "You're liable to get more chances than you want to prove you're a latter-day Wyatt Earp, but get some sleep while I'm still in the mood to stand guard."

"Thanks, Blake," DeWitt said sincerely.

"For what?"

"For scaring off that German. He might have been headed right for my pit. I would never have heard him."

Blake laughed. "Think nothing of it, chum. Just put me in your book."

"I will, Blake. I surely will."

Then Blake Hunter was alone again, staring into the darkness of his pit.

Why had he lied? he wondered.

He had never found it necessary to boast before. His exploits had spoken for themselves. He had taught himself to fly, using a pusher, then a hydroplane, and he'd flown under bridges, barrel-rolled at a hundred feet up, raced cars, swum in shark-infested water. Done a hundred things more dangerous than crawling a few yards into the night.

So why had he lied?

He stared out into the darkness and he knew.

7

I T WAS a gray dawn, days later, when Franklin
DeWitt awoke with a start. Jolted from a dream,
he grabbed his rifle and looked wildly around, his
finger on the trigger.

There was nothing to see. No movement to the
front and around him only the voices speaking in
French and English as the legionnaires awoke to another day on the line.

Overhead, German and French observation planes
passed one another, the men in the rear seats taking
pot shots at each other with rifles. The French pilots
were equipped with revolvers or .30-30 Winchester
carbines which had been designed for fighting Indians
in the American west.

On the ground, the Gopher Gang boys lay on their
backs and fired a few rounds at the German aircraft,

enjoying the sport until a handful of six-inch steel darts were tossed from the cockpit.

The rain of *fléchettes,* as the French called them, jabbed harmlessly into the dirt, but a few came close enough to the infantrymen to make them hunch their shoulders, as if trying to shield their entire bodies beneath their helmets.

The darts had taken the sport out of sniping at the aircraft.

That's where I should be, Franklin thought, with the eagles instead of the moles.

Blake Hunter spoke to him from the next rifle pit. "Did you hear they're going to put machine guns on the airplanes?"

Franklin was dubious. "How?"

"Mount them on the top of the Nieuport wings. Or maybe put them directly in front of the pilot and fire through the propeller."

"The prop wouldn't last long that way."

"I heard they're going to try covering part of the prop with metal that would deflect any stray bullets. I don't think it will work. If enough bullets hit the prop, even if it's shielded, they'd put it off balance and it'd tear the engine apart. But think of it, fighting in the air. Wouldn't that be something? God, I'd like to be up there. I'll bet I could fly circles around those dumb krauts."

Franklin thought of the potential of air battles— what great stuff for the book. He dug out the pad of paper he kept against the skin of his belly.

Until now he had been too frightened to write, even though their section was awesomely quiet. The rain of darts had been the closest his squad had come to danger since they moved into their position. But he could hear the sounds of battle on either side of the entrenchments, which they improved daily. And Teeter was ready with the rumor that the war was going badly for the French. The Germans still threatened Paris and had already crushed the Russian's entire second army. They were creating an aura of invincibility for themselves.

But here the war was a waiting game, so he rested the pad on his knee and brushed away specks of mud from the cover. He flipped to a clean page and began writing about Blake Hunter's first night on the line and his fearless probe into the darkness. The incident was one Franklin did not want to forget.

His typewriter was stored back at the staging area and there was no longer any dry, safe place to keep his precious notes. He would send them back to Brooke Madigan to save for him. He would tell her she could read them if she wanted. So far the notes would only make her think more highly of Blake, but they were a fair accounting. Hunter deserved respect for his performance at the training camp and on their first night at the front.

Franklin did not begrudge his friend recognition. He only hoped he would soon do something equally impressive.

With the last sentence written, he leaned back, his eyes staring at the sky now bright with the full glow of the sun. A bird flew along the lines, dipping and rising, scanning for tidbits of food dropped by the men huddling in the pits.

Franklin was hungry and he turned toward Blake's pit, hoping Hunter or Teeter would know when the food would be brought up. He spotted the Gopher Gang members just beyond Teeter. The New York legionnaires, as green at soldiering as Frank himself, were stretching their cramped bones and standing on their tiptoes, trying to see down into the valley and the German lines beyond.

His curiosity was aroused when they climbed part way from the pit, intending to take a better look at what lay before them. Until now they had been as cautious as he.

Franklin stuck his own head up, glimpsing the scarred but peaceful land that sloped away before them.

He heard it. Three sounds reached his ears almost simultaneously. The crack of what he believed was a German 77 artillery piece, the scream of the 25-pound shell streaking across the valley, and then the shattering explosion in the midst of the five curious men.

He was down, moving instinctively, at the first warning crack. Shrapnel cut the air where his head had been. His face was between his knees and he thought he let out a cry like that of a frightened child.

Men yelled in pain and he drew himself from his protected position to go running along the shallow, twisting ditch. He reached Blake's pit and crawled through, unaware of what his friend was doing. Another shell exploded, then another, and another.

The peaceful morning had been blasted away in the deadly roar of warfare.

Teeter was ahead of him, exposing himself briefly where the ditch was not quite deep enough. A few feet farther and they found five mangled bodies lying twisted and torn. Three were gaping with the startled look of the dead. The other two were bleeding profusely, their limbs broken and folded back on themselves.

"Get this one first," Teeter shouted, grabbing the shoulders of the least shattered of the living.

Franklin obeyed, took up the legs, leaving the shoulders to Teeter, and started carrying the screaming man through the maze of trenches, pits, and shellholes. The shells continued dropping dangerously close to the two Americans with their wounded burden. More than once they dived for shelter, protecting the Gopher as best they could as they continued to carry him deeper and deeper into the rear area. In his headlong dash to the *poste de secours,* Franklin was not aware of the stretcher-carriers running toward them until they were taking the wounded man from his grip.

"Come on, city slicker," Teeter was shouting. "Got to get that other son-of-a-bitch. Stuck his head up just like a red flag in front of a bull, the stupid ass."

Franklin pivoted and reared back. The line of rifle pits and shallow trenches they had just come through was like a lake with heavy raindrops pelting every inch, but spattering mud and pieces of men instead of water from the surface.

"My God!" he said aloud. Had he run through that? But he must have.

"Come on," Teeter was bellowing, "got the other one to get out."

The Cowboy hadn't stopped; he had partially given up the flimsy protection of the ditches. He leaped a trench, sprinted across the flat surface, dove into a pit when a shell came whistling in, and then re-emerged above ground again for another bolt across the open.

It didn't make sense at first. What the hell were they going back for? One wounded man. Through the smoke and the dirt-laden air, Franklin could see fresh bodies tossed out of the pathetic defense works the previous unit had left them. There must be dozens of wounded now, countless dead.

So what were they going back for? he asked himself as he raced across open ground, cutting back and forth, hoping to dodge the incoming shells and still catch up with Teeter.

Why? he wanted to know. He was risking his life for what?

"Down here." A hand reached up from the ground and grabbed DeWitt's leg. He tumbled into the pit where Teeter was struggling to pull the second wounded Gopher from under the corpses.

Frank bent down, saw the wounded man's mouth open in a terrified scream, not from the pain of his wounds, but the claustrophobia of being pinned beneath the dead. When he was freed, he bit his lip and groaned while the other two Americans carried him among the deafening explosions surrounding them. Shrapnel cut at DeWitt's sleeve and Cowboy's helmet was knocked from his head. Still alive several hundred yards and a miracle later, they were out of the worst of it.

When they were finally beyond the barrage and aid men took charge of the second wounded man, the two collapsed. Teeter dropped on his back, stared at the sky and gasped for air. Frank hunched over, the pains in his chest unbearable. He couldn't breathe.

It was long minutes before he became aware that other men were emerging from the trenches. Alone or in pairs, they were bringing out the wounded. Some of the rescuers went down in the flame and smoke of the explosions, their human burden lost with them.

And Frank finally understood Teeter's primitive code.

The two wounded they had carried out were theirs. Their responsibility. They had been closest.

Others were somebody else's worry.

With a new respect, DeWitt looked at the crude, lying westerner. He was sitting up, retrieving his helmet, then slowly standing erect. The shelling had stopped.

The smoke was clearing like morning mist nudged along by an incoming breeze. The dirt was settling to the earth, its disruption over for now. And the valley between the opposing armies became calm again.

The sun was warm, the sky clear.

A stunned man walked by, stumbling over the wounded and dead, until an aid man caught his arm and directed him toward one of the ambulances that were now backing up to the aid station like trucks backing against a dock to collect their cargo for the day's run.

"First blood," Teeter said.

Franklin frowned. "What?"

"Your arm."

Franklin raised his upper right arm where he could see it. A sticky red goo was smeared on his uniform, mixed with the mud. Alarmed, he clutched the muscles with his left hand, searching for the wound.

"Relax, boy." Teeter inhaled deeply and exhaled. "Ain't your blood. You'll get to know yours from the others."

"How?" Frank took his hand away and studied the mess in his left palm.

"Your own always looks more important. You'll get to know." Teeter swung around, spotting something that interested him at the edge of a woods on the reverse slope of the hill. "You hungry, dude?" he asked.

"Yes."

"Sit a spell. I'll get us some grub, better'n the shit we'll be gettin' in the trenches."

"How?" Franklin asked.

But Teeter was gone, swinging onto the running board of an ambulance and riding along the road that led past the woods. Twenty minutes later he returned, bearing two new mess kits steaming with hot stew and an empty beer bottle that was black with warm coffee.

He passed a kit across to his friend and sat on the ground, his legs crossed under him, grabbing the hot meat with his dirty fingers and pushing pieces into his mouth. The gravy he drank like soup.

Franklin settled beside him, eating hungrily, unconcerned with where it had come from until he had finished and was sipping coffee from the bottle.

"Where'd you get that?" he asked. "That's the first good-tasting food I've had since I signed up."

Teeter wiped the empty bowl-shaped tin of the mess kit with the elbow of his uniform. "Officer grub," he said.

"But how did you get—"

The Cowboy laughed. "Scroungin', boy! Scroungin'."

"What's scrounging?"

"Ain't you never heard of a scrounger, pencil-pusher? Jesus, scroungin's more important than shootin' in any man's war. I swear, boy, sometimes I don't think you even served in that there Salvation Army. No matter—I do the scroungin', you do the thinkin'."

"Whatever you say." Frank stood and looked across the shelled area where teams were gathering the dead.

He had been under fire.

It seemed incomprehensible. The shelling had started so quickly. War had been nothing but boredom during their first days on the line. Boredom mixed with a slowly waning fear. Then he had heard the scream of shells and saw men—men he knew—blasted apart, limbs severed from the torsos, arms and legs broken. In a second the Gopher Gang had been erased from the roster. How could it happen so quickly?

He had at last seen war, and he had been engulfed in abject terror, yet he had functioned, carrying the wounded to the rear. How had he been capable of thinking or acting under such a threat to his very being? He didn't know.

Thank God for Teeter. The squad considered him nothing more than a bald-faced liar, yet he had been the stimulus that had made Franklin act like a man under fire.

"We'd better get back," he said. "The shelling might signal an attack."

"Naw, they'd've been on us by now. Krauts ain't damned fools. Best way to attack is right behind the fuckin' artillery barrage. Besides, that fancy friend of yours got himself a visitor and I promised to take him to Hunter."

A slightly older version of Blake Hunter climbed from an ambulance and came forward to meet them.

He spoke to Teeter first. "You the one who said you could take me to Blake Hunter?"

"Yep. Just follow my ass, mister. If I throw it in a hole, don't wait to hear the shell. Just toss yours in after mine."

"You're Duncan Hunter," Franklin said as they started back toward the trenches.

"Yes. You know Blake?" the ambulance driver asked. His hair was lighter than his brother's, but he was lean and tall, too, a couple of years older than Blake, and more serious. He wore a mustache and had the same hazel eyes as Blake.

"Franklin DeWitt. Yes, I know your brother." The two shook hands and followed the Cowboy along the ditches, many of which where half-filled with dirt and debris now, providing even less protection than they had before. "I heard you were coming up from Monaco to drive an ambulance. This your first show?"

Duncan Hunter shook his head. "They had me on the line days after I signed on. Actually, I'm on a waiting list to get in the air service."

"Join the crowd. Three of us here are waiting, too. Your brother is especially anxious."

"I can imagine he is. Looks like you boys got a little wake-up call from the German alarm clock this morning. I hope Blake's okay."

Teeter suddenly leaped for a shell hole, landing flat on his belly, face down. Hunter and DeWitt followed him like links in a chain. An explosion hurtled chunks of metal just above their heads. Another dozen shells landed around them. None of the three moved for a while after the shelling ceased.

Bulldog was up first, peering about cautiously, then climbing out with no more concern than he would feel rising from his bed in the morning back home. But Franklin DeWitt felt chilled. He had not even heard the incoming shell until it burst five yards away. If he had not followed Teeter's example and plunged into shelter without questioning, he would have been dead.

Duncan Hunter was as unconcerned as the Cowboy. Closer to the main line, though, they stuck to the ditches, crawling when necessary to keep below the protective dirt until all three tried to squeeze into the cramped pit where Blake sat with his rifle between his knees, his eyes fixed straight ahead.

He emerged from his trance with a smile.

"Duncan, you old son-of-a-bitch!" he said exuberantly, clutching his brother around the shoulders in a bear hug, then pushing him back so he could see his face. "How did you ever find me?"

"I just asked the French where I'd find *les sommolviches.*"

"The what?"

"The sons-of-bitches. Apparently you guys use the expression so often, the French think it's a synonym for American."

"Them fuckin' sons-of-bitches," Teeter groused. "Them frog bastards swear every fuckin' bit as much as we do."

"Anyway, you're here!" Blake grinned. "You should have arrived a few minutes ago. Really something, wasn't it, boys? I had to run clear across the front of our troop, keeping the boys down. First time under fire. Only natural some of them panicked." He paused and scowled at his friends. "What happened to you two? Get rabbit fever?"

Frank started to object, but Teeter spoke for both of them. "Damned right. The dude here and I took off like jackrabbits the minute we heard the first shell comin' in. Found us a nice safe place on the hind side of the hill and sat out the killin'. Had us a hot meal, too, didn't we, dude?"

"Yes, yeah, that's right," Franklin slowly agreed. "We hightailed it first thing."

"Well, you boys sit 'round and gossip," Teeter said. "I'm going back to my own hole and dig her clear down to China. The Jerries start shellin' us again, I'm gonna sit out the noise with my head on the lap of some cute slant-eyed geisha girl or whatever the hell they call 'em down there."

Teeter slithered on his belly to his own pit and from the way the dirt began flying over the edge, he meant what he'd said.

Bake gestured toward the Cowboy for his brother's edification. "Big talker. Runs with the first shells. No surprise, of course. But what about you, Franklin?"

DeWitt didn't answer. His mind was on Teeter. After all the big tales, the Cowboy had brushed off a heroic act as if it hadn't happened. There was no understanding the silenced raconteur.

He returned his attention to the two brothers, listening without comment while Blake extolled his own exploits during the shelling. The older brother said little.

For a minute, it sounded too heroic, running across the front of the line, saving men from themselves, but then another Yank crawled through the ditches.

He was a Southerner, red-haired, red-faced, with the big callused hands of a hill farmer.

"Wanna thank you, Hunter," he said. "Plumb lost mah head when them shells started booming. You all saved mah life, pushing mah backside down where it belonged."

"Forget it," Blake said magnanimously. "You weren't the only one who needed a little nudge."

"Yeah, well, you all can push mah head down anytime you want." The Southerner started to crawl away again, but he looked back, his eyes lighted as if he had an earth-shaking idea. "Why these Frenchies oughta make you an officer, Hunter. Anybody keeps cool in all that noise, that's officer material, I tell you. Real officer material."

"Thanks. Maybe they will," Blake replied.

"They sure better. Well, you come see us, you hear? Ain't but four or five pits away. Don't imagine I'll be goin' much of anywhere for a while."

"Sure, Johnny Reb, I'll be around. You need anything, you just call." Blake's expression was a model of modesty. He seemed anxious to change the subject away from himself. But before he returned to his brother, he frowned at Franklin. "I expected those hillbillies to head south as soon as the fighting started, but what happened to you, Franklin?"

"I—"

"You needn't have worried. I'd have taken care of you. Next time stick close to me. Okay?"

Franklin nodded.

"Duncan, God it's good to see you, although I think you're crazy. A married man in this mess."

"I'm just driving an ambulance," Duncan said apologetically. "I had to do something."

"Why?"

"Why? With you and Allison on the front lines?"

"Allison on the front lines?"

"Well, that's an exaggeration, but she's not far from here. She's staying at a chateau a few miles south of Cuiry-les-Chaudardes."

"The regimental rest area?"

"Yes."

"But that's not safe."

"You know Allison—where there's men, there's Allison. She was among the taxi drivers who rushed the troops to the front when things looked worse than they do now."

"But Cuiry-les-Chaudardes. So close. What a coincidence."

"No coincidence. When she decided to stay near the front, dad found out where you were and she drove up in your car. She heard you might be pulled off the line eventually for a few days' rest. So Allison took a job—volunteer, of course—translating for the French officers and medics. They were having difficulty communicating with the English-speaking wounded and the foreign correspondents stationed at the headquarters. The French were glad to have her, what with the legion on line all through here. There are other women in the field hospital and helping in a dozen other ways. They're all French of course."

"Allison came up alone?"

"There's another girl with her. She's helping, too."

"Brooke Madigan?" Franklin asked quickly.

"Yes, that tycoon's daughter. Crazy as Allison. You'll be seeing them when you get relief."

"If I'm still alive," Blake remarked. "But don't say

that to either one of them. Tell them I'm way behind the lines, safe and sound."

"They know better."

"Well, then give Allison a kiss for me. And tell the Madigan girl that I'll get this damned fool war over with soon so I can take her to dinner in Paris."

"You know her?"

"Know her?" Blake laughed. "Don't I know them all?"

His brother merely grunted.

"Well, you'd better get off the line, Duncan. No use in two Hunters risking their lives. Maybe I'll see you when I get relief. We're only supposed to be on the front four days, but I have a hunch these frogs will leave the legion up here forever and save their own men. Will I be able to find you if I ever do get off here for a few days?"

Duncan nodded. "The hospital's close to Cuiry, too." He started to stand and his brother pulled him down.

"Not that way, brother. So far this morning, Fritz has stuck to shelling, but it wouldn't surprise me a bit if he's got machine guns zeroed on every inch of this hill, just waiting for us to get careless."

"Okay. See you later, Blake. And be careful. You too, DeWitt."

Self-consciously, Franklin said, "Say hello to Brooke for me when you see her."

"You know her, too?"

"Vaguely," Blake answered for his friend. "Tell her he's doing fine up here. Shaping right up. I'll make a soldier out of him in no time."

Duncan Hunter crouched and disappeared toward the rear.

When he was gone, Blake rolled over on his belly and put his rifle on top of the parapet. "Don't worry, Franklin. Lots of guys break with the first barrage."

"But, I didn't—"

"Hey, you don't have to excuse yourself to me. This is old Blake, remember? Your buddy. I'm not going to tell anybody. Matter of fact, I'll write my father today, ask him to get you into the air arm, too. They probably won't let you fly, but you can be my mechanic. I'll tell the French you're a genius with tools. Doesn't matter anyway. Give me a plane and I'll figure a way to get it up in the air, so relax. The worst is over."

Franklin DeWitt tuned out his friend. His thoughts were far back of the line, with Brooke Madigan.

She was so close. He hoped she would see him when she met with Blake during their rest period. Of course, he probably did not stand a chance with her. Blake was too much competition, but Franklin wanted to see her again. He had felt more relaxed with her than he had with any girl he had ever known.

8

B LAKE WADDED the letter from his father into a
ball and pitched it out of the trench. It soared
out of sight over the mound of dirt which increased in size as the men spaded deeper into their
protective craters. They were preparing their battle-
front lodgings like burrowing animals that dig and
hoard before a hard winter. Logs and ammunition
crates had been laid along the bottom of the long,
narrow pits so that the men could sit and sleep above
the ever-present mud and water. Places to stand had
been cut along the leading edge of the trenches and
small firing holes had been bored through the dirt
mounded on the side facing the Germans.

The officers were somewhat more secure. They had
actual bunkers cut deep as caves and reinforced so

that shells would not collapse them except in cases of repeated direct hits.

All the troops had exercised their ingenuity, plotting the trenches in a zigzag fashion rather than a straight line. With that design the shrapnel from a shell would be confined to a few feet rather than slicing like a deadly scythe down an open corridor. Barbed wire was being brought up and patrols went out at night and placed a serpentine fence some twenty yards from the front line. Tin cans with stones inside were placed in the snarls of wire to act as alarms when the Germans probed closer. Night after night the jangling chorus increased as if a colony of tinny rattlesnakes was multiplying in the fence.

At the first rattling sound the legion combed the wire with rifle fire. In the mornings after such blind target practice a dead German or two sometimes lay in the wire. At first they were left where they fell. Then when the stench became unbearable, a white flag was raised and men from both sides went forward during daylight and buried the dead where they lay.

A passage through the wire was made every night the French legionnaires went forward on patrol, and the gap had to be mended upon return. The patrols became routine, each gleaning bits of information as to enemy positions which the artillery could use for spotting new targets.

Later both sides set up outposts beyond the wire. The poor bastards assigned to the forward listening positions had little chance of survival. Too often they gave their positions away during the day and the enemy shelled until the occupants of the forward positions were dead or forced to make a break for their trenches. Few made it.

The Germans employed more machine guns than the stubborn French high command permitted. Also, the Germans were willing to waste forty or fifty shots to bring down a man or two, while the legion was expected to make each bullet count.

Eventually, the outpost personnel occupied shell holes during the night, scarcely moved during the day and even played dead when observation aircraft flew over. The fatality rate dropped somewhat.

Both Blake and Franklin served on night patrols and in the forward listening posts, but their turns had proved uneventful. Other nights they had lain in their trenches listening as friends went exploring. If there was gun fire, it usually erupted into a full-scale battle with flares lighting the plain between the two forces and artillery or mortars used to drive off the patrols.

To Blake, watching from his trench, those night scenes might have been a childhood nightmare replayed, a nightmare taking place in some vague purgatory where silhouetted spirits played in the murky light. They would dart forward and stop and then dart forward again, and sometimes they disappeared in a boom and a sudden puff of smoke, as if Hecate had decided the playful wraiths should return to her underworld kingdom. At other times, between the occasional explosions of a shell or the crack of small arms fire, the night scene became a movie screen where the dreamlike action played itself in silent unreality.

Only a few who fell were carried back to safety.

Too many were left to suffer through the night and into the next day. On occasion, when the casualty was visible, one side or the other finished him off.

In Blake's area the job fell to Mulligan. No one suggested the prizefighter put the wounded out of their misery. He did it the first time, and whenever the problem arose after that the men stared at him until he did his unassigned duty.

Afterward all he would say was: "There." Then he would sit and look straight ahead for a while.

Occasionally one side would shell the other for ten or fifteen minutes, destroying trenches and killing a few of the enemy. Since the positions had been held for more than a month, hitting a particular point with accuracy was not difficult. The artillerymen had ranges to each point plotted and sighted in. The limiting factor was whether their officers would allot shells for the minimal gain achieved by intermittent shelling when other sectors were locked in bloody charges and counterattacks in which ammunition supply was a key factor. Also, the legionnaires as well as the Germans were stockpiling supplies, knowing that one of them would soon be ordered to strike hard at the other.

Blake resolutely pushed thoughts of the coming attack out of his mind. Until now, he had expected to be kiting around in the air long before orders came to charge across no-man's-land as an infantryman.

Today was quiet and the mail had come forward. For most it was an exciting moment, but the letters from Blake's mother, sister, Brooke Madigan, and several girls from home were stuffed unopened in his pocket. The only mail he wanted was the response from his father concerning his transfer to the air arm of the French forces. He had waited months for the letter.

His father had refused to intervene.

"Diplomatic ethics," Bill Hunter had written. The United States was neutral; he could take no stance in his son's role with one of the belligerents.

"Bull," Blake said aloud. His old man was afraid his youngest son would show him up again, make more of a name than anyone else in the family. Jealousy was something Blake could not accept.

"Blake," Franklin said, crossing the crude walkway they had built. "Get any mail?"

"A fistful." He patted his pocket, smiling. "The girls must have nothing to do except write letters."

"Allison?"

"And Brooke Madigan and girls you don't know. I'll never have time to answer them all. A war must bring out sentimentality in women. The letters ar. positively gushing. How about you?"

"I got a few." He dismissed the subject and went on to what was uppermost in his mind. "We're going over the top this noon, according to rumor," he said.

"Attack?" Blake took the second blow of the day as a personal affront.

Franklin looked grim. "They've spread the word to the officers. It's supposed to be a surprise attack. The boches will never expect us to attack at noon."

"Splendid," Blake said. "About time we saw some real action. Maybe they'll give us the relief they promised if we take a few yards for the general."

The sound of an engine drew their eyes upward and they saw a German observation plane flying parallel to the trenches, ignoring the puffs of anti-aircraft fire exploding around it in the cloudless sky. The ground troops watched it warily. The Germans had taken to dropping artillery shells on the trenches recently. Most of the shells had landed off target and failed to detonate, but now fins had been added which kept the nose pointed to the ground.

Having experimented on the front line troops, the aircraft had grown bolder and were bombing areas to the rear, beyond the range of accurate artillery fire. In defense, the groundhogs raised the barrels of their artillery pieces at the airborne intruders, using timed fuses for air bursts. So far they had scared the German flyers but had failed to knock any of them from the sky.

The plane reminded Franklin of something. "Oh, Bill Thaw got his transfer today."

"To the flying service?"

"Yes. He left this morning so he'll miss the attack."

They knew Thaw only vaguely, having shared no more with him than a common desire to get out of the infantry. Otherwise, he was a stranger.

"Damn!" Blake exploded. "Why the hell did he get his transfer instead of me? He must have paid some French officer on the side, or he had influence in high places. I'd make a better flyer than he would. That's where I belong." As soon as he had spoken, he regretted the selfish outburst. "I mean, I could do more good up there than I can here."

"Did you hear from your father?"

Blake sighed. "Never wrote him."

"But I thought you said—"

"Couldn't bring myself to take advantage of him that way, use his influence. I thought I could get a transfer on my own for both of us. Teeter too, if the crazy nut wanted to come along. But . . . they turned me down."

"The French?"

"Yes. They have enough of their own people wanting to fly. I don't mind for myself. But for you and Teeter, this isn't right. You particularly. I got you into this mess."

"No, you didn't," Franklin insisted.

"Nice of you to let me off the hook, buddy, but I know better. You wouldn't have joined up if I hadn't. Worse yet, I misled you, thinking I could get us into aviation. Sorry. Take care of yourself today. If you got hurt, I couldn't live with it."

Franklin ran his hand down the length of his rifle.

"I can get transferred," he said.

"You?"

"The DeWitts are very influential in Washington. My father's quietly helping organize an American volunteer squadron to fight alongside the French."

"But they said—"

"It would be good press for the Allies, an unofficial endorsement of the French. The military may not be too crazy about the idea, but the government is. They'd take a few of us into the regular air arm first, then form a special squadron later."

Blake slapped his friend on the back. "Bully for you, old boy. Glad you're getting out of this hellhole."

"I'm not going," Franklin replied. "Not unless you and Teeter are accepted, too. And your brother."

"Don't be a fool. I wouldn't have stayed here if you hadn't made it."

"Yes you would."

"You flatter me. I can't let you miss your chance."

"Too late. I wrote my father as soon as the mail came in. All four of us or no one."

Blake stared at the muddy, sober-faced young man opposite him. Such loyalty astounded him.

"Stay behind today," he said quickly. "Pretend you're sick. No sense getting killed when we're . . . you're close to getting a chance at flying."

Frank shook his head. "No thanks," he said.

His response was lost in the thundering roar overhead. The shelling in preparation for the attack had begun.

Their sergeant, a short, bookish man who had won promotion because he was fluent in several of the languages spoken in the legion, hurried up to the men. "Prepare to move out! Prepare to move out!" He ran along the short portion of the line occupied by his squad. Over the clamorous booms of the outgoing shells, he shouted through cupped hands in order to be heard, and even then the men had to relay the message.

"*Baïonnette au canon.*"

Blake, the first to repeat the word, assumed authority.

"Fix bayonets. Move to the ladders."

With a flourish he drew his blade from its scabbard and attached it to the end of the rifle. In a brief instant of quiet the ominous clicking of metal against metal rattled the length of the trenches as bayonets were rammed into locking lugs.

This is it, Blake thought, bitter at first. No. A new adventure. Think of it that way. A new experience, great stuff for his letters and later for back home.

He stepped in front of the crude ladder of tree limbs between his and DeWitt's position.

"Two to a ladder," he reminded the men.

For some the ladders were no more than footholds chopped into the dirt. For others a sloping ramp had been cut from the mud to make for an easy exit. "Stay right behind me, Frank," he cautioned his friend. "If I get hit, don't risk your life trying to save me."

Halfway up the ladder, crouched and twisted so his head was just below the dirt, he watched for the signal from the sergeant. The stench of exploding gunpowder stung his nostrils.

There would be a whistle, then the advance to the wire, which had already been cut in many places. They were to charge straight forward at the double, firing as they ran, making certain their magazines were still full when they reached the German trenches. Once there, they were to use bayonets if necessary. They would take the first enemy trenches, moving into the reserve line if possible, but they were to keep their eyes on their sergeant for the signal that they had accomplished their objective. Then they would dig in to stay. It sounded so simple.

Blake felt no fear, but then he had not expected to. He just needed a cigarette, and when it looked as if the order to advance might be delayed for more artillery fire on the enemy emplacements, he took out his gold cigarette case and lighter. It had lost its glitter. He lit up and offered a smoke to DeWitt.

"No thanks." Franklin's voice quavered. "Blake, I don't think I can do it."

"Of course you can, buddy. Stay behind me. You'll

be all right." The young writer had to go; if he
blew this, turned yellow, he'd ruin all their chances
of getting out of the infantry.

"It isn't that. I just don't think I can kill anybody."

Relieved, Blake dragged on his cigarette. "Well,
hell, who's going to notice if you kill someone or
not? Go along for the experience and shoot your
weapon once in a while. Great material for your
writing."

Officers were checking the area. German shells began to whine in toward the attack force, shrieking
and booming. The din penetrated the body and became part of it. The officers reached the lip of the
trenches, exposing themselves to heavy machine gun
fire. One tumbled back into a rifle pit and was gone.

Whistles blew.

"*En avant! En avant!*" the officers called in har-
mony. "*Pour la patrie.*"

"*En avant,*" the sergeant shouted.

Blake was first out of the trench, his body charged
with adrenalin. Others followed, but as he glanced
around him he realized there were fewer than he
had expected. The line was pathetically thin. He
heard shots behind him. Thousands of troops were
crawling reluctantly from their dirt cocoons. The
noncoms were firing warning shots, or perhaps even
hitting a few of the slackers.

Now there was nowhere to go except forward, and
their best ally was speed. The cratered expanse between them and the Germans was the most dangerous of all. Machine gun bullets and incoming artillery
were turning it into something like the bubbling
mud beds of Yellowstone Park, only now the mini-

eruptions in the earth's surface were caused by man-made explosives rather than gases from the core of the planet.

Blake saw a man near him fall, then another and another. Those behind stepped over the dead and wounded without so much as a glance.

"Keep moving. Faster. Faster," the platoon officer barked at Blake's left. The officer was sprinting in front of his troops, waving his pistol in an arc over his head. When a shell burst directly ahead of him, he ran through the cone of dirt and smoke, emerging with his uniform dirtied and tattered. There was blood on his left shoulder, and he stumbled, caught himself, and continued advancing.

It was then Blake noticed the incongruity of the officer's dress. He had put on a clean uniform for the charge, complete with spotless white gloves. Until the shell burst in front of him, he had been carrying a swagger stick in his left hand; it had vanished in the cloud of dirt.

Urged on by the officers and sergeants, the untried troops had increased their pace. A terrified Moroccan jumped into a shell hole and put his hands over his ears. The sergeant jumped in behind him and kicked the Arab in the rear. The frightened man scrambled from the hole, started to charge again, took three steps and fell, bullets bending both knees back as if the legs had decided to retreat in defiance of the sergeant.

A shell exploded behind Blake, its concussion like a plank shoved into his shoulders. His first thought was of Franklin, and he turned sideways as he ran.

His friend was nowhere in sight.

Blake slowed. My God, he couldn't let anything happen to DeWitt. In the chaos, though, it was hard to recognize anyone. The squads were beginning to blend together as the unlucky casualties were culled out.

"Keep going," the angry sergeant called.

Hunter blanched at the rebuke. No one could call him a coward.

He ran again, faster, trying to regain his position at the front. It was then he saw Franklin DeWitt, ahead rather than behind him.

The *Feldgrau*—German foot soldiers—were a few yards ahead, climbing from outposts and running down the communication trenches that stretched to the main line of resistance. One clambered over the top and tried to make it on the surface.

Raising his rifle, bringing his cheek down against the stocks, Hunter lined up the sights. The man was sprinting straight toward safety. He did not zigzag or even angle to one side or another, which might have required Blake to lead him by a foot or more. There was no wind to take into consideration. The range was short.

It was too easy.

Hunter fired. The German's left shoulder swung around ahead of his torso, and he spun, faced his assailant for an instant, then completed his three-hundred-and-sixty-degree turn. He took four faltering steps before falling face-up.

Blake ran forward again. Around him others were firing, some into the communication trenches, others in the direction of the main line or at machine gun nests. While much of their fire was less accurate than Blake's single shot had been, they were making it difficult for the enemy to expose themselves enough to cut the withering fire that had taken such a toll when the charging force had first advanced.

A bullet missed Blake by inches, then another, and he thought some German had singled him out as a target. He had reached the man he had wounded, however, and the war narrowed down to the two of them. The German was flat on his back, a small, heavy-set man with blood flowing through his uniform. His left shoulder was deformed from the wound, but his rifle was in his hand. He did not raise it to defend himself, but he might have.

Blake felt a chill start at the base of his skull and run down his body like ice water. With leaden, strangely stiff arms he lifted his rifle and pointed it at the German's head.

The man on the ground screamed. Instead of raising his weapon as Blake had expected, he threw his good arm across his face. It was too late. Blake's finger had irrevocably begun its backward motion against the trigger. The gun bucked and the plump face and the hand merged into red pulp.

I had to do it, Blake told himself. I couldn't leave the bastard behind to shoot one of us in the back. He shuddered.

"Keep moving," the sergeant yelled, but even he stopped to look at the dead man. There were bodies scattered around and behind them, but this man was different. His killer was known.

Death by shrapnel or sweeping fire from an entire line of riflemen was easier for the sergeant to accept. This had been an execution—justified though it was

—not the impersonal, random death of those who had fallen thus far in the attack.

Blake's spirits rose from the depths. He could kill. It was easy.

9

FRANKLIN DEWITT crossed no-man's-land in a daze. He wished he could toss away his rifle and use his notepad. He needed time—now—to record the vivid images, the sounds, odors, the feel of battle. They should be written down before time sanded off the sharp edges of reality.

In the man-made storm of battle the sky was perversely cloudless, a beautiful blue dome set like a glass lid over a pot bubbling with violence. The ground between the two lines had been plowed with shells, great furrows carelessly cut and scummed with water. The trees that remained stretched skeletal limbs up from the soil. On one a single leaf clung, tremulous and naked. If there had been grass, it had been turned under in the mottled, grayish soil. A few weeds poked up and here and there was a poppy, still budded and green.

Off to the right the foundation of a house, or perhaps it had been a farm building of some sort, had been battered until it rose no more than a foot above the ground. It was rather like a grave with cement borders, except that the remains—shatters of mortar and stone—were scattered both inside and outside its margins.

Even before the first new casualties began to fall, the offal of war was all around him.

Empty rifle cartridges seeded the battlefield. Hunks of black shrapnel protruded from the dirt. A German spiked helmet lay on its side next to another that a Frenchman had worn. A bayonet had been shoved into the ground, holding up the rifle to which it was attached. Live artillery shells stood in the soft ground where they had landed without detonating. Binding it all together were the strands of barbed wire stretched between four-foot sticks or twisted in thorny clumps.

There was other uglier litter. A dead cow, a mud-caked shoe, bits of uniforms, a foot sticking up from the bottom of a hole. There was no way of telling whether the body that was probably below it was French or German.

The scene was far from static. It seethed like a boiling stew. Minute by minute shells created new craters, reshaped others, tossed men aside or into the air, redistributed the soil and licked it with dragon tongues of fire and smoke. Amid the bombast of artillery, small arms fire was reduced to punctuation marks: brief dashes of inch-long flame and little periods made of white smoke puffs. Under it all the

earth heaved and writhed and belched with the abuse
of the opposing armies.

Now the soldiers were swarming over the devasta-
tion like hungry locusts, moving low in search of
something living to devour. From the German side
rifle fire swatted at the invaders, felling one, two, then
more with quick, sharp blows.

Absorbing the sounds, Franklin heard an enormous,
dissonant symphony tuning for performance. Against
the tympany of artillery, rifles twanged like strings
plucked in too-strong pizzicato. Tramping feet merged
into the bass section; shells whistled like brass; the
cries of the wounded were the high-pitched cry of
the reeds.

An unruly choir of voices lost itself in the cacoph-
any: officers bellowing orders, sergeants threatening,
men cursing, the wounded crying.

There were two mutually pervasive and offensive
odors—those of putrescent flesh and acrid cordite.

Franklin's mouth had gone dry; he could taste
nothing, but he could feel the concussion of shells,
the wind of bullets whistling close, the moribund
brush of a bloodied comrade touching him as he
pitched into the final, deep pit of death. The American was aware of his feet pounding the earth, jolt-
ing his body, his cartridge belt cutting at the top
of his pelvis. His helmet kept slipping over his eyes,
and it weighed more than it ever had before. The
rifle was heavier, too, and he clutched it until his
forearms and fingers hurt.

Three-quarters across the stretch of hell, he still
had not fired his rifle, and the sergeant raged at him.

"Shoot! Shoot, damn you!"

He fired wildly, at nothing, to shut the man up.

He knew there were men who would refuse to fire in the worst of battles in order to avoid cleaning their rifles. Afterward, if they survived, they would be caught by a sharp sergeant's inspection and sent to repent on the next patrol.

But he could not shoot at a target. When he did see a man he could identify as the enemy, he hesitated too long. *Could he kill? Could he?* Before he reached a decision, the target would be gone. He could not face the test.

The Germans ahead were no longer a faceless enemy; they were men, just like him.

What if the one he killed was as aware, as alive, as obsessed with the future as he? What if he killed a German who could see the blue sky in all this hell, someone who could write or paint the horrors the two armies were inflicting on each other, who could say it so graphically that the world might pause before marching into such insanity again?

There was another possibility, though. Suppose that by killing he were to rid the world of a monster? On both sides there were men who did not fight on principle but rather for the thrill of legalized murder.

Like himself? he wondered. By God, he was among the worst. He had come into the war with no altruistic motive. His purpose was to observe, to take his notes, to make himself into a writer. The rest were fighting to protect their country or at least one they loved, but he was the same observer of life that he had always been.

Could he become a participant now? Could he kill?

A sudden lessening of the noise shocked him from his introspection.

The shelling, from both sides, had stopped. The continuing sounds were those of machine guns, rifles, and the voices of men shouting, screaming, crying, and grunting from exertion.

At this point neither side's artillery could go on firing without endangering their own men as much as the enemy.

Franklin recognized the meaning of the quiet. There was no longer a wide expanse to separate him from the foe. Only yards remained, hardly more than seconds before the two groups would be fighting man-to-man.

"When the blast of war blows in our ears, then imitate the action of the tiger. Stiffen the sinews, summon the blood." In one of those incongruities of duress, the quotation inserted itself into his bookish mind more as thought than words.

He had the blood for the battle. He was not frightened for himself, at least not enough to run. But could he imitate the action of the tiger?

No! his conscience shrieked as they topped the first trench and he was eye-to-eye with the Germans. They were pressed back against the rear wall of the dug-out defenses, giving themselves space in which to wield their weapons.

Blake saw young faces. Old faces. Thin and puffy fat. Flesh grimaced into wrinkles of anger and terror. Mouths open in silent screams.

There was a final rattle of gun fire and men on both sides crumpled in about equal numbers.

With proximity came new sounds. Grunts, groans,

the thud of a rifle butt against a skull. Then the dull, puncturing noise, like a knife makes when it is plunged into a watermelon. The bayonets had been put to work.

In the wildness of battle, Franklin DeWitt had somehow reached the lip of the enemy trench. He stood there in numb fascination, watching a German choking another man. A bayonet cut through the strangler and pinned him to the floor of the trench.

Teeter shoved his foot against the dead German and extracted the blade. Blood geysered as if a can of red paint had been punctured.

"Mon dieu! Aide-moi!" Franklin recognized the anguished voice of his sergeant pleading from the bottom of the pit.

The sergeant was on his back trying to hold the end of a German rifle so the man wielding it could not push it home.

DeWitt turned, positioned himself to fire at the enemy's head just as the face looked toward him.

It was a young face. Frightened and gaunt. Helpless.

DeWitt hesitated. *Shoot, shoot, shoot,* part of him cried.

No! His finger was paralyzed on the trigger.

"Leave him alone!" he yelled. "Surrender!"

The sergeant's strength gave out and his arms jackknifed. The bayonet plunged into his chest. His dying eyes glared up accusingly at the young American.

The hesitant finger moved on the trigger. Part of the German's back was blown away. Aghast at what his hesitation had cost, Franklin jumped into the trench, stabbed the enemy soldier with his bayonet, twisted it free, and rolled his victim over with his foot.

The face was not young. Nor was it frightened or gaunt.

His imagination had created what it had wanted to see.

The man under his foot was a battle-hardened veteran. There was a bandage on his face from a recent wound, and he had the prognathous jaw of a bulldog. His mouth was open, lips pulled taut over long, jagged teeth. A glint of triumph lingered in his eyes in the instant before pain took over.

Franklin reversed his rifle and smashed the butt into the German face. He kept pounding and jabbing until he had pulverized the gloating mouth into something inhuman.

"Enough!" he heard a voice say.

A hand grasped his rifle, and he turned to see Teeter restraining him. The Cowboy must have seen it all. The deadly indecision, the violent reaction . . .

Around them the trenches had emptied of Germans and the battle had settled into sporadic fire down the communications groundworks to the German reserve line.

Franklin DeWitt sank to the wood flooring under him and tossed his rifle aside.

He had done it. He had killed . . . twice. The sergeant by hesitation. The German in fury.

10

As THEY MET and passed their replacements by night, Franklin wondered if the newcomers went forward with the same doubts he had. He was a shadow that plodded toward the rear with shoulders slumped more from relief than from the weight of the pack strapped to his back. And like him, the replacements were only unknown shadows, too, so impersonal they might almost have been the enemy. Somehow it seemed wrong. Forced to share the common consuming experience of war, they ought to feel some closeness, some kinship. But there was nothing. Just shadows of things, scarcely human, in the night.

He had left the trenches because he was ordered to. The prospect of returning was as unwelcome as had been the initial trip to the front. How could he go back to the hideous shelling and the stench of bodies rotting in open graves from which they could not be retrieved? He would have preferred to stay until his time was up, until he would never have to return again. Going back would be the worst punishment of all; he now knew what organized barbarism waited in the trenches.

Compared to what he had come from, the rest area was a resort. A misty rain softened some of the damage wreaked on the shattered village of Cuiry-les-Chaudardes. Despite the rain, most of the townspeople were in the street, gathered behind the priest, shaking their fists at a major who had decided to keep his men busy during their respite from war.

Ropes had been hauled to the top of the church steeple, wrapped around the cross, and dropped to the uniformed men below. Grunting, slipping in the mud, the men tugged and strained, ignoring the women beating at them with their fists and the old men spitting at them as the steeple finally gave way and crumpled into the road.

Wailing and muttering their disgust, the people sloshed off toward their homes. The soldiers looked at their work without interest, left the ropes and headed for shelter.

Probably the major was right, Frank acknowledged. The steeple would make an easy target for enemy artillery if they advanced more than a mile on their next attack.

It would not have been a pleasant duty for the major. If he had made his own hard decision quicker, Franklin thought, the sergeant would be alive.

With the cold rain dripping off his helmet and soaking his leggings under his greatcoat, he followed the seven survivors of his squad through the slippery, sucking mud. When they reached the house where they were to be quartered, a surly old woman opened the door and immediately began to scold them.

With much shouting and flailing of arms, she made herself clear. She wanted them to take off their shoes and their outer clothing before entering. The weary Franklin was about to accede to her wishes when Bulldog Teeter pushed her away.

"Go fuck yourself, ya old bitch." He stomped to a makeshift counter made with a board set between two chairs. It was covered with tinned jam, sweet biscuits, *vin mousseux* and other luxuries the men had craved on the line. There were cigarettes, too, and Teeter snatched up a pack along with a bottle of wine.

The sparrowlike, hook-beaked crone spat obscenities at the Cowboy when he did not pay quickly enough.

"She wants a sawbuck," Blake told him. "That's outrageous. Haggle with her, Teeter."

"Naw. I'll give her what she wants," Bulldog grunted. Holding the cigarettes and wine in one hand, he poked the other deep under his outer coat. He passed her a five-dollar bill. She studied it, puzzled, then followed him toward the stair leading to their second-floor quarters. "*Spécial,*" he told her. "*Dollar de valeur.* Here, have more." He rolled off more bills and waved at the men behind them. "*Vin pour tout le monde.* Somebody tell her. It's special money. Worth more."

Most of the Americans recognized the money quickly enough.

It was Confederate.

Franklin's first impulse was to challenge Teeter's petty theft, but Blake snatched up a pack of cigarettes, too, and then a bottle of wine. The old woman protested, ready to turn violent in response to the mischievous legionnaires. By the time she had hoisted a wine bottle as a weapon, Teeter finally came to a regular American dollar bill in his bankroll and her eyes lighted with recognition.

"Aw, you don't want none of that Yank shit, ma'am," he said, tossing the bill over his shoulder and finding another Confederate five for her.

He plunked heavily up the stairs while she still gaped at what she held in her hands.

Smiling for the first time since he had gone on line, Franklin took a bottle of wine for himself and went up the rickety stairs behind his two friends. Morning was sending spears of light through one wall of the house, and he could see it had been blown away by a shell. Ill-fitting boards patched the hole.

"Where the hell did you get the Confederate money, Bulldog?" Blake asked.

"Never travel without it. Looks as good to me as the dag-blasted, ass-wipin' paper these foreigners use. You let 'em cheat you on the change, and they're happy as a red squirrel in a hickory-nut tree."

The small group crowded into the room Teeter selected. The floor was covered with straw, and rain was dripping through holes in the ceiling. They stacked their rifles in the center and dropped packs along the wall. Greatcoats were stripped off and spread on the straw to dry. A rough fireplace had been built along one wall, and although rain came in around the chimney made of sawed-off shell casings, there was dry wood that looked as if it had been torn off one of the wrecked houses in the village. Pooling their meager supplies of toilet paper, they soon had a fire going.

When Frank looked around minutes later, the tired veterans had arranged themselves against the walls, their helmets off, their shoes drying near the fire. Most of them were leisurely smoking cigarettes or sipping from the wine bottles. The only exception was Blake Hunter. He had to fill his gold cigarette case before he extracted one and lit up.

He jerked his head up as if a thought had just occurred to him. "If anything ever happens to me," he said abruptly, "I'd like to leave you two something."

"I'll take whatever smokes you got," Teeter said obligingly. "Ready-mades or the makin's."

"Franklin?"

"The cigarette case," Franklin said somewhat absently. His mind had been an ocean away.

"It's personally engraved. From a girl."

"Doesn't matter," Franklin answered. "None of us is going to get out of this alive anyway."

Teeter laughed. "Maybe you ain't, but I sure as hell am."

"Me, too," Mulligan, the prizefighter, said from across the room. "Gotta be more to life than there's been so far." He closed his glazed eyes and retreated into the silence where he spent most of his days.

Blake did not speak again. Warmed by the fire, relaxing for the first time, the seven survivors closed their eyes or stared ahead, each nurturing his own thoughts.

How many of them were reliving their moments in battle as he had so often since he first killed, Frank-

lin wondered. Some, perhaps. But then he had come
as a student, one who must live and experience before he could commit truth to paper. He had come
to study war more than to fight it. And what had
he learned so far?

His mind answered with a quotation from Proverbs.
*"The wicked flee when no man pursueth: the righteous
are bold as a lion."*

"What?" Blake asked from beside him.

Franklin had not realized he was thinking aloud.
"A quote from the Bible," he answered.

"In this mess? I don't think God would send His
only begotten son to this place even to be crucified."

"Blake, did you kill anyone during the attack?"
Franklin asked. "Anyone that you knew you killed,
not just a figure at a distance that might have fallen
by coincidence when you shot?"

"Do you mean is my conscience bothering me? No.
Like your Bible says, *'The last enemy that shall be
destroyed is death.'*"

"I don't get the connection."

"You will."

" 'The last enemy that shall be destroyed is death.' "
Frank repeated the quotation from Corinthians. He
could grasp the apparent *non sequitur* in its Biblical
context, but he was certain that his friend had given
it another meaning.

"Speakin' of killin'," Teeter said without opening
his eyes, "any you bastards see DeWitt smashin' that
boche's face when he jumped into the trench? When
he was done, that hun's mug looked like an egg
stepped on by a fuckin' big Texas longhorn."

"Yeah?" The hillbilly was interested. "What about

it, DeWitt? I gutted one of them buggers, but I never did nuthin' to his face."

Franklin knew the Cowboy meant well, but dredging up the memory sickened him.

"Too bad the sergeant bought the farm," another voice said from across the room. "I was just beginning to understand his lingo."

Teeter said, "DeWitt just about got to the little son-of-a-bitch in time. If'n he'd had another second, he'd a had it. As it was, he moved faster'n me, and I can take a shit on a coiled rattlesnake b'fore he can sting my ass."

So the Cowboy was forgiving the delay, Franklin thought. As he would have forgiven anyone else's indecision under the same circumstances.

But he could not forgive himself, and he picked up his greatcoat and put it on along with his helmet. At the bottom of the stairs, he bought a pack of cigarettes at the scrawny woman's blackmarket prices and lit up before he went out into the cold, dreary rain. He rarely smoked, and he had difficulty keeping the ready-made lit as he walked through the devastated village.

Slick as melted chocolate, the street was empty save for a few soldiers who stood in the protection of doorways and stared into the steady downpour.

He would have to remember that. The way men stood and stared at nothing so often after they had escaped alive from a battle. The veteran knows he is going to die in a different way than the average person. Even though he might feel confident that there would be stays of execution until after the war was over, the soldier continues to live on death row.

Eventually, regardless of whether he survived the fighting, Franklin _knew he was going to die_ and the thought could never be tucked away and ignored again. It was an uncaged enemy that would stalk him for the rest of his days.

Walking helped, though, and he felt better when he was alone on the road, heading nowhere in particular except south and west away from the fighting.

His feet didn't hurt and it felt strange without a pack or rifle weighing him down. Trying not to look to either side, purposely avoiding reminders of battle, he was content to stare into the rain or ponder the rivulets of water eddying around his boots.

He recognized the three-storey building taking shape in the distance. It was the Chateau de Blanc Sabbon, a well-known landmark in the countryside. The Germans had shelled it on several occasions, but like the village it lay out of range at the moment. A wall of mortised stone surrounded the garden and the woods that hid some of the towers and gables of the aging mansion.

At the entrance the gates sagged from broken hinges and he kept on walking down the graveled road through the woods, following vehicle tracks that detoured around shell holes. Along the road lay unkempt gardens, shredded hedges and decapitated statuary beside fountains choked with leaves and moss.

Although one wing of the chateau had collapsed under the weight of war, the rest of the structure was intact. Some of the windows were boarded up. It was probably off-limits to all except officers, he thought, but he continued to the door, prodded by curiosity. It opened before he knocked.

A stooped old man in a butler's uniform peered out cautiously. In one hand he held a single-shot dueling pistol. He aimed it to one side of the unwelcome visitor.

"Go away," he said in French. "The countess is to be left alone. The general's orders."

What general? Franklin wondered. He was not even certain which general he served under. The top echelon ranks seemed to change with more regularity than the *sous lieutenants*, who had the shortest combat life-expectancy of any group in the legion.

"Who is it, Jacques?" someone asked in English from beyond the foyer. He knew that voice!

"Allison? Allison Hunter?"

"Who is it? Is that you, Blake?"

The door swung farther open as Blake Hunter's sister ran across the parquet floor.

"Franklin! My God, I might never have recognized you. You look awful. Come in! Please. Come in!"

"I'm a mess," he apologized. She was chic as ever, looking as if she was ready for a rendezvous in a Paris café.

"Don't be foolish. Come in out of the rain." She looked past him. "Is Blake with you?"

"No."

"He's all right?"

"Yes. I just went for a walk. We're in Cuiry for rest."

"We've been waiting for Blake . . . and you . . . to come off the line."

"We?"

"Brooke Madigan is here with me."

"Oh!" Franklin felt alive, more so than he had since he left Paris.

"She was anxious to see Blake, too."

Did she have to put it that way?

He had entered the large entryway of the chateau. It was in surprisingly good condition. Family portraits stared down from walls, a few at cock-eyed angles that shelling had a way of giving to everything it brushed, and there was a carpet on the staircase leading up the second floor. An old woman was coming down.

"The countess," Allison explained. "She won't acknowledge you exist. She pretends there's no war. That's why she stayed here against the military's advice. They would have commandeered it as a headquarters, but I understand even the Germans left her alone when they occupied this sector for a time."

The old woman, walking with a cane, reached the bottom of the stairs, looked at Frank long enough to make out the uniform and then disappeared through a door into another room.

"Jacques," Allison said to the butler, "have the stable boy go into the village and fetch my brother." She looked at Frank for directions.

"First house still standing, on the right as you enter the village from this direction."

She repeated his instructions. Her French was more polished than his.

"There are only three servants," she said. "Jacques, the cook, and the stableboy. Of course, the horses were taken in the first few days of the war, but there's plenty of food stashed away in the cellar. Not even the Germans found it."

"But how did you get to stay here?" he asked.

She led him down the entry to a door, opened it, and motioned him into the study. Flames danced in a fireplace and the floor was carpeted with valuable, if worn, Persian rugs. There were soft chairs and oil lamps, shelves of books, and a desk.

"A German officer used the desk for a few days, I understand, but the old countess must have influence on both sides. The German picked up and left quickly when he received a message from somebody. A superior, I suppose."

"But you . . ."

"We drove up with the taxicabs the first time. You heard about that?"

"Yes." He was uncomfortable, physically and otherwise. He felt like a clod, his muddy feet on the rugs and rain dripping from his coat. He took off his helmet, feeling a kind of reverence for the fine old house.

"The sector commander insisted Brooke and I return to Paris immediately, but we came back after I met the countess's son. I promised we'd look after his mother if he allowed us to stay with her for awhile. So the commander relented and now I don't think he could get along without us."

"I heard you were translating."

"Yes. When the war correspondents or foreign military attaches are in Cuiry, they bring their rations here and the cook fixes them a good meal. We help them get the news from the French officers. We entertain, too—Brooke plays the piano and I sing for them. It's the only entertainment they get."

"The *poilus* get nothing."

"Yes. You and Blake should have demanded commissions. They wouldn't have dared refuse you. It might have influenced my father."

"We're still hoping to get into air service."

"Yes. Before winter sets in. Take off your coat, won't you?"

"Blake!" The door behind him burst open and an exuberant Brooke Madigan swept in. Her expression changed when she saw Franklin. "Oh! I heard Jacques saying there was an American here. I assumed it was Blake."

"He'll be here shortly," Allison remarked. "I've sent the stable boy for him."

"Then he's finally in Cuiry, too?"

"Yes," Franklin said. "I don't know for how long. Our battalion took quite a few casualties. We'll have to be fleshed out again before we can defend so much as a hundred yards. And I suppose the officers will be displeased to find I've wandered away from the house where we're quartered."

Brooke Madigan gave a little laugh. She sounded more sophisticated than he remembered. "You don't know Allison. She has the French . . . Well, don't worry. You'll be staying here, not in those hovels in the village."

"Yes, Franklin," Allison concurred, "we're expecting you to stay here, too." But she looked at him with distaste. "You'll have to get out of those clothes, though." She sniffed, and he realized how he must smell to her. His nostrils had grown accustomed to the stench of men who never bathed and whose clothes were smeared with blood and mud and all manner of other soil. "Go upstairs to the far room at the end of the hall. I'll send the cook up with water—a few pitchers are all we can spare, but leave your clothes outside and she'll wash them for you."

"But I'll . . ."

"There are men's clothes in the room, silly," Allison

laughed. "The old woman's grandson lived here. So did the boy's father, but he must have been more Blake's size."

"I'll feel like a thief."

"Don't be ridiculous. The countess will think you're her grandson. She'll like that. He's dead and I think he was her favorite."

A dead man's clothes. Why not? he thought. After killing another human being, he could stop being squeamish about the long night someone else had entered.

Embarrassed by his appearance, he half-smiled at Brooke Madigan as he passed. She was more beautiful than he remembered. She looked older with her long, dark hair snugged into a chignon at the back of her neck.

She returned his smile and said, "Franklin, I'm so glad you're all right."

Perhaps he misinterpreted, but he thought he detected a genuine interest. It set him hoping.

"Thank you."

"I'm honored that you've been sending me the notes to save for your book." She seemed reluctant to let him go so quickly. "And those first chapters are marvelous."

"Then they have been reaching you?"

"Yes. Via the embassy. You'll never know what an influence they've had on me. A good influence."

"All that about dying?"

She shook her head. "No. I saw war as ugly and stupid when Allison and I first drove troops to the front. Then I read your notes."

"You find something uplifting in them?" he said, puzzled by her words.

"Not exactly uplifting. Enlightening is more accurate. War brings out the nobility in ordinary men, doesn't it? That part about Teeter saving those men and never mentioning it. And Mulligan ending the agony of the wounded . . . It can't be easy for him, but he does it anyway."

"And Blake running along the line keeping the men down when the first shelling struck us," he put in, curious to see how she would react. But he could read no change in her expression.

"Yes, that too. There's a certain beauty in courage. It's easy to hold a flower and admire its color, but to wallow in the mud and find life worth saving, or to end a man's pain when to do so goes against everything we've been taught takes a true eye for worth. You gave those moments stature with your words. I'm not as bitter about the war as I was before I started reading your material."

Not bitter. After reading his material. Strange. He had written what she read, but the words had not affected him, not like the experience itself had. He was just an observer, a camera taking the picture. The viewer would see whatever he or she wanted in what he had portrayed as faithfully as he knew how.

"Perhaps you'll tell me more of your experiences," she said.

"I'd rather listen to yours."

She smiled. "There'll be time for both. You and Blake will surely get a long rest if your battalion is not up to strength."

He remembered she had probably come to Cuiry in the hope of seeing Blake.

He went up the stairs suddenly dejected . . . and surprised that he could feel anything except exhilaration. He was off the line and inside a real house. Wasn't that enough?

11

BLAKE HUNTER arrived at the chateau in a Fiat motor car commandeered by the military. It was chauffeured by another private, who, although he might have wondered why he was according such service to a peer, opened the door for him with the same respect he paid high-ranking officers. Blake accepted the obeisance with the nonchalance of royalty.

He was glad the rain had stopped because he wore a parade-clean uniform and shining boots muddied only at the soles. With his usual elan he carried his rifle, bayonet attached.

He set it aside as his sister ran along the hall to throw her arms around him.

"Oh, Blake dear. Thank God you're safe!"

"It'll take more than a few huns to give me trouble," he laughed. Easing her aside, he let his smile include Brooke Madigan a few steps back and Franklin DeWitt on the stairs, looking like a bumpkin in ill-fitting civilian clothes. "Brooke! How wonderful that you're here!" He strode across the entry, his boots clicking on the oak parquet, circled his arms around her tiny waist and lifted her from her feet. He kissed her warmly, his alert eyes sweeping the stairs and the room around him. "I can't believe it . . . your risking your life to see me." He held her at arm's length. "Let me look at you. More beautiful than ever! How are you? It must be awful here for you."

"It's been quite peaceful actually," his sister said, "except we can hear the cannonading when the wind is right."

"Franklin's here, too," Brooke said. "He's upstairs." She turned, surprised to see that he had changed and started down.

"Good. We're lucky to have you girls here to provide us with such fancy lodgings. We'll miss our muddy holes and rat cellmates. Old Frank," he said, grinning up at his friend, "can use a rest. He's been through a lot. If there's not room for both of us, I can spend the nights in the village . . ."

"Oh, come now, Blake," Allison scoffed. "Did you look at the size of this place when you drove up? There's space for the whole foreign legion."

She turned as the countess appeared in the foyer, and then started the introductions.

"Countess, this is my brother, Blake Langley Hunter."

"A *poilu* in my house! Get him out!" the old woman stormed in French. Thin white hair trailed back from her forehead, straight and wispy as a cirrus cloud stretched in the wind. The bluish veins in her hands twisted and lumped under her skin like the maze a mole digs just below a close-clipped lawn. She leveled her pale, imperious gaze on Franklin. "Pierre, get this man out of my house!" Only officers were human in her mind.

"Of course," Frank said in French, but he did not move as she laboriously climbed the stairs, passed him, and disappeared down the hallway.

Allison smiled at her brother. "She'll accept you as soon as you change to civilian clothes. She thinks Franklin is her grandson already. You'd better go right up. Franklin, will you show Blake to the room next to yours? That was the countess's son's room. There should be something there that will fit."

"Sure."

"Wait," Blake laughed. "Not so fast. I haven't even had time to say a proper hello to Brooke." He opened the door into the study, took her hand, and pulled her inside. Closing the door behind him, he said, "There. That's better. I like a little privacy."

He pulled her into his arms and crushed her mouth under his. She stiffened, and when her resistance increased, he stepped back, surprised. He was not accustomed to rebuffs from the gentler sex.

"What's wrong?" he asked. "You came all this way to see me."

"Not really." She sounded uncomfortable.

"I don't understand."

"I mean, I'm glad you're safe," she stammered quickly, "pleased to see both you and Franklin, but I didn't come chasing after you. Your sister and I—"

"Brooke, my darling, you don't have to explain." He stepped in close again and she retreated to the fireplace. Silhouetted against its flickering light, she was more appealing than ever. He felt desire stir in his body. He had been without a woman since his race in Monaco months before. Not one to satisfy sexual compulsion the way many of the men in the trenches released their craving, he needed her more than he needed food and drink. There was no solution in the village; the whores had been driven out.

"I'm not being coy, Blake. I'm just saying I came up here on a whim with Allison. Paris . . . it's a ghost town, unless you like the taverns where women dance naked while the soldiers get drunk. America is being so neutral, there have been no parties at the American embassy since the war started. It just seemed a good place to get out of for a while."

"You're trying to say there's nothing between us."

"No. Nothing isn't the right word, but—"

"You wrote. Your letters were—"

"I only wrote once or twice, Blake. I . . . you'll have to give me time."

"There's someone else?"

"No . . . well, maybe, I don't know. I met you and Franklin and the war took you away so quickly, and . . ."

He inhaled deeply, trying to put things in place and regain control of his emotions. Franklin? Could she prefer that mouse to him? He could not bring himself to accept it.

"If you'll excuse me," Brooke said.

He spoke before she reached the door. "Don't go yet, Brooke. I've got to talk to you first."

"Oh?"

"It's about Frank." Posed against the backdrop of the fireplace, his foot on the hearth and his arm resting on the mantel, he took a cigarette from the gold case and tapped it against the back of his hand before lighting up. He might have been modeling for a portrait that would one day hang above the fireplace. "He was my roommate, you know. My closest friend. And he's . . . well, he's not quite the Franklin we knew in Paris."

"What are you saying?" She sounded angry.

"Don't misunderstand, please. He was brave as most of the new men on the line. They were all just boys. None of them had done things—faced death, taken risks, however you want to put it—as I had. You can accustom yourself to fear, you know, but war doesn't give a man time to adjust."

"You're saying Franklin was a coward?"

"No. No, never. I said no such thing. I saw him kill a man myself." Well, it was almost true.

"Don't! I don't want to hear it."

"Then bear with me. Give me time to help him. He's my friend. He would have died to save me, I know, if I had needed help."

"What are you suggesting?" Brooke asked.

"Very little. Just don't be alone with him for a few days."

"Alone? I didn't say I came here to see Franklin, either."

"Of course you didn't. I didn't mean to intimate that you did. But I need your help to get him off the front lines. He can't go back. I'm afraid of what it would do to him."

"But how can we keep him from being sent back into battle? Is he so sick they'd release him from duty?"

"No. And he wouldn't allow it. But we could get him into another branch of the service."

"The ambulance corps, for instance?"

"No. That's just as traumatic as the front lines."

"Then what?"

"The air service. Where he could soar above the rubble and see the tragedy in the miniature he could bear. We must get him transferred into the flying corps."

"My father could help," Brooke thought aloud.

"Yes, I suppose he could. And I have already suggested to Frank that he ask his own father to seek a transfer for him. Lowell DeWitt made quite a name for himself in the navy. The French might find it expeditious to grant the request of an American military man. As a soldier, I don't have access to the telegraph, but you—"

"Using my charms," she said cynically.

"Don't put words into my mouth," he objected. "I'm merely saying that as a civilian, you could have a wire sent from Cuiry to your father. Within hours, he could contact Lowell DeWitt. If your message sounded urgent enough, Franklin might be transferred before we're even ordered back on line. I'm trying to save my friend's sanity. If sending a telegram is too much to ask, then I apologize." His jaw tightened and he straightened his powerful shoulders.

"I'll do it, of course. I'll talk to the commandant at Cuiry and ask that Franklin remain here until we get a response."

"Good."

"But you think he'll be able to manage in the air service?"

He flicked his cigarette into the embers. "It's my

last hope," he said heavily. "It's dangerous, but perhaps I'll be lucky and get to go with him. I have a request for transfer in myself. I could keep an eye on him."

"I'll mention you to my father, too."

"No. Absolutely not. I have no intention of imposing myself on your father's good offices. I'll serve where I'm assigned."

"You have a duty to your friend, too," she reminded him.

He sighed. "I suppose you're right. But the most important thing right now is to get him off the line."

"He's lucky to have a friend like you."

"It's settled then. And, please, do remember what I said. Try not to be alone with him just yet. If he hurt you he'd never forgive himself." He joined her at the door. "You'll get the wire off as soon as possible?"

"I'll write it now and send it in with the stable boy. It will be on its way before dark."

"You're a wonderful girl, Brooke. I realize how you feel now, but I want you to know I'm wild about you. If you ever change your mind, let me know."

He had his arm around her shoulders when they re-entered the foyer. Franklin and Allison were just coming out of the sitting room. Blake brushed his lips against Brooke's cheek as they approached.

"Ah, Frank, old chum," Blake said, clapping a hand on his shoulder. The dark-haired man's handsome uniform was in sharp contrast to the wrinkled garb that hung on Franklin's muscular frame like castoffs from an unkempt great uncle. "Will you show me to my room now? I think I've said my hellos properly." He winked at Brooke and followed his friend. "Wonderful girl, that Brooke," he said when they were in the upper hall.

"This is to be your room, I guess," Franklin said. Blake heard the depression in his tone. "They said you'll find civilian clothes in there that are supposed to fit you."

"Good. Want to look dandy for the girls, you know. Great of them to have us here, isn't it?"

"Yes."

Blake walked into the large bedroom. It was a world apart from what they had known these previous weeks, despite the fact that one window was boarded up and the furnishings were old and dusty. He went to one of the two large closets and pulled open the doors. It was filled with elegant clothing for a male.

"I'd better go back downstairs and see if there's anything I can do to help," Franklin said.

"Stay, old buddy. I'm bubbling with love and I need a pair of ears."

"Brooke?"

"You know anyone more desirable? Anyone more beautiful? And talk about spunky! Imagine her coming this far forward and waiting so long for . . . us."

"You're in love with her?"

"Mad for her. And I know what you're thinking. Just another of Blake's dalliances. Well, let me tell you, you're wrong. This time it's different. I'm really in love."

"Does she love you?"

"You expect a girl like her to tell me that when we've known each other such a short time? Of course, war has a way of speeding up things. What do you think, is it too soon to ask her to marry me?"

Franklin had sat down on the edge of the bed. At the mention of marriage, his head jerked up sharply.

"You might not make it back. I suppose that's more important than how long you've known her."

"Make it back? From the trenches? Hell, man, a guy with my experience could live forever in the legion. It's the careless ones, the men who haven't tested their courage and their reflexes in adventure, that don't survive the infantry."

"A stray bullet, a shell you can't duck . . ."

"With my luck, no chance. No. I have no qualms about asking her to marry me as long as I'm on the ground. Now flying, that's different."

Franklin lifted his blond head and studied the man whose braggadocio he half admired and in a way envied. He wished he had some of his friend's self-confidence.

Blake thought he read a glimmer of hope in the young writer's blue eyes, and he continued maneuvering. "Flying is another story," he said. "I've done enough of that to know that no matter how good you are, your machine can always fail you. Yes, if I thought my transfer to the air service had a prayer of being accepted, I'd stay away from Brooke. It wouldn't be fair to her. Too risky."

"But you're in for a transfer."

Blake shook his head. "No chance. For you, yes. You have pull, but I don't."

"Your father could do something."

"I told you, I'd never ask him. It wouldn't be right."

"But if you get a chance, you'd give up Brooke?"

"Until after the war, yes. I'd have to. We signed

up to help the French. We have to serve where we best can. College men like us on the front line are a waste. Any manual laborer can dig a trench and shoot a rifle. We're being cowardly by not pressing for transfers more forcefully." Blake had put on a formal dinner jacket and was knotting a black tie. He looked elegant, impossibly so, this close to the front line. He ran a hand over his black hair and smiled at himself in the mirror.

The mirror told him what he knew: he looked good enough to get what he wanted from a woman, just as he always had. He did not quite understand why Brooke Madigan had not capitulated already. Until a few minutes ago, he had assumed she had, but there would be time for that later. Right now he had to get transferred off the line. To win that objective he could forgive himself a bit of subterfuge. As in military planning there was strategy involved.

"Don't repeat anything I've said to Brooke, Frank," he said in a conspiratorial tone. "I haven't even hinted my intentions. I've discouraged her, actually, and I will until I get the final rejection of my request. I have your confidence, I hope."

"Of course."

Franklin rose and followed Blake to the stairs. They were halfway down when they saw Brooke handing something to the stable boy and sending him out the front door.

"Well," Blake said. "I feel civilized again." He referred to the clothes he wore. "How about it, Allison? Any word yet on when the States are going to get into the war?"

"Wilson is being quite firm about neutrality. I think he's running for re-election already. And there's a big division at home, I hear. Pro-Germans and those who favor the Allies."

"Pro-Germans," Blake said with disgust. "Who could be on the kaiser's side?"

"They probably think they're in the right, too," Frank said magnanimously.

"Nonsense," Blake scoffed. "In any case Wilson better send help soon. I can't hold off the huns alone forever." He laughed at his own boast. "God, how many months have we been here as it is?"

Frank shook his head. The days and weeks and months were blending together for him as they did for the other men in the battle. Those who counted days seemed to be the first to die.

12

THEY SAT AROUND the long table in the main dining room of the chateau with the countess in the hostess chair. To Franklin the entree tasted suspiciously like horse meat, but he marveled at the contrast of the room's elegance to the filth of the trenches they had just left. There were candles in the chandeliers hanging from above and in the candelabra on the table. The china was exquisite Bavarian which had survived the scroungers of the two armies that had fought near the house during the first fluid days at the beginning of the war.

Tapestries hanging from the walls helped retain the warmth from two fireplaces; Franklin could feel it at the back of the delicate heirloom chair in which he sat.

Outside the night was stormy. Lightning flashed

through the French doors and rain pelted the glass as if trying to pound its way inside.

The old woman did not speak, but Brooke addressed her periodically and helped her cut the meat. As a courtesy the four Americans spoke in French. It was also a necessity since the cook, who helped the butler with the serving, spoke not a word of English.

Franklin found himself adrift in the tide of conversation, as usual an observer rather than a participant.

"The hems will be shorter again this year," Allison was saying.

And Blake, always conversant on every topic, added, "I understand the Paris designers are going in for transparent skirts for the spring. Quite daring."

"Silly," Brooke giggled, "they will reveal nothing more than patterned linings."

"A pity," Blake joked. "And with high-button shoes covering the ankles, the designers have blinded us men again. Might as well look at a Picasso as thumb through a fashion magazine these days."

"Oh, Blake, behave yourself," his sister laughed.

Frank's thoughts drifted away from the table, his ears tuned to the volleys of thunder that came and went outside. At first they seemed to vary in intensity and then he recognized the distant rumble that bridged the louder reports after each flash of lightning.

Without excusing himself—he constantly forgot his table manners—he pushed back his chair and went to the French doors. Opening one, he felt a splash of cold wind on his face. Rain spattered around his feet.

"Franklin, good heavens," Brooke complained. He was chastened, wounded as easily as a sparrow—he, a man who had run through shellfire. "You're letting in the rain."

"Sorry." He started to close the door. Then he swung it back again. "That's not thunder," he announced.

"Of course it is," Blake said, assuming the protective role. "Come on, buddy. Watch the nerves there."

Frank saw the two girls glance at each other as if they thought he was shell-shocked, a term that seemed to have originated in the legion. It referred to those who went into seizures or catatonic states at the first loud noise after they had been exposed to the real thing.

The sound came again and Hunter cocked a more alert ear. "By God, you're right. That isn't thunder!"

He hurried to the door and stood where the rain swept in.

Franklin saw the flashes at the same moment as Blake did. It was not lightning. Electrical discharges arced across the sky, but the lights they saw were individual explosions.

"That's shellfire," Franklin said matter-of-factly. "I thought you said the artillery never reached this far."

"It doesn't," Allison responded.

The girls joined them in the doorway. There was no doubt; the long-range artillery fire was dropping far behind the lines. It might have been aimed at the rest area in the village, but in the storm, with no observers to correct the aim, the explosives were straying closer to the chateau.

"What do you think, Blake?" Franklin asked his friend.

"Is there a cellar?" Hunter asked his sister.

"Yes," Allison said quickly. "Under the entire house. But surely you don't think the shells can reach this far."

"They wouldn't hit the chateau," Brooke said. "The countess has influential friends on both sides."

As if in answer an explosion struck close enough to rattle the glass doors.

"Well, I doubt that her influential friends are loading and aiming those guns," Franklin said. "Hurry. Get the countess downstairs. And, Jean," he said to the butler, "douse all the lights." The last he had to translate into the French before the servant understood.

The cook appeared, eyes wide with fright, and the stable boy burst into the dining room, chattering so fast that none of the Americans understood him. Taking charge, Blake hustled everyone including the confused and reluctant owner of the house through the kitchen and down steep stairs to a dank cellar. With only one candle for light, Blake designated the protective areas for his charges.

"Minimizing casualties," he called it, as he put the cook and stable boy together beneath an old table and found a place behind stored furniture for the countess and the butler.

"Here in the wine cellar, Frank," he directed. "Keep an eye on Allison for me."

The candle went out and Franklin realized his friend had taken Brooke off somewhere in the dark by himself. The acoustics of the cellar, broken by partitions that created storage rooms, and the combination of thunder and shelling outside precluded overhearing whatever they might be discussing.

Within minutes Franklin realized that the shelling had stabilized. Although it still rattled the house and shook the stored contents of the cellar, it was coming no closer.

"I don't understand," Allison said, clutching his arm for reassurance. "Why on earth are the Germans shelling this far back and in the rain?"

There was no explaining artillery. He had sat in the front line more than once and heard shells roar overhead, exploding a thousand yards away in an empty field. Poor intelligence, he supposed, a reason aircraft were becoming more important. They could pinpoint roads, rail lines and troop movements far beyond the vision of ground observers. As for firing in the middle of a storm, war was impervious to day, night, and weather. While a rain might make a muddy field nearly impassable to foot soldiers, officers seldom called off an offensive, be it a major or a minor action. Patrols went on schedule regardless of the misery. When the top-ranking man was a corporal, however, quite often the assigned squad progressed just beyond the wire, found a relatively secure hole, and stayed there until the scheduled time to return.

Any good infantryman could make up an elaborate report of what had been discovered on such static patrols.

"You're not afraid, are you?" There was curiosity and surprise in Allison's voice. She had pressed close to him, and he could detect the light scent of her perfume over the musty smell of the cellar.

"The shells aren't going to reach this far," he predicted, concentrating on the intensity of the muffled thumps. Obviously the shelling had accomplished its objective, whatever it had been, and was no longer advancing. "Probably some kraut officer punishing his battery by making them work on a miserable night."

"You shouldn't be so reassuring," Allison said.

"What?"

"Blake is over there shielding Brooke in his arms, soothing her and telling her how he'll save her from the dastardly huns, of that you can be certain."

A picture of Blake holding the girl in his arms flashed across Franklin's mind. There was no denying the jealousy that stabbed through him.

"You are shy, aren't you, Franklin DeWitt?" Allison asked.

Why deny it? "I suppose so."

"Ever had a girl?"

"Of course." He had had women in the extreme sense of the word, but love had never been involved.

"You need a girl who's forward. Who'll take the initiative until you're ready."

"They're scarce in the trenches," he said with a wry chuckle.

"Oh, you are naive."

"Oh?"

"Tell me how you're going to protect me from the big bad Germans," she teased.

"Well, I'm going to insist that you and Brooke return to Paris. I didn't think the Germans could reach this far with their guns." He cocked his ear. "There. They seem to have stopped firing."

He started to rise.

"I can still hear them," she insisted.

"That's thunder."

"Don't be foolish. Blake's not going to light that candle again for an hour. You'll see. Obviously you don't know my brother as well as I thought an erstwhile roommate would."

"I could find our way upstairs."

"Franklin, you stop it. I'm not that much older than you. Two years does not a mother make."

"What does age have to do with finding the stairs?" He was enjoying himself now.

"Oh, God," she said. "I believe you are stupid, too." A clap of thunder gave her an excuse to throw herself against him until she was almost lying on his lap.

"They're firing again!" she squealed. "Protect me, Franklin."

"That was thunder. You can tell by—"

Her lips silenced him.

The kiss was surprisingly exciting and when she might have pulled away, he kept her close with a slight tightening of his arms. "I think you're right at that," he said. "It is the artillery."

He pulled her close, pretending she was Brooke. Although in his heart he cared only for Brooke, his body could accept the substitute. Allison was the kind of girl he could cope with, one without pretense when it came to male-female relationships.

He cradled her head on his arm and kissed her with hard, seeking lips. Her lips parted under his and he felt her tongue testing his lips tentatively, asking if she would be allowed to caress the inside of his mouth. French kissing, the guys on the line called it. They talked a lot about sex. He had learned more in a few days in the legion than he had in the years he had gone out with "easy" girls.

She twisted in his arms and at first he thought she was uncomfortable. Then he felt her breasts against his chest.

"Buttons," she whispered. "They hurt."

She undid the buttons of the civilian jacket he wore and ran her cold hands in beneath his shirt to touch his bare chest. At her touch his shyness vanished; it would have seemed ungracious had he not slid his hand away from her back to cup the full firm breasts that rose to welcome his fingers.

There was that to say about girls like Allison: they didn't humiliate a man by making him self-conscious. She did not object to his touch, nor had he expected her to. That's the way it had been with the few girls he had dated. He thought of them as tramps, but the term obviously did not apply to Allison. She was well-born, several cuts above the girls he had known.

"I've been thinking of you like this since I first saw you," she said against his ear.

"I'm glad."

"I'm not like this with other men. I don't know why I'm acting this way."

He was flattered. He lost track of time as his body reacted in the age-old chemistry of man and woman. After awhile he realized her elbow had slipped off his leg and rested on his groin.

Did she know where she touched him? He knew the answer, and he tried his hand on her leg. There was no rejection when he let it rest near the knee at first. Then he slid it toward her hips and she made small moaning sounds and inhaled sharply as his touch became more intimate.

Once she held his hand back for a moment before allowing him to resume its exploring.

Hell, he thought. First time he had kissed her.

But that was the way it was sometimes. He recalled guys in the legion telling about heated love affairs that took no time whatsoever to develop. Then, too, there was the shelling. Of course she had heard it before, had been frightened before when she was helping the French officers with translating chores at the headquarters located even farther forward.

Then it was no longer her elbow touching his groin. She was massaging him gently with her arm. When her hand enfolded his swelling organ, he hesitated no longer and moved his fingers to the warm soft place between her legs.

He wanted to stop thinking but his observer's mind would not be denied, and he found himself analyzing his emotions and sensations. There was no right word, though, for the warm glow inside that blazed under her touch and made his heart thud hard in his chest.

Allison excited him more than any woman ever had before. He was laying her on the stone floor and sliding down on top of her when Blake spoke from across the cellar.

"Well, I guess the shelling is over," he said cheerfully.

The gold lighter Hunter carried sparked into flame and ignited the candle. Fortunately, the illumination did not extend to the wine cellar, and Frank climbed off the girl and scrambled to his feet. He was helping her up when Blake led Brooke and his entourage toward the stairs.

Back in the study with the fireplace snapping again, he noticed the sooty mess on his trousers. Allison was brushing dust and mildew from her dress, too.

Brooke noticed. "Whatever happened to you two?" she asked.

Frank was speechless, but Blake's sister answered without a beat. "We heard a rat."

"Are there rats down there?"

"Well, at least we thought it was. I tried to move and tripped over something . . . oh, look at the countess. She's asleep in the chair. Blake, would you help me get her upstairs? She tends to stumble when she's drowsy."

"Of course."

She seemed to whisper something to Franklin as she passed him. "Good night all," she said sleepily. "I'm going to bed. That was an unnerving experience."

"I'll be right up, too," Brooke said.

Franklin watched the brother and sister lead the old woman from the room.

He stood behind the piano. His stubborn body was still in erection and he did not want Brooke to notice.

Allison had a good shape, he was thinking as he watched her provocative behind leaving the room. She was quite a nice girl. He felt at ease with her.

"I'm surprised to see Allison so shaken," Brooke said. She stood up, stretching and covering a yawn.

"You've heard shellfire here before then?"

"Yes. Much closer."

"But you shouldn't be here; it's too dangerous."

She looked at him with serious eyes. "Not everyone can flee, you know. There are nurses and aides, farm women who stayed behind to help their husbands get in the crops. Old women like the countess . . . She stayed in the chateau when the Germans swept into the area and when the French swept them out again. Many of the people in the village went into their cellars and waited out the fighting. I guess the Germans came this way in 1870 or whenever it was they last invaded France. The older people like the countess remember vividly. They would rather stay here than become homeless refugees."

"But that's no reason for you to endanger your life," he said.

"Oh, we're quite safe. Besides, I have no more intention of sitting out the war than you do. I may not be allowed to fight and I know very little of nursing, but there's always something a woman can do."

"Yes, I suppose."

An awkward pause settled over them, the way the front line quieted occasionally for no apparent reason. Brooke seemed to feel a need to speak.

"Blake thinks a great deal of you, doesn't he?"

"Yes," Frank agreed.

"He's quite protective."

Too much, but he didn't say it.

"He says he wants to be sure you come out of this alive so you can finish your book and tell people what war is really like. He says maybe your words could make this the last war. Wouldn't that be something, if you wrote a book and so many people read it that there would be no more wars?"

"I'm afraid only the dead know how horrible war is," he said, "and they don't live to write about it."

"You'll come through all right. If you and Blake stick together."

"Yes. I—"

"Frank!" Blake called from outside the study.

Franklin delayed answering. He did not want to leave Brooke. They were just beginning to have a real conversation. But his friend persisted.

"Excuse me," he said to Brooke. Stepping into the foyer, he saw Hunter at the top of the stairs. "Yes, what is it?"

Blake seemed surprised. "Well, nothing, friend. I just thought you'd want to get to bed early. It's been a long day. You've been through a lot these last few weeks."

"I don't—"

Brooke spoke from behind him. "I'm coming up, too. If the shelling starts up again, we might have to go back to the cellar, and I don't think I could sleep much down there. Not if there are rats around." She shuddered.

Upstairs, Blake walked Brooke to her room. Franklin paused at his door, not wanting to leave the two alone.

"Good night, Frank," Blake said. "See you in the morning."

"Yes. Fine."

"Good night," Brooke smiled.

"Good night." He stalled as long as he dared but they out-waited him and finally he went into his room, leaving the two of them alone in the hall.

Once he was inside, a disquieting thought struck him. You don't suppose Blake and Brooke had . . .

were like he and Allison . . . in the cellar! He hadn't wanted the thought to form in his mind.

Not Brooke. She was not like Allison.

Or was she?

13

THE YOUNG WRITER lay naked under a feather com-
forter. His body was cold. He should have kept
on his long underwear, but he was free of lice
and the longjohns might harbor a few of the pesky
beasts.

He stared into the darkness, writing a scene in his
mind. He was standing at the edge of a glen in the
spring and Brooke Madigan was coming through the
open field, holding her wide-brimmed hat as she
drifted closer and closer to him.

In his imagination he caught the cool breeze, the
smell of grass, saw the buds on the trees, and her
lovely face. But he could find no words for what it
would be like when she reached him. He had a pencil and notepad beside the bed, and he would have
lit a lamp and written if he had been able to imag-

ine her lips on his, her breasts pressed against him. He tried, but he could not force his stubborn brain to conjure up the words she would use to say she loved him.

"Because she doesn't," he said aloud.

She loves Blake Hunter. Who could blame her? He was tall, handsome, charismatic, a true friend, tender and strong. What more could a woman want than Blake?

How could he, the quiet, shy observer, write a love story about a woman who at most thought of him as a casual acquaintance? In any case, she had tried to be gracious to him, he would give her that, and she hadn't flaunted her preference for Blake, perhaps because she sensed how he, Franklin, felt about her. She was the kind who would try to make life easier for him, unwilling to hurt a soldier who would soon return to battle.

He wished he were back on the line.

He had joined up to collect experiences for his writing. No sense staying where the experiences were both depressing and negative, where he had to watch the girl he wanted love another. Besides, he needed sexual relief. Unlike many of the men, the trauma of war had not stimulated his desires, but seeing Brooke Madigan had. He could control his impulses —forever if there was hope—but to see her every day and to know there would never be anything between them was too painful.

A sound jerked him from his reverie. The door to his room opened slowly. There was no light from the hall, and if he had brought his rifle with him, he might have shot the shadow coming in slowly, cautiously.

"Franklin?" The voice was Allison's.

He was not surprised. She was straightforward. He knew what she was like, not that he condemned her. He was no virgin himself, and had taken what a few women had offered him, for experience, he had told himself in the beginning. A writer had to know about life. But for relief mostly, he admitted later.

"Come in, Allison," he said.

She was surprised. "You were expecting me?"

"Yes."

She closed the door behind her.

Now the room was dark again. Snow was falling, as it had intermittently for the last two days. When it was not building the first drifts of winter, the sky was a moody gray. The moon could never penetrate the cloud layer, and he wondered if the men who replaced him were going into the hellish cold on patrol.

He felt her reach the bed and sit on the edge.

"I didn't think you'd expect me," she said.

"I'm not totally naive," he said.

"In other words, you know women."

"Somewhat, yes. If a man ever knows a woman."

"You guessed I was easy." He let that comment go without response, and she laughed at his silence. "All right, I'd be a whore, but I don't need the money."

"And there's no one else. You can't very well sleep with your brother."

"Don't demean yourself," she said. "You're an attractive man."

She had risen from the bed and was probably stripping off her clothing. When she slipped beneath the covers with him, her body was smooth and cool.

"You like Brooke, don't you?" she said. "Well, she's too sweet on Blake to ever do this for you."

Her hands had reached his groin. They warmed quickly to his body temperature and his penis lifted in obedient response.

That was strange, he thought. A man could love one woman but be as easily aroused by another. The need, perhaps, was even greater than it would have been with Brooke. His body throbbed with it.

"Oh, now, not so fast," Allison protested. "Touch me, suck my breasts. You have to earn me even though I came to you. And you have to take the precautions. You brought something, didn't you? All you optimistic soldiers carry them around with you."

"A sheath?"

"Yes."

"Yeah, but to hell with it."

He rolled on top of her, feeling a sudden anger.

"Frank, don't. I can't afford to take chances. Franklin!"

He covered her mouth with his and thrust his tongue between her teeth. It was Brooke under him, and he was punishing her for loving Blake.

Allison squirmed, tried to cry out, but his mouth stifled her, and his knee forced her legs apart. He was about to plunge into her; then he stopped himself. This was not his way.

But Allison was laughing. "Don't stop now. Do it! Rape me. I like it this way, too."

He drove his hardened member into her and her hips lifted to help. In frenzy he stroked in and out, on and on, the need driving him wild, but the juices inside him seemed clogged from disuse, and the end would not come. When finally it did, he lay limp and emotionally exhausted atop her.

It was probably only seconds but it seemed an eternity before he heard her curse him in a whisper sibilant with anger.

"Take it out, damn you! Take it out. I don't want to get pregnant!"

He withdrew quickly and she rolled out of bed, snatching up her night clothes.

"I'm sorry," he said.

"Next time you use something," she said. "I'm not taking any chances."

Then she was gone and he was left to stare into the darkness again.

In his wide-eyed blindness, he could imagine words printed across his vision in bright white letters, words that described what had just happened to him.

Desire, depravity, disgust, despair.

They said it all.

14

THE MAJOR who came to the chateau was not pleased. He had ridden in a staff car through the layer of snow that remained after a brief thaw. A lorry arrived with him, but he was alone when he rapped on the door of the study.

He scowled at Blake and Franklin in mufti, and he ignored their crisp salutes.

"Private DeWitt," he said in faltering English. "Get your gear together."

"Sir?"

"You've been transferred to Pau."

"For aerial training?" Franklin was shocked.

"Yes. You apparently have . . . how is it you say . . . pull in high places. You won't have to go back on line with the rest of us."

"Sir, I did seek a transfer, but with the understanding that my friends go, too."

The major consulted a list. "Two brothers . . . Blake and Duncan Hunter?"

"Yes, sir."

"And that unsavory character, Teeter?"

"Yes."

The major looked at Blake. "Get your things, too, Hunter. You're getting a free ride."

"Sir, I did not use 'pull,' as you put it, to get a transfer," Blake objected.

The major looked toward the stairs. Brooke and Allison were at the top.

"Take the two women with you. The general has decided they are interfering with military matters."

"Sir, I don't understand," Franklin said. "Neither of the women has anything to do with my requesting assistance."

"Take them and get out."

"Yes, sir. But what about Teeter and Blake's brother?"

"The scoundrel Teeter is in the truck waiting. He is going with you."

"And my brother Duncan," Allison said, coming down the stairs. "Is he going into the air service, too?"

"That I do not know. He is not under my command, but from the influence Private DeWitt seems to wield in military matters, I presume he too will be honored while real men are skewered on the bayonets of the *boches*."

"That's not fair," Allison interrupted. "The observation duty is as dangerous as a position on the ground."

"Allison, please," Blake said. "This is strictly a military matter."

"Be on your way within the hour," the major told Blake and Franklin. "I do not want your whereabouts to be known when I take my men back up on the line tonight. It will be difficult enough getting them to return without knowing three of their own escaped because two of them are highborn."

The major pivoted, whipped his swagger stick up under his left arm, and stormed from the house.

Blake shouted with joy. He threw an arm around Frank and yelled, "You did it, old buddy! You got us transferred where we belong." He looked up at Brooke and winked. "Girls, how soon can you be ready to go? Dress warmly. It will be a miserable, cold ride before we reach a train."

"Is there a town near Pau where we could stay?" Brooke asked.

Blake's exuberance was boundless. "Of course. It's far behind the lines. I'll feel safer knowing you're back where you belong."

"Then we're going with you," Allison said. "We'll get jobs as translators as we did here."

"Fine. Right, Frank?"

Franklin agreed, somewhat dubiously.

The women had gone back upstairs when the door opened and Bulldog Teeter peered in.

"Come on in, Teeter. Close the door." Blake slapped him on the shoulder as the Cowboy looked at the paintings.

"Reminds me of a place I owned once in Virginia City. Won it in a crap game from this here miner fella. Struck it rich three times and blew it three times on craps and poker."

"You owned a chateau?" Blake scoffed.

"Weren't called no fancy name. Met me a woman and let her move in. Next thing I knowed, she had the place swarmin' with fancy ladies. Sluts they was. You paid two dollars downstairs and got a coin the size of a silver dollar—stamped 'Bulldog's Place—Good for One Screw.' All the whorehouses used tokens like that them days. Couldn't keep the ladies honest otherwise. Sold them in the livin' room and gave the girls their share when they turned in my tokens. Burned down, though. See, this big miner was chasin' this little filly all over the top floor, wantin' to do somethin' to her with a candle—a lit one—and next thing we knowed the whole damn place was burnin'. Damn women of the town wouldn't let their menfolk start a bucket brigade until it started burnin' the church next door. And by then, I was out in the cold again."

"Frank, you could learn something about story-telling from this raconteur—liar to you, Teeter. You're without a doubt the damnedest twister of truth I know." Blake laughed in quasi-admiration.

"Lord's truth." Teeter raised his right hand in testimony.

"We'll see when we get to Pau. You say you can fly a plane already. You'll get your chance to show us you aren't full of shit."

"Take you up for a spin first day, less'n you're scared as a prairie dog in a grassfire."

"You're on," Blake agreed. "Providing there's dual controls."

"Controls. What kinda controls? You mean like reins on a horse?"

Blake gave the Cowboy a good-natured push and crossed to the stairs.

"You boys heard the 'hot stuff' about this here Sergeant Frantz?" Teeter asked.

His friends stopped on the stairs.

"No," Blake said for both of them.

"Took hisself up in a Voisin."

"The pusher?" As Franklin remembered, the Voisin was one of twelve airplanes the French had when the war started. With a forty-eight-foot wing span, it had a crew nacelle that looked like a baby carriage jutting outward from between the wings. The nacelle rested on four large, wire-spoked wheels. The observer rode in front, the pilot in the rear.

"Frantz had his observer tote a Hotchkiss gun along a few days back, maybe a month, I don't know."

"A machine gun?"

"Yep. And they done shot a German Aviatik clean outa the sky when they crossed trails."

Blake exploded with enthusiasm. "I told you somebody was going to figure a way to fight in the air!"

The news of the French flyer's success followed months of frustration. Until then experts had been lashing Winchesters and Brownings to the wings and some enterprising aviators had strapped on rifles pointing to the rear. None had proved successful.

"First one shot down, I reckon. Bet we'll all be gunnin' for each other by the time we're puttin' the spurs to them Nieuports."

"Come on, Frank," Blake said. "Let's get our things."

Franklin hesitated and then asked the question that was uppermost in his mind. "Does this mean you won't propose to Brooke?"

Blake winked. "Not today, buddy. Not today."

15

A T Pau the "rollers" scooted along the frozen ground like kiwis, their wings too short to lift them into the air. Officially called Blériot Penguins, the clipped-wing machines were meant only to teach the men to taxi in a straight line.

To Blake Hunter, practicing on a land-bound aircraft was an insult, and he avoided the sessions whenever he could.

To Bulldog Teeter the craft were distant relatives of the bronco, and he wheeled around the field missing other trainees by inches and nosing over when he persisted in pulling the throttle full out in order to jump a ditch between the field and a road. When the tail rose perpendicular to the ground and a bursting gasoline tank almost engulfed him in fire, Teeter leaped free and strode through the French sergeants and officers who rushed over to berate him for destroying an expensive piece of equipment.

"Fix that dang roadrunner, will yuh, while I get me one with some power," he said, ignoring the waving arms and angry shouts of the Frenchmen.

For Franklin the "rollers" were a welcome relief from the hours of hard-to-follow lectures about the art of military flying. He mastered the controls quickly and awaited training aloft.

To the fourth new American in the squadron the roller was not so easy to master. For Duncan Hunter, recently pulled out of the ambulance corps to join his brother, the flightless bulk was a significant obstacle. Too often he worked the wrong controls. He tipped two of the craft over, collided with another, and somehow managed to repeat Teeter's mistake without benefit of a ditch.

When he had been extricated from the up-ended plane, he was called into the commandant's office and given an opportunity to resign. Rather than face his brother and his friends, he left a note and took the first transportation in the direction of the ambulance group serving the 289th.

Later, watching Blake read the farewell note from his brother, Franklin wondered if he detected a hint of satisfaction in the younger Hunter's reaction.

"Too bad Duncan didn't make it," he said, "but it's better he learned he wasn't fit for air duty here than to find out over the front lines."

With the end of preliminary training, the future pilots were given passes and allowed to go into the village for the first time. Although the food at camp was better than the cold, grease-glazed mixtures they had eaten on line, they were hoping to enjoy some good meals with Allison and Brooke.

The two American women had spent little time in the small house they had rented in town. Both were busy with volunteer work, translating for headquarters personnel forced to deal with Americans now that the air service had chosen to allow them in the training program. Twice weekly the girls visited a military hospital nearby, where they read books to English-speaking wounded or wrote letters for them if they could not do it themselves.

Although Allison took the work as an adventure, Brooke found it both sobering and maturing. Death was a new experience for her, and a hard one to deal with. One day she had sat beside a boy from Nebraska, hardly older than she, while he dictated a letter to his parents, telling them how sorry he was that they had quarreled before he left for France.

"I know now it was a mistake," he said. "I should have stayed home and . . ."

He stopped mid-sentence and fell asleep.

But when she looked up his eyes were open.

"Soldier, do you want to rest now? I could come back later. Soldier? Soldier!"

Actually, deep inside she knew he was gone, but she dropped the letter and went screaming out of the ward. Somehow it would have been indecent for the living to accept another's death without protest. Even when the doctor came and leaned over the boy briefly before pulling the sheet over the vacant eyes, she continued to flail at the bonds of mortality.

"Oh, no," she cried foolishly, touching the doctor's arm. "Please, can't you . . .?"

"No, but you can finish the letter," he said curtly. He strode from the room, leaving her to agonize over the last message to his parents. She searched for words to make it right, to make it more acceptable than the terse cablegram the French would get around to sending eventually.

That night and for countless nights to come the boy would return to her thoughts. He must have experienced so little of life. Childhood on a Nebraska farm. A few months of excitement in France.

He should not have wasted a day of his brief time, not an hour. Neither should she, but how did you avoid letting life slip through your fingers an hour, a day, a year at a time? Where did you start? The fact that there were no answers depressed her.

The news that Franklin and Blake were coming lifted her somber mood. They were in high spirits and they stood around the piano singing, with an *obbligato* of snores and snorts from the Cowboy, who was on the couch sleeping off about a fifth of cognac.

When they played the victrola and danced, Franklin suffered every time they exchanged partners and Blake ended up with Brooke.

Once, unwilling to go on watching her in his friend's arms, he had gone out into the kitchen on the pretext of getting a cup of coffee. A few minutes later Brooke found him there alone at the table, the cup still full but no longer hot. She joined him and they tried to make conversation.

"I hear the British troops are having a bad time at Gallipoli," he said. Brilliant opener, he thought sarcastically.

"Where's that?"

"On the coast of Turkey."

"I guess I don't understand what they're doing over there."

He shook his head and ran a thick, strong hand over the dark stubble at his jawline. For the first time she noticed his dark eyebrows in contrast to his wheat-colored hair. "I don't know either," he said. "Somebody said the Allies are trying to knock Turkey out of the war so we can connect up with the Russians."

"The Allies would have the Central Powers surrounded then, wouldn't they?"

"Yes. But it seems the British landed on the beach at the foot of a cliff and they're getting the hell blown out of them. Excuse me. I seem to swear more lately."

"I can understand that." She studied her hands for awhile before she said, "I saw a man die recently."

His gaze fixed on her face. He had not thought of her being where men died.

"At a hospital?"

"Yes."

"Do you want to talk about it? Or . . ."

"No, it wasn't that . . . well, terrible . . . for me. I was taking down a letter to his parents and halfway through a sentence, he just stopped. The worst was finishing the letter to his parents."

"That had to be hard."

There didn't seem to be anything more to say and the conversation stalled again.

Finally she took a deep breath and blurted, "You like Allison, don't you?"

"Of course. She's been wonderful. Generous . . ."

"No, I mean . . . really like her."

"Yes."

"You, uh, you know what she's like, don't you?"

He shook his head. "I'm not sure what you mean."

"Well, what I mean is—and I don't mean to criticize her—but you aren't the only one. Who likes her, that is."

He laughed. "I know. I'm not that naive."

"But you could be finding a girl of your own."

"Like who?"

She backed off, worried that he would think she was suggesting herself. "There are plenty of French girls in town who would give anything to know an American. You're good-looking and—"

"Hey, you two," Blake interrupted, poking his head into the kitchen. "You're spoiling the party. Come on."

Brooke followed him quickly, but Franklin lingered over the cold coffee, unwilling to break the spell of pleasure he had felt being alone with the girl he thought he loved.

The evening ended with Blake staying behind a minute, probably to kiss Brooke good-bye. The other two waited in the imported tin lizzie Brooke had bought so that the boys could get into town more often.

With the start of flight training, the men lost themselves in the thrill of soaring with the eagles.

They trained on Caudron G3s, modified two-seaters with dual controls. The planes were ungainly snarls of wires and struts, with four-wheeled undercarriages and twin rudders set on long booms running aft from the main fuselage. Although the trainee's visibility was limited by the top wing resting on his head, they could fly 70 miles per hour and they were magnificent machines to the men who trained in them.

With his first flight Franklin's apprehension was swept away in the gusts of excitement. He had the sensation of gliding on a sled across a lake of mirror ice. The wind, cold and bracing in his face, made him feel like an arrow slicing through the sky.

On his first short flight he saw a bird and waved to it, wondering how it felt about the huge invaders in their domain.

Only the dead-stick landings bothered him. With the engine off, the plane plummeted through space like a dead bird. The ground rushed at him with alarming speed, and although he learned to control his nerves, he was far from comfortable with the maneuver.

Blake of course was soloing after the first two hours aloft, and Teeter claimed he was ready after less than six hours with dual controls.

"Easier'n steerin' a herd a cattle," he bragged. "Give me a chance and I'll show all you Frenchies what a Yank can do."

Irritated by his boasting, the instructors turned him loose on an outmoded pusher returned from the front lines as too obsolete to be of value. With the entire camp as an audience, Teeter took the pusher down the runway at full speed, got her off the ground, came down again, bounced twice, banked with her left wingtip inches off the ground, and flew straight into the side of a barn.

Climbing out of the wreckage, the undaunted Cowboy launched a verbal offensive against the Frenchmen he expected to wash him out of the service.

"You frog bastards didn't tell me the controls was all ass-backwards on that thing," he bellowed.

The instructors sputtered in Gallic fury, but he stalked away, marched to an old Caudron G2, yelled at the mechanic to turn the prop and climbed into the cockpit. Before the officers still inspecting the wreck realized what he was doing, he had the second plane roaring across the grass field.

The plane lifted off smoothly and went into a climbing turn. It gained altitude, made a circle, and came sweeping down across the field, wheels no more than ten feet from the ground and aimed directly at the heads of the instructors. It dropped three feet more, forced them to flatten themselves in the dirt, and then climbed again for the pallid late-winter sky. For twenty minutes he performed acrobatics with the clumsy craft, before he set her down easy and taxied into the original position.

He skinned off his cap and isinglass goggles and strutted off into the pilots' lounge.

Behind him a gallery of admirers stared in amazement. Blake expressed their unanimous opinion.

"By God, that Cowboy can fly!"

Franklin shook his head and laughed. "Whe-e-ew! I never thought he'd make it." Then he turned and asked to try his luck next.

The Frenchman nodded, still stunned by the success of the man none of them believed capable of anything more than braggadocio.

Taking no chances that the *sous lieutenant* would change his mind, Franklin rushed to the same aircraft Teeter had used and climbed in, snugging down his cap, his goggles, and tugging on heavy, fleece-lined leather gloves.

A fleeting shiver of uncertainty gave way to the challenge of testing himself against the machine. As the mechanic turned the prop and the engine sputtered into life again, he thought of Brooke Madigan. If he couldn't have her, there seemed no reason to fear real danger, much less the minimal risk of soloing.

Maybe he wanted to die.

Or perhaps he was just trying to become a participant in life.

He gave the thumbs-up signal and the chocks were pulled from beneath the wheels. More throttle and the Caudron moved forward tentatively. A light wind rushing past him grew to a howling gale as he picked up speed. Gently, the way he had been taught, he pulled back on the stick. He was using too much space, he realized. There were trees in the distance, and if he didn't clear the ground in time, he would plow directly into them or clip their leafless branches.

More throttle. Climb. Climb. His lips formed the words.

His fingers squeezed tight on the stick, the plane lifted, and the wind lay against him like a wall. The wings shuddered. The struts seemed about to snap. Meaning to ease off, he cut the speed too much; the undercarriage smacked the ground with a jolt that bounced the craft up again. It was sinking for a second time when he clenched his teeth and gave her the throttle she needed.

He was climbing at a steep angle. Too steep. He could feel the sickening sensation he got when the instructor had deliberately stalled the training craft to show him how to correct for the mistake. But they had practiced that thousands of feet in the air. With only several hundred feet between him and the ground, he wondered if there was time for the only maneuver that would save him from killing the engine. He had to put the nose down and accelerate. If he was too low, he would plow into the ground nose-first.

Gamble. It was the only way.

Pushing the stick forward, he nosed down from the climb and plunged at once into a dive. The ground came up as if viewed through a telescope. He felt like a pedestrian trapped on a trestle with a locomotive bearing down on him. He wanted to close his eyes, to try to pull out of the headlong plunge, but he knew he would crash if he acted too soon and stalled the airplane.

At this speed instinct superseded instrument. He hauled back on the stick and gave the plane full throttle.

Nothing. The plane rushed faster toward doom. Then as he braced for the end, the plunging bird lifted her beak and began to rise. Twenty feet above the ground he had her horizontal to the field with trees looming ahead.

Chancing a stall again, he banked, clipped a few top branches with his wheels and surged up into the milky blue.

Franklin DeWitt inhaled, perhaps for the first time since he had started taxiing.

The air felt good, cold and clean. He let his hand relax on the stick, flying straight, keeping the wings level before he tested himself in banks and turns. Finally he climbed higher, and found himself suspended in a brilliant puff of cotton cloud. He stuck his hand out, half expecting to get some of the white stuff to stick to his fingers; what he felt was the damp spindrift of the surf. In the next instant he was above the clouds, looking down.

The world was more beautiful and orderly than he had realized. Everything was toylike, sharply defined. A road became a straight line, a village divided by right angles.

He had seen it all before; alone at the controls, however, he viewed the panorama anew. Everything seemed brighter, cleaner, in sharper focus. Here he was his own man, with no war, no mud, no stench to dim his perception.

And no Brooke Madigan. For the first time in his life he had done something that really mattered to him, and he wanted to share it with her. He had to know if she would care.

Nosing down again, he scanned the countryside for the landmarks that led him back to the field. He circled twice and finally brought the airplane down with only a couple of bounces before he cut the throttle. He did not try to taxi back to the hangar. Instead he sat in the cockpit, grinning inwardly, while his friends and instructors ran forward to congratulate him.

They helped him from the plane and into a waiting truck that took all the men who had soloed that day, plus Blake Hunter, to the nearest tavern. They stormed in, shouting in a variety of languages, and tossing money on the counter.

"I ought to go," Franklin said more than once to Blake, but the others bought him one drink after another. He was getting drunker by the minute.

"Wanna tell Brooke," he said, his tongue thick and clumsy in his mouth.

"Watch it, buddy," Blake laughed. "Don't get our girls mixed up. I wouldn't want you to lay the wrong one. Allison is yours. Remember? Here, you better have another drink. It'll clear your head." He pushed the bottle toward Franklin, then picked it up and filled the glass for his friend.

Franklin bent over the drink and felt his head swimming. His mind was fuzzy and he wasn't thinking too well, either. Maybe he should tell Allison. She'd be more impressed. They'd been close here at Pau, had made love several times, and he liked her candor. Why did he persist in wanting Brooke?

She was Blake's girl. Should forget her. She was hard to relax with, anyway. They never did get around to subjects that would give him a chance to say what he felt. On the rare occasions when they had been alone together, they discussed things like Booth Tarkington's latest books. As the voice of adolescent America, some of his novels told of boys who were in love and incapable of telling a girl of their feelings.

Franklin wished Brooke would see the parallel between him and the younger heroes of the popular writer. Instead she turned their conversations to Harold Bell Wright's *The Eyes of the World,* a righteous protest against artists who prostituted themselves for money.

"Don't let that happen to you, Franklin," she cautioned. "Write the truth."

"When I know it," he had said.

But I need help with the love story, he had wanted to add. Why hadn't he said it? What would she have said? He had thought about putting it in a letter to her, about telling her he loved her. But then he had never been satisfied with a sentence he had written; why then would he *write* the most important thing he had to say?

Maybe tonight, buoyed with the day's success and the false confidence that liquor brings, he could do it. He'd tell her about the flight and then . . .

"Gotta go," he said, tossing off a glass of cognac as a chaser for the champagne and wine that had gone before. "Gotta tell Brooke."

He was still mumbling when his friends bundled him into the truck and drove him back to the base.

16

Brooke sat in the bleachers along the edge of the airfield and watched the band march by and then the new aviators. When their lieutenant gave the command, the flyers came to a disciplined halt and right-faced toward the audience and the aged general who had come to do the honors.

Blake stood at the far right of the troop, the position of distinction marking the high scores he had attained in proving his skills as a pilot. He was undeniably handsome, she thought, dashing actually, tall and dark in his aviator's outfit with the Sam Brown belt and the khaki pants bloused in his knee-high boots. Like the other men he wore a white scarf around his neck and new sergeant's stripes on his sleeve. Each carried a swagger stick, making them in-

distinguishable from the officers except for the desig-
nation of rank on their shoulders.

They were the emerging elite, the _chasse_ . . . the
combat flyers. The military recognized them as far
more skilled than the average foot soldier, yet the
French brass was reluctant to let the bulging ranks
of aviators into the officer corps directly.

They were made sergeants, therefore, kept in a sort
of limbo, but they were proud and happy as the general pinned the silver wings above their breast pockets.

Brooke smiled and applauded when Blake received
his wings. She did the same for Franklin. He saluted
the general smartly and then turned his eyes to where
she sat, and she was surprised to feel her heart doing
funny little flip-flops. A wave of pride swelled within
her.

He was a pilot; he had made it. Obviously she had
been right in asking her father to intervene, to use
his influence in obtaining the transfer for the sensitive young writer. Despite what Blake had said about
his nerves, he had shown no sign of strain during
the weeks of arduous training. For that matter, she
would never have known he had a problem if Blake
hadn't warned her. Sometimes she almost wondered
if it was a fabrication Blake had designed for his
own aggrandizement; she knew that he was not above
denigrating others now and then.

For some reason Franklin had not come to the
house often since she and Allison had come to Pau.
That had disappointed her. And he had gotten drunk
on the day he soloed, waiting until later in the week
to come to the cottage and share his triumph. Blake
had apologized for him the first night, and had taken

her and Allison out to dinner at the hotel's small but excellent restaurant.

By the time the ceremony was over and the new flyers were moving toward the stands to greet those who had come to watch, Brooke had made up her mind. She was returning to the Sorbonne, perhaps to the States if the school would not admit her so late in the term. She was giving in to the letters of rebuke that arrived almost weekly from home.

"A cheap camp-follower," her father had called her. He could not abide her trailing two soldiers around, even though one of them was Allison's brother, and he had threatened to cut off her allowance. It was funny, too; her mother had been running around alone writing about the war down in Cuba for the publisher William Randolph Hearst when her father had met her. He apparently thought none the worse of her, but then fathers were different where daughters were concerned. It did hurt, though, especially when he knew she did plan to go back to school. Thank goodness her mother understood how it felt to be young and in the midst of history as it was happening.

She would not let her father spoil today. Franklin and Blake were flyers now. They would not have to die in some bloody hole or be forced to bayonet some German youth like the one from Nebraska who had died while she sat beside his bed.

Like many others, Brooke did not equate flying with war and killing. It was glamour. It attracted exciting men like Blake, men who were fun. Of course Franklin was . . . well, intriguing was a better word. He was too quiet and moody to be fun, she had to admit, especially lately. Now that he could use his typewriter again he was even quieter, more engrossed in his writing. And he didn't ask her to read it anymore.

With the ceremony over, Blake and Franklin, along with the roguish Teeter, came running across the field, waving envelopes and shouting that they had their orders.

"No leaves?" Brooke asked Franklin when he reached her.

He was grinning broadly. "No. But I made it, Brooke! I made it!" In his elation he grabbed her in his arms, swung her off the ground, and kissed her quickly.

He put her down and stepped back, embarrassed. "I'm sorry," he said. "I guess I got carried away."

"Don't be sorry," she smiled. What would Allison say to a man as indecisive as Franklin? She gathered up her courage and gave it a try. "I enjoyed it."

"You did?" His surprise seemed genuine.

Before she could respond Allison was there. "What about me? Don't I get a kiss?"

I was wrong, Brooke thought, as Allison hooked her arm through Franklin's. I should have told him to kiss me again.

Blake and the jubilant Teeter were making plans for the evening.

"Just like the night after a round-up," Teeter announced. "No keepin' us in the bunkhouse!"

"Remember, we leave early," Franklin warned.

"For where?" Brooke asked, her throat suddenly constricting.

He didn't know, and Teeter didn't care. "You can stay in the barracks, but this ole boy is burnin' up

Pau tonight and the ladies is welcome to come along, if'n they're so inclined."

"Of course we are, aren't we, Allison?" Brooke responded quickly.

Did she imagine it or did Franklin disapprove? He didn't fault the impetuous and forward Allison; why should she be different? She was disgusted with herself. What do I care what such a prude thinks anyway? she thought.

"Naturally!" Allison said enthusiastically. "Don't be such an old poop-in-the-head, Franklin. You'll have days to nurse your hangover."

"Well, sure I'll go," Franklin said. "It's just that with orders out for tomorrow the town will be wild tonight—not much of a place for you girls, probably."

Brooke tossed her head impatiently, swishing the silky black mane that she had let hang long and loose around her shoulders that day.

They ate at the hotel, drank good wine, and toasted everything American from President Wilson to an Indian maiden Teeter had begged to marry him until her father came after him with a tomahawk. From the hotel they wandered across the street to a café where only aviators were allowed. Tonight there were a number of women present, too, some of them dates of the regulars.

For Brooke it was a memorable experience. The floor was more dirt than stone, and broken bottles crunched under their shoes. If there were windows they were not visible in the dark bar or near the stage at the other end of the room. The unsteady tables had legs of various lengths and straight-backed chairs that had been shaped with no regard for the human body. The chairs worked for the management, though, by forcing the drinkers to hunch forward over their glasses of cheap wine and watery bar liquor. The air was heavy with the smell of cigars and cigarettes, cheap perfume and the castor oil used in the airplane engines.

There was a round-shouldered piano player who won applause when he played "Dark Town Strutter's Ball" or "Yankee Doodle" and ducked live cigarettes which the men tossed when he played something less popular. Periodically some girls in lumpy tights pranced around the stage, collecting a variety of tossed coins and catcalls until they wiggled their ample *derrières* in an inexpert cancan.

Several of the women at the tables sat in the men's laps and drank and giggled while their dates ran appreciative fingers along legs and thighs.

Blake brushed aside the sordid surroundings with an offhand, "It's war, what can you expect?" But Franklin wanted Brooke to leave.

"This is no place for you." Then he added lamely, "You're just too young."

"Why?" she countered. She tried to join in the wildness, but a few minutes later she felt his hand on her arm. "Please, Brooke. Let me walk you back to your house. I don't feel right with you here."

Allison raised a sardonic eyebrow at her friend's sudden acceptance of Franklin's request and then turned back to the distinguished major she'd been flirting with.

Talking little, Brooke and Franklin walked out into the cold spring night, the boisterous talk and laughter dying away behind them.

They were almost at the cottage when he broke the silence.

"You'll be going home or to Paris, I suppose. Allison said your father was giving you trouble about neglecting your studies."

She laughed. Neglecting her studies was more than a euphemism. She had neglected her life, acted like a tramp. She had followed two men around the country when she was not even certain that she cared about either one of them. Maybe she was wilder than her mother, although she had managed to stay a virgin.

Sometimes she wondered why she was saving herself and, more important, for whom.

"You ought to go home," Franklin said flatly.

"To the States?"

"Yes. I really wonder if the French can hold out much longer. No telling what these Germans would do with women they took prisoner. You've read the atrocities they've committed in Belgium. They used flame throwers to burn women and children and they have that Big Bertha."

"The one they named after Mrs. Krupp?"

He nodded. "They'll be shelling Paris soon from seventy-five miles away."

She had reached the cottage door and was unlocking it. "But with the zeppelins who'll be safe anywhere? London? The United States? Who knows?" She went in without inviting him, wondering if he would follow.

She lit a lamp. He had come in and closed the door. He was painfully bashful. Why did she bother with him? He obviously thought of her as little more than a younger sister.

"Well, I'm safely home now," she said.

He did not take the hint.

"Brooke, I had to see you tonight."

"Oh?"

"I interfered in your life," he said, "when I had no right."

"Oh?" She sat on the old-fashioned sofa while he stood with his cap in hand. She waited, hoping he would finally get to the point.

"I knew you and Blake . . . you know . . ."

She made no effort to help him. "No, I don't know."

"Well, I know you belong to Blake—I can't blame you. He's good-looking, a lot of fun, a good friend."

Her patience had worn away. "Franklin DeWitt, I don't have the faintest idea what your point is, but I do not—I repeat, do not—belong to Blake or to anybody but myself!"

"I didn't mean anything wrong, Brooke. I know you wouldn't do anything . . . improper."

"Well, thanks for nothing!"

"I mean, he was going to ask you to marry him."

"*Marry* me? Blake?" Even to him the incredulity sounded real.

"You sound surprised."

"Shouldn't I be?"

"I don't know, but you see, I stopped him. He was going to ask you and I interfered. In a way I took advantage of him."

He walked to the couch and sat down somewhat tentatively, with one cushion separating them, the distance between them a Great Wall of China, a Verdun fortress, a Rock of Gibraltar.

"He would have married you if he had stayed in the infantry where he was more confident. He knows aircraft, recognizes that it's even more dangerous than ground duty, and I made his transfer possible."

"My own father helped. You were just doing a friend a favor."

"I didn't do it for him."

She cocked her head quizzically. "Then why did you help him?"

"To stop him from marrying you."

"You didn't think I'd be a good wife for him?"

"No. Nothing like that. You know better."

"Then why, Franklin? Just once—just this once—answer a question directly."

"Because . . . because I hoped it . . . I wanted you for myself."

"You?" She laughed. She was filled with pleasure and relief until she saw the hurt in his eyes.

Surprisingly, he lashed back at her. "Yes, damn it. I may not be as good-looking as he is. Maybe you're too rich, too spoiled for me. But yes, Miss Madigan, I was fool enough to think I had a chance with you myself. If you find that amusing, I'm glad I provided you with your entertainment for the evening."

He rose and stalked toward the door.

"Franklin," she called. "Franklin!"

Wordlessly, he slammed the door and headed back toward the café.

She followed him a short distance, calling after him. "Franklin, I wasn't laughing at you. Truly I wasn't."

If he heard her he gave no sign, and when someone came out on to the porch next door she retreated into the house. In a town inundated with carousing flyers, a ruckus in the street was not to be taken lightly. In a moment the gendarmes would be summoned.

She was angry but elated—angry because he would not give her a chance to explain, elated because at last he had spoken out, and although confessions were supposed to bring catharsis to the speaker, the words had relaxed a tightly wound spring of tension inside her. *Franklin cared about her.*

All the restlessness that had sent her traveling around a country at war drained out of her; a cold place inside had thawed.

She lay down on the couch and snuggled into the pillows, wondering as she did if she should go after him. No. He should assert himself. He would. He would come back and they would straighten things out.

She'd tell him . . . What would she tell him? That her father's wealth and power, her family's social position, didn't mean that he was below her? No, that wouldn't do. That he was intelligent and attractive and she hoped they would see more of each other, that she wouldn't go back to the States after all? No, he wouldn't like it if she was too bold.

But why had she been staying in France? It had grown old and ugly with the war.

You've stayed here because of Franklin, she told herself. Admit it. Admit you're interested, infatuated. In love? Certainly not in love. They had spent so little time together.

But wars had a way of compressing time. A few years ago the motor car had seemed a modern miracle, accelerating life into a new phase of speed. Now men were soaring with the birds.

Her Franklin was flying. She liked the sound of that.

She closed her eyes, half expecting him to come

back at any moment. Probably after he had a few drinks to give him courage. Funny. A man could fight in the front lines, kill another with the butt of his rifle, fly airplanes, but he'd need alcohol to talk to a woman.

When he came back, she would scold him . . . just a little. A smile of anticipation lifted the corners of her mouth as she pulled the afghan off the back of the couch and drifted into a dreamless sleep.

When she awoke it was the sound of the front door that startled her.

"Franklin?" she asked.

It was Allison, quite drunk, her hair and clothing disheveled. And there was daylight in the street behind her, the sound of lorries moving through the street.

"Ooh," Brooke said, stretching. "What time is it?" She looked at the pendant watch still hanging around her neck.

"It must be morning," Allison mumbled. "I feel too awful for it to be night."

Morning? It couldn't be morning.

"You weren't out all night, certainly."

Allison blinked and sank into a chair.

"Why ask me? You should know. You were the one who was here."

Brooke looked out into the street where a lorry was making a turn at the end of the village.

"Franklin—is he gone?"

The unsteady Allison looked at her through glazed eyes. Thinking was painful. "I remember I kissed him a lot. Yes, I think he was going somewhere. He and the others. And the major." She giggled. "Especially the major."

Brooke felt her body tighten with apprehension and regret. She had let Franklin go without saying good-bye, without breaking the barrier of misunderstanding between them. She did not know where he was going or when he would be back, or if he would be back at all.

17

D URING THE REMAINDER of winter, spring and into summer they flew Caudron G3s. In the two-seater aircraft they were no more than taxi drivers for the observers who helped make range adjustments for the artillery and gave warnings of impending charges by the Germans.

While the flights lacked excitement at first, the enemy soon improved their special anti-aircraft cannons, throwing projectiles at the aerial intruders. For Franklin DeWitt the first close encounter came while he was ignoring the puffs of ground-based fire that had seemed so harmless in his early forays across the line.

This time a strong jolt shook his plane. A hole appeared in his right wing. The shell had pierced the

fabric, breaking two ribs of the wing without exploding on impact.

He stared at it, his mind and body numbed. He
should be dead. The thing should have exploded and
torn him and the plane to pieces just as shells shredded everything in their paths on the ground. He felt
cold. A shudder shook him. Then just as suddenly,
as if to revitalize him, a red-hot flush tingled in his
cheeks.

After the numbness came panic. It was a new sensation. Until now—with the odds stacked against the
enemy in the vast arena of the sky and with the
noisy engine blotting out the bursts of 77 and 105-
millimeter shells—the anti-aircraft fire had not worried him. His euphoria was over.

In the next instant, the engine quit. The plane's
heart had stopped. Her punctured gas tank spewed
gas like an old mare emptying her bladder.

Franklin swallowed hard against the fear that rose
inside him and tightened choking fingers in his chest.

With the engine dead he could hear his observer
screaming. "Do something!" he shrilled in French.
"We're going to crash!"

Damned right we're going to crash, Franklin
thought with perverse superiority. He didn't need to
be told you can't stay airborne without an engine.

In a way it was a seductive moment, something so
memorable it should not be erased by death. For
brief seconds he was a hawk gliding down for the
kill, eyes boring into the mushrooming landscape that
grew as if a magnifying glass were lowered over it.
Green patches became trees; stamp-sized shapes took
on the dimensions of buildings, flat places mounded

into hills. The only sound was the whistle and roar of wind as the huge bird soared toward death.

Enemy machine gunners, who should have been concentrating on the infantry about to overrun them, raised their barrels and started shooting at the aircraft gliding slowly earthward. At its reduced speed the Caudron was an easier trophy, an eagle turned turkey. Bullets jabbed the wings and fuselage like so many sewing machine needles on canvas.

To Franklin, gazing downward, the earth seemed to rise. Ant paths were roads now; insects had become trucks. The young pilot swept the scene below with frantic eyes.

No place to land. Couldn't maneuver if there were. Must not lose speed—need it to land. Heading right into a skirmish. Cannons, small arms' fire. Open space between the trenches. Ground gray-white and muddy. Every hole a wallow. Coming fast. Men running . . . barbed wire, pickets . . . ground blurring . . . parapet ahead . . .

No great thoughts before I die? No truth?

The plane hit with a joint-splitting thud, ran its nose up against the parapet, and lifted its tail like a scorpion.

Franklin felt himself tossed as if in a barrel at a carnival funhouse. A hard jerk across the upper part of his legs stopped the churning motion and he was suspended upside down. With unsteady fingers he grabbed the carbine from its scabbard on the inside of the cockpit, unfastened his belt, and dropped into the mud.

Bullets twanged past him; the plane and its occupants were easy targets. A spiked helmet charged in from the left and Franklin stopped him with a single shot.

"Get out," he yelled at his observer, but the man was in the other seat, hanging upside down and cursing the pilot as if he were to blame. Two more Germans had emerged from behind the one lying inert beyond the plane. Discouraging them with shots in their direction, Franklin stuck his head up into the cockpit and tried to unfasten the trapped man's belt. With the Frenchman's full weight on the belt and the clip wedged between his legs, the man was impossible to free unless he aided Franklin's efforts. "Unbuckle it, you dumb shit! Unbuckle it!" the American bellowed.

The hysterical observer was still flailing ineffectively and hissing oaths at his ally when half of his face blotched red. His hands fell, dangling below what was left of his head in a kind of bloody, inverted surrender.

"Shit!" Franklin grunted. The fool was dead; served him right. He should have concentrated on saving himself; you don't stay alive cussing fate or your pilot on a battlefield.

Franklin pulled himself away from the plane and rolled into a shell hole. He lay there with his carbine as waves of French soldiers rushed over him. Some grinned down at him as they ran past into the chattering machine guns. One jumped into the hole, shook his hand, and climbed out again to resume his headlong thrust toward the enemy lines.

No one asked him to help, and so he sat there until dark when the futile attack had spent its human ammunition and the stragglers came stumbling back. He joined them, found the communication trenches and crawled along until he located a lorry that would take him to his base.

Dropped off a mile from his headquarters, he had to walk in, and he felt like a fool when he entered the pilots' mess.

"I got shot down," he said before anybody could ask.

"From the ground?" Blake asked.

"Yes."

"But nobody gets shot down by anti-aircraft fire!" Hunter roared.

"You do if you draw to inside straights like the kid does sometimes," Teeter observed.

Franklin kicked mud off his shoes. "I had to shoot my way out like a goddamned *poilu*."

"What happened to your observer?" somebody asked.

"He got killed."

"Oh!"

For the dead man, the single word was both elegy and epitaph.

The group chose to continue joking about DeWitt's bad luck. It was better than thinking it could happen to any of them, on any mission. The sense of invulnerability given them by the lofty heights at which they worked had been badly marred.

In the morning they returned to their flying, the dead man forgotten. Some, however, gave wider berths to the German aircraft they passed occasionally, and flew around areas that were known to be heavily stocked with anti-aircraft weapons.

On the ground the war settled into a gruesome stalemate, while the air battle took on new dimensions. Germans began fixing machine guns to all their aircraft and sent one French plane after another down in flames. The surviving flyers held elaborate funerals for their dead comrades . . . until they began to come too frequently.

Finally, with the inventiveness that grows out of need, machine guns were positioned for the observers, and the first German to attack the newly armed Caudron made the mistake of approaching Blake Hunter's aircraft. Instead of turning back toward his own lines the moment an enemy plane was sighted, as had become the custom, he looked back over his shoulder.

The dark shape was coming up from the rear. The bastard would be expecting an easy kill, Blake thought, already savoring the pleasure of gloating to his comrades, already basking in anticipated glory.

Behind the American pilot, the French observer loosened his seat belt, leaned far forward out of his cockpit and hit the pilot hard on the shoulder. There was a look of terror on the kid's face; although he had practiced with the gun, he had hoped he would never be required to test his skill.

"Yeah, I see him," Blake shouted, nodding vigorously, for his words were lost in the sputtering of the engine.

"Shoot him down!" he yelled, pointing to the movable weapon.

He put the Caudron into a steep dive, forcing the observer to pull himself back into his seat before they leveled off again. The German, in a new Fokker, seemed to relish what appeared to be his quarry's attempt to escape. The difference between what he got and what he expected was the difference between hooking a game fish that dove and thrashed against the hook and pulling a bottom fish off the ocean

floor. After a few tugs, the bottom fish would suffocate when its internal pressures exceeded the weight
of the surrounding water. Its guts would burst outward; death would come quickly, without a struggle.

But the German had a marlin on the hook. The
Caudron was swerving and twisting, flying as close
to the ground as it dared. In recognition of his catch's
frantic maneuvers, the German gave him line and
played him, diving behind him and attacking from
above and slightly to the rear. What the unwary
angler did not know was that it was he who was
being played.

Even the violent maneuvering was part of Blake's
calculated plan; the German was doing just what he
was supposed to. By playing scared, Hunter would
lure the complacent German close enough to nail
him with the first fire from the hidden machine gun
that the Jerry did not know was aboard the French
craft.

"Come on, baby," Blake coaxed his machine. He
put the Caudron through its tough paces deliberately,
forcing both the German and the observer to hold
their fire.

He glanced over his shoulder; that too was part
of his plan. When the German was close enough to
make out the shapes of the men in the two-seater,
he would think he had his targets terrorized, a slice
of drama that could make him neglect the newly in-
stalled drum-loaded machine gun.

At the last second Blake caught the attention of
the man in the rear seat and formed the word "now"
on his lips.

The Frenchman understood. He nodded and while
the Caudron continued to play for position, the

Frenchman settled down behind his gun and waited.

At the last moment before the German would have to start shooting at the darting two-seater, Hunter straightened her and held her on a deliberate course. He could visualize the German throttling back, fixing his sights on the target, moving his finger to the trigger.

Before the Fokker could fire his first burst, tracer bullets stabbed streaks of light first above, then below him, and finally, as the Frenchman bracketed him, straight into the German's engine. The propeller disintegrated. Parts of it tore back into the engine and in a blinding, orange flash the fuel tank burst. The Fokker became a ball of flame that stopped abruptly in place; then it was a meteor, a central cluster of fire trailing its wide, burning tail of smoke and debris.

"Good show there, Sergeant Hunter," Blake said in smug self-congratulation.

He held up a thumb in recognition of the gunner who had made the ploy a success.

For Blake, the expectation of reliving the triumph was what made the victory worthwhile. As expected, word had spread already and he was met by mechanics and fellow pilots who ran to the plane. Any evidence of success was a moment of triumph for the all of the squadron, all of France.

Nothing had gone well for the Allies. The kaiser's force had reached the channel and were blockading the islands with submarines. The Turks had entered the battle on the side of the Central Powers, offset by a feeble Italy that came into the war on the side of the French and English.

Blake's triumph, therefore, was a boost for the entire escadrille. Although the actual kill had been made by the gunner, the Yank absorbed the glory, telling and retelling the story of the maneuverings that had made the machine gun effective.

"Make them attack from above and behind," he said, demonstrating with his hands. "It's suicide for them."

"Even with their own weapons?" Teeter asked. "Sounds like a Mexican showdown to me."

"You're wrong," Blake said emphatically. "The Fokker had to maneuver his entire plane to change his aim. My gunner had a stable platform from which to fire. Like I said, coax them to come in from above and behind. They'll never get you from that position."

He swung his white scarf over his shoulder and started to enter the barracks.

Franklin DeWitt was coming out, sullen and depressed, the way he had been for months. There was no secret about his glowering attitude. Brooke Madigan had not written since they left flight school, nor had he. What little he knew of her he learned from parts of letters she and Allison had written to Blake, who shared the news selectively.

"Hey, Frank," Teeter called, "you hear what our boy Hunter just did?"

"No."

"Shot down a Fokker, he did."

DeWitt's response was a dry "Congratulations."

"Easy," Blake started. "I—"

"Later. They're sending me up to look for that long-range gun the Germans are using. I got a photographer waiting."

"You going up this late?" Teeter asked.

"Yeah. Orders."

"What if you don't get back before dark? Momma ain't gonna leave no light in the window for you, y'know."

Franklin shrugged.

"Better listen to what I have to tell you, Frank. If you get attacked, your cameraman can use the machine gun to—"

"There's no gun. They took it off to make room for the camera."

Frank elbowed his way through the crowd.

They watched him go, and Blake shook his head. Once inside, he stripped off his helmet and flight jacket and then went over to headquarters to report his triumph. Having absorbed all the accolades available from that quarter, he stayed in the barracks long enough to write to Brooke and his sister.

They were in Paris again at the embassy, and they were bored. Brooke, however, had been refusing to accompany Allison on another foray into the battle zone. Blake's efforts to lure them to a town near the base had proved fruitless, and as he closed the letter, he thought of something that might serve two purposes: put an edge of modesty on his . . . well, colorful account of the air battle and also perhaps entice Brooke into changing her plans about remaining in Paris.

There was no point in kidding himself. Brooke was infatuated with DeWitt, whether she would admit it or not. Some women wanted a loser, somebody they could mother. Allison had written letters full of adjectives and interjections about dates she had arranged for her friend with French and British staff officers. Nothing had come of them.

Both the war and his love life were at a stalemate, Blake had to admit. He had screwed the whores in town—several of them hadn't even insisted that he pay—and had made love to a few of the nicer girls around Pau, too, but he needed to see Brooke. If he did, he would be able to convince her that she was concentrating on the wrong man, a weakling, more boy than man.

At the bottom of the letter he wrote the bait:

"Unfortunately my success today has had a negative effect I failed to foresee. Apparently still trying to compete with me, Frank has volunteered for a photography mission deep behind enemy lines, starting too late to guarantee a daylight return. I fear my friend puts little value on his life, forgetting there is still hope for the courageous and wise, but no more than a fiery death for those who overrate themselves."

That should do it. Brooke would come running if she thought she might be responsible for his friend's reckless behavior.

He posted the letter and ordered a driver to take him into town to the club where the flyers from the dawn patrol were beginning their daily ritual of drinking and whatever came after. It made a man feel good to have a reason for wild, boisterous behavior. Blake always became the center of the celebrants, those whose aircraft had served them well for another day.

Ready to retell his own story, he was surprised that other news superseded his. A pilot named Bill Thaw, the first American to fly in combat against the Germans, had returned from a brief stay in the hospital with a report that the French were going ahead with plans to form a squadron strictly for Yanks.

"Norman Prince is working on it," Thaw said, with obvious relish for the concept. Prince, another of the early volunteers scattered through the French air service, had gained a name for himself with his persistence.

"They're thinking of calling it the 'escadrille américaine.'" Thaw said. "You interested, Hunter?"

"More observation flying?" Blake was sick of flying above the enemy lines while his observer peered at the ground. Even the puffs of anti-aircraft fire bursting around him and sometimes even punching holes in the fabric of his plane had become mundane. He was confident he could outrun any of the new single-seat Fokkers the Germans were putting into the air. Today was the first fun he had had in weeks.

"No," the American called Cowdin replied. "Fighters. I said leave me out if we don't get fighters."

"Nieuports?" Blake asked hopefully.

"Sooner or later," Cowdin assured him. "The Vanderbilts are putting up twenty thousand dollars to back the plan and the Germans are raising hell, saying it violates American neutrality. But what the shit, they sank the Lusitania and sent a couple of hundred Americans to the bottom of the sea. I say neutrality is just President Wilson's political weapon for re-election. The Democrats will stop bragging that he kept us out of war as soon as he wins his second term. Then all those pacifist and German Bund members will have to come in on the side of the Allies. So, I'd like nothing better than to fly in an all-American outfit."

"Count me in." Blake said. It would be an exclusive club; he would want to belong if it ever came to fruition.

"Me, too," Bulldog agreed. "I been in this man's army nigh onta two years and I still don't get the hang of the lingo. The other day I gave a slut five bucks and asked for a fuck. You know what I got?"

"A dollar bill in exchange," Cowdin guessed.

"Right. She hands me a buck, tells me to buzz off, and calls the gendarmes when I tried to take my rights. That ain't legal. When I ran a whorehouse, a guy got what he paid for. If he couldn't come, we gave him a different girl or a refund. I got respect then, more'n I do with these friggin' Frenchies. Count me in."

"What about DeWitt?" Cowdin wondered.

Blake thought about the letter he had written today. It wouldn't do much good unless he and Frank stayed together. Besides, he felt responsible for him. Often he veered off his mapped course to draw German anti-aircraft fire away from Frank or even to make Fokkers choose between two targets instead of one.

Of course, DeWitt and Teeter did the same. It caught all three of them hell once in awhile, but they had been freezing their asses off through their second winter for the French and no one could blame them if they looked out for each other.

"Yeah, put him down," Blake said. "He'll go along with Teeter and me if he doesn't get killed on this damned fool mission this afternoon."

Photography missions were among the most dangerous. The pilot had to fly low and on a steady course that made ground fire far more effective. He wished his friend had not been chosen for the task.

In his present mood, Frank was likely to relentlessly pursue the mission with dogged, detached determination, the kind of attitude that could cost him his life.

18

THE AFTERNOON SKY was clear, the temperature cool. Franklin DeWitt flew with a map open on his lap. An edge was tucked under each leg to keep the wind from tearing it out of the cockpit. In the seat behind him was a former newspaper photographer who had joined the military and had been flying missions since the beginning of the war. A native of Paris, he had arrived at the squadron earlier in the day with orders for the solitary mission.

The Caudron had fuel for four hours aloft. Fuel would be no problem as they probed deeper into German territory; time was the limitation. They'd had less than three and a half hours of daylight left when they took to the air.

Visibility was good, the sky dotted with cirrus clouds at twenty or thirty thousand feet, and they encountered no enemy aircraft. If the mission failed today, the next pilot and photographer could expect a more alert enemy.

What they were trying to find was a 380mm gun that had been lobbing shells into the French city of Nancy. For an hour they flew uneventfully; then Franklin changed course, heading on a northeasterly angle toward Hampont, where the big gun was supposed to be hidden.

From below came the signals that the Germans suspected his purpose. They were waiting for him with eight-pound shrapnel shells as he approached the suspected gunsite. The sapphire sky blossomed black with explosions while Frank dropped to a lower altitude and began making passes over the woods, starting at one edge and working his way back and forth to the far side of the tree line.

The photographer seemed to ignore the chunks of metal flying around him; his main concern was the camera. Shielding it with his body, he tripped the shutters at regular intervals, capturing on film as much of the ground as he could. He had to fight the wind to change the flat, heavy plate-holders that he slid in and out behind the lens of the camera.

Halfway through the picture-taking, the ground gunners found their range. Shrapnel bit holes in the wings. Machine gun bullets with tracers assisting arced up and zinged around the slow-moving Caudron. A few riflemen, perhaps bored with their position so far behind the lines, joined in, plinking at the airborne target.

Franklin DeWitt accepted the danger with a certain detachment, as he had for weeks. Why not? No matter how close the enemy fire came he would con-

tinue to make the necessary passes until the required
pictures were taken or until they were shot down.
So why sweat it? Anyway, for him life was *sans con-
séquence*, not worth extraordinary measures to preserve. While he blamed his attitude on Brooke Madigan's harsh rebuff, he knew part of it was the sheer
fatigue of constant flying. The other pilots solved it
with liquor, occasionally earning themselves a day
off with hangovers that the commanders condemned
but also understood. Frank never missed. Weather
permitting, he was in the air. He had even begun
to neglect his writing, although the book had started
to take rough form since he had last seen Brooke.
He had learned even in rejection. Now he could
write with understanding about the psychological ef-
fects of unreturned love as well as the thrill of war
in the sky.

As if to rekindle the experiences that filled the first
half of his novel, the anti-aircraft fire suddenly became effective.

A bracing wire snapped. Then another broke loose
and vibrated in the wind, singing a single, high-
pitched note. Jagged steel kited over him, and he
ducked involuntarily. Another hunk shattered a strut.
The whirling propeller spit chips off one of its blades.

A slight chattering started in the pistons after
damage made the engine shaft turn unevenly. Minute by minute the unwelcome sound grew. A speck
of oil splattered on the windscreen like a drop of
blood, the blood of the engine that kept them airborne and alive.

"Turn back!" the French photographer shouted.
When he couldn't make himself heard, he hit Frank
on the shoulder with the swagger stick he carried

with him even in the air. A lieutenant, he considered himself the commander of any airplane he boarded. He was the reason for the mission; the pilot was merely his chauffeur. "Turn back," he said again, forming the words carefully with his lips as observers and pilots had learned to do. "I have all the pictures."

Frank nodded.

He moved the stick and the aircraft shuddered. The fabric on the right lower wing was shredded, pieces of it flapping in the wind like streamers.

More of the 77mm shells pierced the Caudron's airspace. Two interwing struts were cut, and the rudder cables hung by strands. Franklin knew the aircraft could fold itself like a broken kite at any moment and plunge to the ground. He had seen others do it when less damaged than this one.

The engine was threatening to shake itself apart; airspeed was dropping. There was no longer any hope of getting back to the field before dark.

The lieutenant, checking his expensive wristwatch, tapped Frank on the shoulder again. When the pilot looked back, the photographer was pointing at the ground. He wanted to take a chance on a crash landing.

Frank looked over the side. Several of the fields below looked flat enough, but he passed over each, coaxing the engine along, gripped by a compulsion as if he had a duty to the plane. When a German airfield showed up to the south, the lieutenant hit him smartly with the riding crop and then pointed toward the strip. He wanted to land and surrender. The pilot acknowledged receipt of the message—and ignored it.

Hell, he thought, he'd been shot down from the ground before. Other pilots managed to fly through shrapnel time after time without taking a hit on their aircraft. He would not crash-land again; he'd fly the damned plane home or die trying.

He felt excitement melting the doldrums that had frozen his emotions for so long. He had a challenge: how long could he keep the ship in the air?

Toy-sized Fokkers were moving on the field below. That did not bother him; with luck, darkness would force them back before they reached him.

He was flying into a red and yellow sunset, a creation so beautiful that it defied description. He caught himself trying to put it in to words, while his plane continued to tear and quiver around him.

"Splashes of reds, yellows and luminous green streaking out parallel to the horizon," he said, trying to memorize his own words, "emanating from an orange ball that beckons as it sinks below the landscape. The sky darkening from blues into charcoal. Then it's gone like one man's life, all men's lives, leaving a faint glow for awhile, before it fades into night."

The sky flicked on a few stars, but there was no moon to help him with landmarks. Lights in the villages below were useless to him since he could not see to match them with his map. He had to fly by dead reckoning.

It didn't matter. He would fly until the wings cracked and tore away completely, or the engine conked out, or the fuel was gone. Then he would select the darkest terrain and try a dead-stick landing. Maybe one or both of them would survive. The photographs might escape destruction. If they did the French could push toward the woods and force the Germans to withdraw the long-range artillery piece. Perhaps the city of Nancy could still be saved.

He twisted around, hoping that he could make the photographer understand what he intended to do.

He was shocked by what he saw. The lieutenant was standing on the seat trying to pull himself out. He was going to jump.

It wasn't a reaction that was uncommon to pilots in burning planes. When death seemed inevitable, they jumped. This was different, however; the lieutenant was choosing suicide simply because he could not stand waiting to die. Frank yelled at him and motioned for him to sit down. When the Frenchman did not comply, the pilot pointed the craft's nose into a climb and relied on gravity to push the photographer back into his seat again.

The maneuver, successful as it was, was costly. More of the fabric shredded, and they began to lose altitude. The windshield was thick with oil. Fire spat out of the cowling.

Slipping the aircraft to the port side, Franklin let the change of wind direction douse the fire, temporarily at least. But the stick jiggled in his hand like chattering teeth telling him that he had to find a place to land before the damaged ship did it for him.

Then, ahead, he saw parallel lines.

Although he didn't recognize what they were, they provided a target and he aimed for them. It was not until after he allowed the nose to come down below the level, that he figured out what the lights were.

Signals.

He hoped.

Bonfires built along either side of the field, lighting his way home.

"Goddamn!" he breathed. His fatalism soared off into the wind.

There were men down there who cared about him, who wanted his safe return, who hadn't given up. They expected the impossible from him. For the first time he felt a part of the camaraderie of the flying service; until this moment it had escaped him.

They wanted him back.

He had a home.

Something new for his novel. A kind of love or affection or bond that existed when people had a common enemy. When he could not have Brooke, he had thought he had a right to let himself die. Now he knew better. He had to live for the squadron; they wanted him back.

He swung around in his seat to tell the photographer the good news. They had a chance.

"Lieutenant! Hey, look, Lieutenant!"

There was no one behind him. He stretched as far as he could without losing control of the stick and tried to reach into the rear seat. Even in the dark he could tell it was empty except for the camera equipment.

"My God!" he said aloud.

The plane shuddered again and the engine coughed. He worked the throttle like a pump, letting his hand tip and turn the stick to correct each uncontrolled movement before it sent the craft canting into the earth.

His mind was whirling. He was with the lieutenant, falling, hurtling downward through the darkness, waiting, anticipating the horrible impact that would come, gritting his teeth, digging his nails into his hands in expectation of that final burst of pain that would explode through his brain, that would register for one awful moment through every nerve in his body. And then, abruptly, the pain would end.

"The fool," Frank said as the lights came up to meet him.

Still, he couldn't condemn the photographer. Nothing was that simple. The man had chosen when he would die, how much agony he would endure in what he considered a hopeless situation.

He could still be right.

The plane was losing altitude too fast, coming down of its own volition. Whether it was responding to the stick or not, whether he was going to crash short of the field—he couldn't tell. It was out of his hands.

As if in reply the stick flopped back; the last control cable must have broken. There was nothing left to do except rear back in the seat, put as much space between himself and the ground as possible, an inch, less than that. A man ought to fight off death until the last, the very last.

God, he thought, let me live to write that. There is hope. Sometimes.

The wheels hit and the undercarriage collapsed. The Caudron went skidding straight down between the signal fires for twenty yards, then turned and rolled over on one wing. Frank felt himself upside down, upright again, and then upside down once more.

There was a loud pop as the last of the gasoline exploded and he was caught, hanging from his safety belt, unable to free himself. Fire snaked along the shreds of fabric, traveling toward the cockpit.

Shit. To come this far and then burn to death.

There was no God. He should have jumped with the photographer.

Faces appeared at the edge of the fire, peering into the heat to see if he was alive, if they should risk their lives to save him.

Bulldog Teeter came running through the crowd. He ducked under the upside-down aircraft, his fingers probing for the lock to the restraining belt.

Then Blake Hunter was there, looking angry, as if he didn't want to take the chance but could not let himself be outdone by the braggart Cowboy.

Whatever his reasons, he was there. So were the others now and Frank was shouting as he dropped to the ground on his shoulders.

"Get the film! Get the film!"

He tried to fight his way into the observer's compartment but he was hauled away. Moments later men emerged from the mixture of flame and smoke and showed him the film holders they had retrieved.

"I'm all right," Frank said, standing away from the supportive hands of his rescuers. His shoulder hurt and he could feel burns on his hands. His forehead felt scorched; otherwise he was all right.

"You made it," Teeter said, speaking over the crackling fire.

"Boy, we got you out of there just in time," Blake said. "What the hell were you thinking of? If I hadn't ordered those signal fires lit you could have come down anywhere."

"Thanks," Frank replied.

What else was there he could say?

"What happened to the photographer?" a Frenchman asked.

Frank took a deep breath. God, he needed a drink. He had never cared much for booze, but now he needed a drink.

"The lieutenant jumped," he said tonelessly.

Then he started back toward the headquarters building. Tonight he was going to get drunk and stay drunk.

19

THEY MOVED to Luxeuil-les-Bains, a resort town less than fifty miles from the Swiss border, six of them at first, then more as the squadron grew. With the exception of the commander, Captain Georges Thénault, his executive officer, Lieutenant Alfred de Laage de Maux, and the famous French pilot, Felix Louis Maurice Happe, the incoming pilots were all Americans.

Above the gate leading into the stone villa confiscated for their barracks, a sign had been painted before they arrived: *"L'Escadrille Américaine—N. 124."* The flags, however, were French. The working language was to be French, too, but English emerged dominant, and the mechanics and orderlies who hadn't mastered the second language in school learned the Yankee version in a hurry. They peppered it with slang and the familiar epithets "bastards" and "son-of-a-bitches." Some accidentally added a southern drawl to their French through association with the indomitable Bulldog Teeter.

For Blake Hunter this was the way wars ought to be fought. He did not concern himself with the carnage of the last battle at Verdun or the premise that the allied high command now accepted. America had to be brought into the war if the Allies were to stand any chance of holding off the Germans. The war was going into its third year, and mutiny marched with the French army. As casualty figures passed the million mark and continued to climb, the fear of execution for cowardice lessened with the near certainty of death in the trenches.

It did not bother Hunter that he and his American comrades were bait—tempting morsels who served two purposes. They encouraged other Americans to seek glory by pressuring Wilson to aid the faltering Allies, and they were the carrot that kept the French *poilus* and the British tommies going. The Lafayette Escadrille, as many called the new unit, was a promise to those living like rats in the trenches that the Americans would be coming soon—millions of them.

As the newspapers and government officials hinted at every opportunity, the flyers were only the forward elements of the American troops that were so desperately needed. Like Hunter, the others in the escadrille did not consider—much less feel any qualms over—the fact that they were being used to lure their nation into a slaughter that cost a hundred thousand lives every time a few yards of shell-pocked real estate changed hands.

The area comprising the department of Haute-Saône where they were to fight was a quiet pool fifty miles and a world removed from the war's violent waters.

Safely behind the battle lines, the elegant villa glistened in spring sunshine. A stone wall enclosed the gardens, which were still tended by an old man who had lived his entire life on the estate. Several other servants had remained behind when the former occupant, a self-proclaimed count who had made the mistake of expressing German sentiments, decided it was safer to spend the war years abroad.

Around the villa were verdant pine-covered hills, where a stream started and wandered down inside the walled garden. Fragrant lilacs posed in mirrored ponds that had been stocked with trout until the owner's abrupt departure. Near the circular drive, weeping birches bowed over plots of tulips and purple pansies.

In addition to the estate's genteel ambiance, there were other notable perquisites for the Americans. Each of them had a room to himself on the second floor. They dined in a spacious, richly paneled hall, stuffing themselves on excellent French cuisine. Privates took care of their clothing, and a car was always available to take them to Luxeuil.

The place fascinated Franklin. "Used to be a spa," he told Bulldog as they drove through the village for the first time. "I'll bet the Roman soldiers used to boil away their aches and pains here."

"But look at all the broads," Bulldog said, indicating the women visible on the main thoroughfare. "Ain't there no men?"

"Don't you know there's a war on?" Blake joked, assuming a prefectorial pose. "All the men are on the line."

"What does that make us?" Teeter retorted.

"Smart," Blake beamed.

To Franklin the village was the first unspoiled stretch of France he had seen in months. Not a single house was scarred by shells, nor did the streets teem with soldiers. The place even lay beyond the sound of guns at the front.

In order to preserve the resort atmosphere, the military had kept building to a minimum. The airfield, the only army installation in the area, consisted only of hangars and storage sheds, and in order to avoid building barracks the men, to their delight, were quartered in the city.

Only a five-minute walk along the cobblestone street was the Hôtel Pomme d'Or where the rich and famous had dined for generations. Since this was their last night before reporting for duty, the three Americans decided to treat themselves. They ate on white linen from gleaming covered dishes of gourmet food. There was an overabundance of wine, and when they left the restaurant, Frank carried two bottles under his arm.

Although he seldom drank, he sat in the villa's main salon and finished both bottles before he staggered up to bed. As common as drinking was among all the pilots, it bothered Blake to see his quiet friend so drunk with duty starting tomorrow.

In the morning, though, Frank was ready for the truck that took them to the airfield. He had skipped breakfast, his eyes were bloodshot, and he had little to say to the others.

Their new commanding officer explained their mission briefly. They were to provide fighter support for a bomber squadron based on another airfield. Their bombardment unit commander also spoke to them. He was Captain Felix Louis Maurice Happe, the most famous pilot of his kind in all of France, better known by his nickname, the Red Corsair. Speaking through a thick beard, he told them he flew a two-year-old Maurice Farman pusher with an added tank to extend his range. He had already flown more than a hundred miles behind the enemy lines to bomb the zeppelin sheds.

A measure of the respect the Germans accorded him was the six thousand dollars they were offering for anyone who could shoot him down.

Happe was infamous for taking risks that he somehow managed to survive while his escort went down in flames. Having lost so many of his own men, he welcomed the Americans, except for one important drawback: they had arrived before their aircraft.

Captain Thénault fired off protests daily and in May six Nieuports arrived in vans. Finding them disassembled, the pilots joined with mechanics in piecing all the thousands of parts together. When they were finished they had Nieuport IIs, the latest French single-seat fighters.

There was a racy top wing that gave them a sportier appearance than the old Caudrons, and they could fly at speeds up to a hundred miles per hour. They were quick climbers too, with a short twenty-five-foot wingspan and 110-horsepower nine-cylinder engines.

Its faults were few. One was the radical engine design that made the aircraft persist in veering right unless the pilot adjusted for the tendency. Another was its speed. With no carburetor, the engines ran at top speed or not at all. An ignition control switch on the instrument panel provided the only solution. With it the pilots could cut off the power as necessary.

The ship lacked one feature the Americans had hoped for—a gun like those on German aircraft, one that was synchronized to fire through the prop, thereby making it easier to aim. Although the French were the first to recognize the value of firing straight ahead from the pilot's eye level, their solution of putting metal on the blades had proven impractical. However, when one of the French planes with the protected propeller had been forced to land behind German lines, the Germans had been quick to recognize its advantages and to improve upon it. They designed a gear that interrupted the machine gun whenever the propeller was in a position to get struck by a bullet. The French, in over a year, had not been able to duplicate the innovation.

The Nieuports were armed with a drum-fed .303 caliber Lewis gun fixed on the the top wing where the fire missed the prop. Five seconds of continuous shooting exhausted the ammunition in the drum, leaving the pilot the tricky task of holding the aircraft control stick with his knees while he rose up into the airstream to replace the empty drum.

"In combat that damn fool design is going to cost some of us our lives," Franklin observed.

"Like goin' to a gun fight and loadin' your Colt after the other guy starts his draw," Teeter agreed. "But she's what we got, so she's what we fly. In a rodeo I rassled whatever horse I drawed, so I won't be complainin' about this beauty."

When several Nieuports had been completed, two of the most experienced pilots, Kiffin Rockwell and Gervais Lufbery, took off on the squadron's first dawn patrol. On the ground, the others worked feverishly throughout the morning to ready their planes, then paused as a courier arrived on a motorcycle and dashed into Captain Thénault's headquarters.

The commander came out gray-faced, and when he spoke his voice was thick. "It's Rockwell," he said. "He tried to attack an Aviatik from behind."

Blake groaned. He had risked his life and the life of his gunner just to prove his theory about attacking an armed two-seater, and on the first day of the escadrille's official operation, one of its key pilots had failed to heed the warning.

"Lufbery is all right," the captain added, "and the artillerymen brought back Rockwell's body."

The captain returned to his office and the men returned their attention to the assembly job, working with new vigor.

Two days later, Franklin, Blake and Teeter were among the aviators who flew overhead and scattered flowers from their cockpits as their comrade was buried near where he had fallen.

While hundreds of thousands had died in the trenches and in the skies, the death of the American flyer snared the attention of newspapers and diplomats throughout the world.

He was eulogized by French and American writers, castigated by the German press as a violator of his homeland's neutrality.

In the escadrille the death spawned a desire for revenge that was frustrated by a stupid shortage of ammunition, a shortage that occurred while millions of rounds were being expended over the Somme in another futile land battle.

Grounded, the pilots roamed the countryside with shotguns, hunting for game, or fished streams for lurking trout.

But Franklin DeWitt drank. He wandered into the village when he awoke in the morning, ensconced himself at a table, and drank until friends half-carried him back to his room.

When their first assignment came, Blake Hunter tried to discourage his friend but to no avail. They were to be part of a massive French and British bombing mission against the factory at Oberndorf, where the standard German 7.92mm Mauser rifle was made.

It was a bleary-eyed Franklin DeWitt who climbed into the cockpit of his Nieuport as sixteen pathetically slow French bombers prepared to join British and Canadian long-range aircraft for the attack. On his left an uncommonly serious Bulldog Teeter and on his right a concerned Blake Hunter watched while their friend went raggedly through the motions of preflight check-out.

He had slipped on the step cut into the side of the aircraft, but managed to get his legs over the padded rim. He ducked his head, suggesting he had strapped himself in. The ship's rudder flipped from side to side. The elevator rose and lowered, and the ailerons on the top wings passed through opposing arcs.

Hunter's mechanic pulled the propeller to suck fuel into the cylinders.

"Contact," the mechanic called.

Blake turned the ignition to "on" and echoed, "Contact."

Once again the mechanic spun the prop, and this time the engine clattered into life.

Frank was already taxiing for a take-off position. He bounced twice, then rose at an abnormally steep incline. On the ground the men who knew him watched anxiously, afraid he would stall and plunge the short distance to the ground. They breathed easier as he continued to climb.

Moments later Blake's mechanic pulled the blocks from the wheels, and the men holding the lower wing released their grip. The Nieuport moved smoothly down the field, the pilot holding the stick forward until he felt the tail rise from the grass. He drew the control stick slowly toward his crotch and the plane lifted like a graceful bird.

Bulldog was behind him. His take-off was rougher, and he climbed fast to join the first plane off the ground. Other escadrille pilots soared up behind them, while at a nearby field the first Farman bomber was rolling down the runway. Then came the awkward Bréguet-Michelins.

At first the Nieuports provided the only protection. They were quickly joined by twenty-four new British Strutters flying in perfect formation, contrasting with the individualism of the *escadrille américaine*.

The air armada moved eastward. They flew without resistance over the red tile roofs of villages that had been untouched by war. Then the sky erupted with bursting shells and streaks of machine gun tracers arching in the direction of the low-flying Farmans. Some turned back; one took a 77mm shell, wobbled a bit, and spiraled down like a wounded quail that fights death all the way to oblivion.

The flight reached the Rhine, and the Nieuports, nearing the extreme limits of their range, began their slow turn toward home. It was not good news when the shelling from below ceased. Blake looked up, anticipating the Fokker E-IIIs that were coming down out of the sun to pounce on the trailing bombers. The Strutters were too far ahead to scatter the attackers before they made their first lethal pass, Hunter reckoned as he weighed the danger of using his fuel reserve to intercept the Germans against the good he might accomplish.

To the east of him one Nieuport seemed oblivious to the fuel problem. It was climbing straight toward the enemy.

"Frank, you stupid-ass drunk," Blake muttered. "Be goddamned if you'll sucker me into the same fool stunt."

On the other side, to the west, planes from the escadrille had already chosen the prudent course and were heading for home. But a second had joined De-Witt in the daring challenge against superior aircraft, numbers, and time as measured by fuel supply.

It had to be Teeter. The big-mouthed idiot was going to make a pass at the Fokkers and take another fable of heroism back to the base with him.

"Shit!" Blake could think of a hundred reasons for letting the two fools kill themselves and none for involving himself, but he banked, came around, and climbed toward the enemy. He depressed the trigger and tested his machine gun; at least it worked.

Ahead of him, DeWitt's plane canted directly into the point of the diving attackers. Hunter could see the Nieuport's gun spitting tracers into the startled leader of the Fokkers, a bold, flaming red target. The first burst hit and the German continued on his course, wings wobbling, the fuselage drifting off into a slow roll, trailing smoke and streamers of fuel.

For an instant the entire diving formation opened up on the foolhardy American, who sailed straight through them and lined himself up behind the falling red Fokker.

"Shoot!" Blake yelled. "Finish the bastard!"

But no further shots came from the trailing French plane. The German, hopelessly damaged, would have to land immediately; the pilot might escape alive.

Franklin pulled away, giving the German the gift of life. Then he came around for another try at drawing the Fokkers away from the bombers.

Now he had to reload.

Leveling off, he reached up for the rear of the gun to bring it down so that the barrel pointed upward. Using both hands and half-standing, he wrestled the clumsy empty ammunition drum loose and lifted a loaded one. He was forced to hold the flat side against the rushing wind until he could seat it on the empty spindle.

It was an operation that a pilot either learned to do quickly or died before he mastered the skill.

The Germans absorbed a second shock when Bulldog Teeter joined them, settled in the middle of the formation, and began pumping bullets into the tail of the wing man to the right of the smoking leader.

"Insane!" Hunter yelled into the whistling wind. "I'm following a drunk and an imbecile!"

Teeter's target veered out of formation and headed for a cloud, its left wing fabric tearing away like a sail. The Cowboy was still in the formation, swinging over to take on the third man in what had been a V-shaped pattern. Behind him a Fokker was trying to get into position to shoot without hitting his comrades in the process.

Blake plunged into the fight from the rear of the Germans, firing at the side of one enemy aircraft, sweeping over him by no more than ten feet and pumping shells into the man on the far side. The enemy formation had lost shape; trained and disciplined men, confronted by suicidal attack, succumbed to panic and turned the sky into a beehive.

A plane zipped in front of Blake; his hand was closing on the trigger when he realized it was Frank with a Fokker locked on his tail. Another was coming at Hunter. What should he do first, shake his own attacker or save his friend? From the course he was taking, apparently in search of a new target, Frank seemed to be unaware that he was about to be chewed up from the rear.

Or didn't he care?

"Shit!" Blake roared again. Why not let the horse's ass go down in flames? He would die a hero, at least, instead of a stupid, love-sick drunk.

A hero!

Ah! The citation flashed across his mind. *"Ignoring an enemy aircraft on his own tail, Aviation Sergeant Blake Langley Hunter heroically went to the rescue of his fellow pilot, the late Sergeant Franklin De-Witt."*

He banked his plane, leveled it and slipped into position behind the German who was shooting at the hungover American ahead of him. My bullets could hit Frank, Blake thought fleetingly, but he fired anyway, using the full magazine of shells in one long burst that he corrected until he saw the pilot slump down in the cockpit.

A second later bullets slashed into Blake's Nieuport. Unlike him, the German taking him on as a target had been afraid of hitting his compatriot; now, with his squadron mate spinning out of control, he could take his revenge.

Blake hauled back on the stick, climbed into a loop and leveled off upside down, escaping the slicing bullets for the briefest of seconds. Next he used the ailerons to put the plane into a spin; his unwelcome adversary stayed right with him.

Again the thought of the decoration he had just earned inserted itself into his mind.

There was only one difference. It was beginning to look as if they would add a couple of words to the end of the citation.

"*Awarded posthumously.*"

Coming out of the spin, he worked the rudder and flew a twisting, turning route that a snake might take across desert sand.

Nothing would shake the German on his tail.

"Where the hell are you two?" he shouted at DeWitt and Teeter. "Where are you when I need you, you goddamned fucking sons-a-bitches!"

He barrel-rolled, his plane retching under the strain, and from his crazy, whirling maelstrom, he thought he saw two planes flying low, heading west.

DeWitt and Teeter. The bastards were on the way home.

"Goddamn," the lone flyer cursed as he tried his last trick. He pulled back on the stick, climbed almost straight up and let the Nieuport stall. The Fokker came after him, missing by inches as the French plane began its fall to earth. The German stalled too, only his situation was worse. For an instant he poised on his tail, then flipped backward and fell like a rock.

Still playing the long shot, Blake pushed the stick forward, prayed the power wouldn't fail, and went through an interminable moment of agony as he waited for the plane to make its choice: nose over and go forward or flip back and follow the German.

When it finally put its propeller forward and down, his problems were only beginning. The ground was rushing up. He had little altitude and probably not enough speed to pull up. He had to wait.

The ground was coming up. Fast.

He had to guess the speed it would take to bring the plane's nose up again. His decision was strictly instinct; when he could stand it no longer, he pulled out sharply, closing his eyes. He had never done that in an airplane before, but there was nothing to see except the ground waiting to kill him.

He opened his eyes to the rattle of a machine gun. He was no more than fifty feet off the ground, skimming along above the heads of the Germans in the front trenches as they tried to utilize the split second they had him in their sights.

Then the machine gun fire stopped.

Now the men in the trenches below were waving at him. He was across the lines and headed home.

"Damn you, DeWitt," he said. His muscles were beginning to relax. "And you, Teeter. We won't even get credit for the kills, you stupid asses."

Then he laughed.

At least he was still alive.

20

BLAKE'S NIEUPORT sputtered in for a landing on little more than fumes from the bottom of its gas tank. The captain was waiting when he climbed down. His greeting was cold, accusing.

"Where were you when Teeter and DeWitt took on the Fokkers?" he asked sharply.

The angry American snorted and pointed at his plane. "Guess," he said grimly. The damage spoke for itself.

The captain was unimpressed. "Did you hear what DeWitt got while you were letting the krauts wreck your plane?" Blake didn't want to know. "He was shooting down the Red Baron, should you be interested."

Blake drew up short. He knew the name, of course. Baron Manfred von Richthofen, the German ace of

aces, had taken to painting his aircraft red. In the
excitement of the flight, Blake had failed to make the
connection when he saw Frank chasing the red Fokker. But, of course, it had to be von Richthofen. No
one else in the German air force would dare imitate
their leader.

Blake was fuming mad. With fool's luck, DeWitt
had bested him again.

"He didn't kill him," Blake said. He sounded more
positive than he was. "I saw the plane crash. The
baron walked away from it." While that was a lie,
he was sure the man would have survived—if he was
the flyer he was reputed to be.

"How do you know?" the captain challenged.

Again the young Yank pointed at his battered
Nieuport. "I was there." He strode away, asking the
mechanics where he could find DeWitt.

"At the hotel," they told him. They might as
well have added, "Where else?"

The bar in the hotel's restaurant had become Franklin's primary lodging. He spent more time there than
he did at the field or in the villa. This time Teeter
would be with him and Hunter was glad; he was
mad as hell at both of them. They had damn near
cost him his life.

He entered the café, slamming the door behind him
with a sharp bang, and then passed through another
into the café. It was too early for most of the flyers;
only one table in the darkest corner was occupied;
he steered a straight course toward it.

"DeWitt, you drunken bastard—" he began. Then
he saw the third figure in the dim light.

"Blake dear," his sister said from the chair between
his two friends.

"Allison! What are you doing here?" The words were snappish with impatience.

She stood and leaned across the table to be kissed. "You invited me, remember?"

That stopped him. In the excitement and frustration of the day he had forgotten the invitation. He shook his head as if to clear away cobwebs, and then he remembered why he had invited her.

"Did Brooke come with you?" he asked.

Her response was giddy with wine. "No, she's being an old maid fuddy-duddy. Doesn't go anywhere. I had to come alone. I think she's mad at one of you. And she has a job at the embassy."

Hunter let the disappointment pass and again leveled his attack at DeWitt. "Just what the hell did you think you were doing up there today, taking on that flock of Fokkers when we were short of fuel?"

Teeter answered for him. "He was doin' his job, chasin' coyote away from the herd."

"Like shit," Blake scoffed, aiming his verbal assault like a machine gun directly at Franklin. "You were too hung over to read your fuel gauge. Admit it, you fuckin' slob."

Allison, shocked by the torrent of invective her brother was pouring on his former roommate, tried to intervene. "Blake, what on earth has gotten into you, talking to Franklin like that?"

"I'll tell you what I'm pissed about. We were supposed to escort bombers this morning. We get to the end of our range and everybody turns back like we were ordered to do—everybody except these two jackasses."

Teeter laughed. "Well, I'll be danged if you ain't

jealous! Frank shot down the Red Baron himself. Drilled a couple more besides."

"Confirmed?" Blake challenged. "Did anybody outside the squadron see it go down? Hell, no. We were so far behind enemy lines and the bombers were so far ahead, you won't get a whisper of credit."

Frank removed the glass just far enough from his lips to speak across it, his words flat with disinterest. "I don't give a latrine full of shit whether anybody saw it or not."

"Well, I do," Blake barked. "Confirmed kills are the name of the game we're playing. All we're going to get out of this is an ass-chewin' for getting our ships shot to hell."

"We?" The Cowboy slammed his glass on the table; luckily, it was almost empty.

"Yeah." Franklin was thick-tongued. "Where do you get off with this 'we' bit? It was Teeter who broke up that attack."

"And who the hell do you think shot that Fokker off your tail?" Blake grabbed a chair and swung it around, sitting astride it as he yelled for the barmaid to bring him a drink.

"Teeter," Franklin said.

Bulldog set his glass aside. "Weren't nobody up there protectin' DeWitt's ass. I was too busy coverin' my own."

"You?" the young writer sounded incredulous, but the truth was beginning to dawn.

Blake said, "Hell, yes. You were so goddamned busy with your own target you forgot to cover your hind end."

"I knew he was there. I just thought what's the difference? You can't live forever."

"You sayin' you came back with us, Hunter?"

"Damn right I am. Didn't you see me?"

"Saw Fokkers thicker'n gnats around a lantern and another Nieuport now and then. Figured it was just Frank and me crazy enough to go back for the sport, what with the fuel we had left."

"I don't understand what's going on," Allison complained.

Franklin sipped his drink without enjoyment. "Your brother is saying he saved my life today."

"And did he?"

"If it wasn't Teeter, then it had to be him. How come, Blake? What did you do it for?"

"Why?" Hunter repeated. A good question.

"Yeah, why?" His despondent friend wouldn't be put off so easily. "You've been taking care of me like a little brother since this goddamned war started. Is that why you did it again?"

"No! Not that you don't need a keeper lately. Lately, hell. You've never been able to take care of yourself."

"Bullshit!" Teeter snorted. "You was just afraid we'd out-shoot you. You been making this a personal contest since the beginning."

Allison giggled. "That sounds like a Hunter. We always have to go everybody else one better. Don't we, Blake? It's a family trait."

Her brother didn't answer.

Franklin broke the lengthening silence, mouthing the realization of his own mistake.

"Shit, we left you back there alone, didn't we?"

"You're fuckin' right you did. Without fuel and a hotshot kraut stuck on my tail like a flea."

"Jesus, Blake," Teeter apologized, "I had no idea.

I wouldn't cut and run on a cowpoke from my own spread. You know that. How the hell did you shake the bastard?"

"Teased him into a stall. He couldn't recover; I did."

"Whe-e-ew!" Bulldog was impressed. "You got two today."

"Two and no confirmation and nobody coverin' my rear when I needed you."

The revelation had sobered Franklin. "Blake, I'm sorry. I didn't know. If I'd seen—"

"Maybe you would have seen if you weren't always pouring this crap into your head." With a sweep of his left arm he cleared the table of drinks, including his own. He rose and stalked off, ignoring his sister's voice calling after him.

Outside, he turned toward the villa, his mind still flaming with anger.

When he reached the house, he tore off his heavy flight jacket and flung it at his orderly, a kid of fifteen, orphaned by the war and crazy about planes. He could see a group of pilots playing poker in the game room, using squares of toilet paper on which they had written their IOUs. One of the older men threw the first jibe at him.

"Hey, Hunter, what happened to that Nieuport of yours today? Some farmer pump you full of buckshot when you tried to fly off with his daughter?"

Blake's tall bulk filled the door, ready for a fight. "I knocked down two Jerries today. Is that good enough?"

"Sure, sure. Only nobody was watching."

"Right," Blake responded, "because you chickens had all run home to roost."

"Aw, come on, Hunter, you didn't get any Jerries today; who you tryin' to kid?" another pilot chuckled.

"The hell I didn't. One without firing a shot. And anybody wants to dispute it, get a plane and meet me at five thousand feet. We'll see who can fly and who just flies off at the mouth."

"Blake, calm down," the older pilot said soothingly. "It's Germans we're supposed to kill."

"I'm telling you I did."

"Okay, okay. From the looks of your plane you sure were into something. Maybe somebody on the ground can confirm it."

"There were Germans on the ground shooting up at me. They're not going to confirm anything."

"But you got 'em. That's what counts."

"Not to me, it doesn't. I want to paint black Maltese crosses on my ship. A hundred of them if I can."

"You will. You're a good pilot. Not like that drunken friend of yours. Lucky bastard shoots down the Red Baron and doesn't even know what he's done. That ought to be worth some pretty good press in the hometown paper." The older pilot had left the table and joined Blake. He switched subjects, obviously trying to calm the younger man. "Say, did you hear they're changing our name officially? The Lafayette Escadrille, after that French aristocrat who helped us fight the British in 1776, you know."

Blake started up the stairs with his orderly behind him. "That damned Wilson is never going to send any troops over, the bloody coward."

"We're going to paint an American Indian head on our planes," the other man was saying. "We're beginning to get recognition. And we're moving out of this sector, too. It's too quiet here. I hear we're heading for the Somme. Lord knows they need us there with another winter coming on."

Hunter heard the last from a distance as he jerked open the door to his room and almost swung it into his attendant's face.

Did he want some lunch? the boy was asking.

"No!" Blake flopped on the bed and folded his arms behind his neck.

"Will Monsieur DeWitt be eating?" the boy asked. He served DeWitt and Teeter, too. They paid him with the money they got from the wealthy Americans supporting the escadrille or with their funds from home. France didn't pay them enough to keep them in cigarettes.

Before he answered, he took his gold case from an inner pocket and tried to get a flame from his lighter, but his hand was shaking. The aftermath of the morning had set in, that special kind of fear that sets in after a brush with death. He had come so close to dying. So god-awful close.

"Sir?"

The obsequious orderly was still awaiting an answer.

The kid was the only one around to absorb his fury. "No! Monsieur DeWitt will not be eating lunch or dinner or breakfast. He'll be at the hotel getting pissy-eyed drunk and screwing my sister until the dawn patrol, and then he'll probably fly off and try to get killed over a girl he could have had for the price of a postcard."

"Sir?" the confused boy asked again.

The kid did not understand at all.

"Nothing. Just get out." Irritated and suddenly enervated, he pitched a pillow at the hesitant youth and then lay back and studied the ceiling as the orderly left the room.

What did he expect to see up there on that ceiling? he wondered. Why did anyone lie and stare at a ceiling?

Somebody with brains should invent an answer machine, and you could lie on your back, stare at the ceiling, and ask the questions that bubble up in your mind. The machine could project answers like the titles on a motion picture screen. The inventor would be richer than DuPont.

But what was the question he wanted answered?

Why had he gone back for DeWitt? If it had been that crazy Teeter, he would probably have let the big-mouthed braggart get killed.

But Frank was different.

Was he trying to protect a friend?

Were they really friends?

Or was he competing, trying to prove he was better? Was Frank doing the same?

I'm a better flyer, he told himself. Better looking, smarter, better educated. Why do I have to keep proving it to Frank? Why do I have to prove it to anybody?

His sister was right: he was as bad as she was, only while she was a glutton for sex, it was praise that he craved.

21

EVEN FOR LATE SUMMER it was unusually hot and
sultry in Paris. Brooke Madigan, in her room
at the embassy, was thoroughly unhappy, as uncomfortable emotionally as she was physically. She
was sticky, itchy and irritated—inside and out. Dis-
satisfied with who she was and where she was, un-
sure of what it was she wanted, she wandered from
desk to window to bed and then back to the window
again. It had been this way since the day Allison
had gone south to visit her brother.

When Blake's invitation first arrived, Brooke had
been tempted to accept. It would serve Franklin right
if she visited his friend and ignored him completely;
he hadn't even cared enough to write. But she had
changed her mind.

Would he think she was chasing after him? That

was something she wouldn't do—for any man. Forget
him, she told herself. She tried but it did not work.
Each day she waited eagerly for the mail; each day
when nothing came, she grew more miserable until,
finally in the depths of depression, she bought a
ticket on a liner heading home for the States.

She would have gone, too, postponing the trip, she
told herself, because it wasn't safe traveling on the
ocean now that the Germans had declared open sub-
marine warfare on any ship approaching the shores
of their enemies. Although President Wilson might
thrash and threaten about tactics that endangered
neutral civilians, there was nothing he could do short
of the war he refused to declare. It was sound and
fury, signifying nothing, as the bard had put it.

Shakespeare . . . school . . . I should at least be
studying if I stay here, she thought. I'm just drifting,
like the war, a great turmoil with neither side moving
in either direction. Yet it seemed silly to sit in class
and read about history when she lived it every day,
swirled in it, felt it, saw it, touched it. So futile to
study the economics and governments of countries
whose borders might be wiped out tomorrow. So dull
to read Greek and Shakespearean tragedies while
France lived out its own. Someday she would want to
study again, but not now.

So she worked in the embassy at a dull job, dating
the uninteresting men Allison kept bringing around.

Then Blake's letter had come and she had been
sorely tempted to go along with Allison. Instead,
pride kept her in Paris. And what did she do now
to keep from going crazy? Knit some more socks that
would somehow wind up being sold in the Paris blackmarket? Or make some more pajamas for the men at

the front—now that she had finally learned how? She had had to remake the last ones with smaller seams. It seemed the cooties were too hard to kill when embedded in seams, and the Red Cross had issued special instructions to foil the little beasties. She picked up the knitting and then threw it down again. She was too nervous to fiddle with that.

Allison had been gone for over a week, and Paris was a prison. Since Brooke had refused to go out a second time with the men Allison brought around for her, there were no dates with her friend gone. And she couldn't go out to a café by herself. She had lost contact with her friends at the Sorbonne when she dropped out. There were embassy parties again, of course, but what a bore! The few young men came with wives or dates; the older men asked her to dance out of duty, and lately she'd been sneaking out early and going to her room.

Thank God for her job at the embassy. It wasn't much but at least it filled up the days. There was still too much spare time to fill, too many nights. The room was littered with half-read books. Lately she couldn't keep her mind on the plots, although she read the best-selling authors: Booth Tarkington, Harold Bell Wright, Winston Churchill, Gene Stratton Porter. Back copies of *The Saturday Evening Post*, *The Ladies Home Journal* and *Vogue* lay on the table beside her bed.

And there were the movies. She saw both French and American films when the Hunters invited her along.

"O-h-h, it's all so . . . nothing!" she said aloud. "I am not going to live like this!"

Resolutely, she walked to the closet, took out her

suitcase, and started packing. Why should she let Franklin keep her from doing what she wanted to do? Even her parents couldn't do that. And certainly Franklin had no hold on her, obviously didn't want one. Why shouldn't she visit Allison and Blake? They wanted her.

"Franklin," she said, "you can just be damned!"

Using the undependable phone, it took a while to get through to the railroad and make a reservation.

When the Hunters issued mild protests about her leaving, she fibbed and said Allison had reported that the town and airbase were safely behind the enemy lines.

"It's a resort," she said. "And I deserve a holiday from Paris before winter sets in."

All the way to the station she reassured herself that she was doing the right thing. And she would show Franklin DeWitt in the process; that alone was worth the trip.

But when she stepped off the train and hailed a taxi, she was no longer so sure. Sitting in the back, she pressed herself against the cushion and held her head away from the window. She wanted neither to see nor to be seen by Franklin.

At the hotel she walked quickly to the desk. "I'd like a room," she said to the clerk. "Preferably one adjoining Miss Hunter's."

She watched the clerk's expression change.

"*Oui, madame,*" he leered. "Whatever you wish."

Then she watched him write in an exorbitant rate on the registration card. Another war profiteer . . . but what could you do?

A porter carried her luggage to her room, and she

rapped lightly on the door that separated her accommodations from Allison's.

"Yes, who is it?" a sleepy voice asked from the other side.

"It's me."

"Brooke!" The key turned and the door flew open. "You're here. I don't believe it!"

The two embraced and went through the usual rites of greeting before Brooke put out the feeler for the information she wanted.

"And how is Blake?" she asked. "Still the lady killer?"

Allison gave her a quizzical look. "They're gone. Didn't you know?"

"They?"

"The whole outfit—Frank DeWitt, Bulldog. Everybody. They left yesterday."

"Where?" Brooke tried to hide the frustration and unhappiness building inside her.

"North. To the Somme, I'd guess. They'll be in that mess through the winter. I'm told it's sheer hell up there."

"Gone!" Brooke sat on the edge of the bed and let the tears roll down her cheeks. Once again her indecision had cost her what she wanted most.

Why didn't I tell him I love him? she thought. I had the opportunity. Why didn't I write to him? What is this dam inside me that holds back the words and won't let me be myself?

In a way Franklin was lucky. He could see his enemy, had been taught how to fight him. Hers was an insidious thing that attacked so silently she was unaware of it. How could you fight yourself, change yourself?

And then a new thought occurred to her. Perhaps Franklin had two enemies—the German and a barrier inside that was much like hers. He had managed to break through it that last night before he had stormed away from the cottage. He had emerged from behind the dam, exposed his feelings and his vulnerability, and she had not welcomed him in from the cold.

Frank, she said to herself. Oh, Frank darling, forgive me. Forgive me, please.

22

FROM THE PLEASANT quarters of Luxeuil, the La-fayette Escadrille moved into the hellish winter of the Somme Valley. It was a shock for the pampered, rich adventurers who swelled the ranks of the original squadron, now arriving by truck at a field southeast of Amiens.

The spirit of Christmas, their third in combat, was chilled by the sight of the tarpaper barracks they were to occupy. The shacks sat in a lake of mud, and the primitive stoves inside lifted the temperature only a few degrees above that outdoors. There seemed to be no plans for feeding them. Men who had volunteered to fight for a country other than their own were little better than beggars at the regular mess facilities of the French airmen in the vast aviation complex.

Day after day, with no equipment available to them, they sat in the huts where the rain dripped through the roof and the winter wind blew out the match when they tried to light a cigarette. With only a few planes available to the fifty-eight pilots and the weather unfit for flying, there was little to do except complain, gamble, drink, and try to make the shacks more livable.

There was plenty of time to decorate their aircraft with Indian heads and to select their uniforms. Since there was no code to go by, Frank chose a black uniform with a red stripe running the length of his trousers and a choke-collared tunic.

Blake dramatized a plain khaki uniform by having a flare added to the breeches and buying laced boots that he polished to a glossy finish. Sometimes, if he slipped off the board walkways into the mud, he shined them more than once a day. As he had before, he adapted the white silk scarf to his uniform, always tossing one end of it over his shoulder. He wouldn't have admitted it to anyone, but to him it was a distinguishing mark of style, a white plume of Cyrano de Bergerac. He took some kidding about it, but he was seldom seen without the gleaming white accessory.

His shirt was a lighter and smoother khaki than his trousers, and his tie was brown. The hat he wore had a beak, braid across the front, and a rakish crushed crown.

Teeter accepted the breeches and bulky knit sweater of an artilleryman, and from somewhere he came up with boots with spurs and a western cowboy hat that his captain could neither abide nor dissuade the American from wearing.

In their quarters the flyers collected a menagerie of pets, among them a half-tame lion that periodically chewed up somebody's uniform or on occasion the arm of an unsuspecting stranger.

When the Germans took to attacking the field at night, Blake secretly rigged his aircraft with cockpit lights and took to the sky without orders if he heard them approach.

Once, when he had been airborne for only a matter of minutes, the lights conked out and he was left without instrumentation. He aimed at the formation of bombers and started shooting at shadows.

His gunsights useless, only the tracers gave him any idea where he was shooting. Time after time he reloaded and blasted away at anything in the sky while the bombers' issue put the torch to buildings below.

Pulling up after an unsuccessful pass, he saw the outline of an aircraft directly above his. On collision course, he depressed the trigger on his machine gun and then blinked at the result—a bursting red and yellow ball.

"Jesus Christ!" he breathed, swinging his craft through the rim of the fireball.

He ducked his head and hunched his shoulders, half expecting the blast to set off his fuel tanks, but when his eyes adjusted to the darkness again, he realized he was still aloft. Glancing aft, he could see burning debris licking at the hull of his plane. For long seconds, not breathing and not blinking, he watched while the wind coaxed the little fires, then blew them out, then teased them into sparks again. In the end, like a cat that tortures its mouse to death, the wind extinguished its fiery playmates, and Blake

Hunter exhaled in limp, grateful relief. He was still alive, still airborne.

"Confirmed!" he yelled at the ground. "Say that one's not confirmed, you bastards. I'm the only one up here."

Suddenly the air around him was empty. He was alone in the sky, in the world; the burning buildings below were no longer in sight. He had drifted away and lost his sense of direction. If the ground crew was lighting the runway for him, he couldn't see its fires. He was lost, like a person newly blinded.

He did not panic at first. Instead he thought about it. Trying to search for the field might send him far behind the German lines. There was only one logical course: he would have to circle, waiting for dawn, in the meantime conserving fuel and flying in as narrow an orbit as possible.

For hours he maintained his aircraft attitude by the pressure he could feel in his buttocks. He tried to steer a course that put a slight pressure on his right side, with no feeling of weightlessness or sudden upward push on his seat. Talking and singing to keep himself awake, he shivered through the night.

With the first light of dawn, he made wider and wider circles until he saw an airfield below. As he flew low, men ran out waving their arms and pointing to the flag.

He was home.

With shaky hands he set the plane down and taxied toward the hangar. Before he could cut the engine, it began to sputter. His tanks were empty.

Mechanics and pilots swarmed around him, cheering and laughing.

"You got one. You got a heinie," they yelled.

Grinning broadly, he sought out the Yanks who had taunted him about his previous claims.

"Want to confirm this one?" he asked. "Nobody was up there but me."

"Confirm, hell," the older of the men joked. "That damned kraut almost fell on our barracks."

"Paint a black cross on my ship," he told his mechanic.

Then he spotted Frank DeWitt and Bulldog Teeter pushing through the crowd. Both were smiling and extending their hands. Their approval meant more than all the rest.

He was king again. Frank had never made a night kill; few of the pilots had.

"Got other good news, too," Teeter said. "We got leave coming."

"Now?" With the thrill of the kill still in him, he was almost loath to leave.

Frank, who was sober for a change, said, "The captain says we're going to be short of planes and ammunition through most of March at least. He says old-timers like us might as well spend part of the winter somewhere else."

"Paris?"

"It's old Paree for me," Teeter grinned. "I'm going to jingle my spurs in the beds of as many mademoiselles as I can."

"And you, Frank?"

"Paris, I guess," his friend said without enthusiasm.

Blake winced. He didn't want to share Brooke with anybody, much less Frank.

"Your sister would be hurt if I took leave somewhere else," DeWitt added.

Satisfied, Hunter slapped the backs of the men on

either side of him. "Great! Paris, here we come! The three musketeers. A month in paradise."

"Then back to hell," Frank said glumly.

"Hell?" Blake said. "You call this hell? I haven't had so much fun since I first took up flying. Up there in the dark, all alone, me against those shadows, what a game! Better than hunting lions and tigers in Africa. I kinda hate to quit even to go to Paris."

Teeter laughed. "Flyin' and fightin' is fun all right, but screwin' is better and I'm more likely to get more fuckin' in Paree than I am at fifteen thousand feet, freezin' my donk until it shrivels like a raisin."

"Paris, then," Frank said, forcing a smile. "And to hell with coming back. When the time comes to return, I will have drunk so much champagne, I'll be too numb to feel the bullets and shrapnel even if the heinies get me."

"That's the spirit, dude," Teeter said. "This war ain't never gonna end until every Frenchman is dead. We're gonna have the whole damned country of women to ourselves. That's why jackasses like us go to war, ain't it? Stirs up the blood, gets the women ta thinkin' they gotta produce more babies to replace the corpses. So I say, let's do our part for France! Let's see how many women we can get pregnant before we gotta come back and kill Jerries again."

23

T HE WHISKY in the flask didn't taste very good but he drank it anyway. He'd been sitting in the cab outside the American Embassy in Paris for quite awhile, smoking cigarettes and sipping from the flask while he waited. It was cold, and he stomped his feet on the floor and rubbed his gloved hands together to keep the circulation going.

To his regret he was sober enough to feel stupid. If he were half a man, he would walk straight up to the door and announce himself.

"Brooke, I'm sorry," he would say. That was the best way. Plain and simple. No embellishments.

So why couldn't he do it then? Funny what the certainty of rejection could do to a man. Change him from a person who faced problems head-on to one who sidestepped and approached from an oblique angle. It wasn't like him, but for some reason, where Brooke was concerned, his emotions knotted him into a mental and physical straitjacket. Even the booze couldn't give him the courage to leave the cab, and so he sat waiting for her to come out with Blake Hunter.

The flying trio had been in the city three days and two nights now, luxuriating in an expensive hotel and dining at fine restaurants.

Blake had been to the embassy twice, Frank only once, and then he had met Allison outside, taken her to dinner, and evaded her broad hints that they spend the night together.

He had begged off, fabricating excuses, and she had gone home angry, leaving him with the worry that she would tell Brooke about their affair. The fact that it was strictly a physical liaison would make it no more acceptable to Brooke—if, indeed, she cared at all. One thing was sure: she wouldn't approve. Although they had not had a lot of time together, he knew her well enough to realize that such casual arrangements were not for her.

But he had to see her, had to settle this thing between them—or was it only within him?—once and for all. He knew he was drinking too much, knew it affected his performance in an aircraft, that it could endanger his partners in the air. Maybe if he could get her out of his mind, he could earn some respect again—from himself and others.

He had snuffed out his fourth cigarette by the time she and Blake came down the steps arm-in-arm and climbed into the cab ahead of him. He tapped his driver on the shoulder and followed them across the city to the Théâtre de Chatelet. When they had gone inside the opera house, he bought a ticket, wedged himself through the crowd, and followed them until they seated themselves in the Hunter box on the upper level.

Feeling uncomfortably like a voyeur, he waited near the exit until he saw her walking out, evening purse and gloves in hand, obviously headed for the ladies' room. He had visualized meeting her as if by accident, but once he saw her there was no maintaining the guise of nonchalance.

"Brooke!" he said with quiet urgency.

She turned, smiling, not sure who wanted her attention.

"Franklin?" She seemed astonished as he emerged into the lighted foyer.

"Yeah, it's me." He was afraid she would walk away and the words stumbled over each other in his need to detain her. "Brooke, I want to apologize. I was a fool. A crazy, lovesick kid who didn't have the sense to . . ."

He stopped. Her words were tumbling out too, merging with his.

". . . wasn't laughing at you . . . should have written . . . my fault . . . I was so crazy in love with you and . . ."

There was a tingling silence while both of them registered the word they had heard from the other's lips: love.

Love. He had said it. So had she.

"Oh, Franklin!" she said, and the warmth in her voice and in the dark, almond-shaped eyes thawed the icy thing that had chilled his life since the war had begun.

Then she was in his arms and they were both talking at the same time, each taking the blame for the misunderstanding that had kept them apart so long.

He kissed her, and the touch of her lips under his, of her body against him, ignited a feeling that was like sunshine touching the center of his being.

"Oh, God, I love you, Brooke. I've loved you since the first moment I saw you. For so long now. I want to say it and say it. To hear it! I feel alive again." He kissed her again and then the words poured forth once more, as if to make up for all the months of silence. "I've been a fool, you know . . . drinking . . . flying badly . . ."

"You shot down the Red Baron?"

"I guess. I wasn't even totally sober. I didn't give a damn about life anymore. If it hadn't been for Blake . . ."

Blake.

Reality returned, disturbing their brief euphoria.

"Oh, dear," she said. "I'm with Blake."

"I know." He shook his head. "I tailed you two. I can't believe I did it. For three days I've been trying to bump into you by accident—on purpose, of course."

She laughed delightedly. "I've been quizzing Allison for months, trying to get her to tell me something about you—without appearing too curious, of course. But she wouldn't. It was so frustrating. Sometimes I would think you were dead, and she just wasn't admitting it. I read casualty lists and sneaked peeks at her letters from Blake. It was awful. Why didn't I just write to you and tell you what I felt?"

"And why didn't I write? There were telephones when we were based near Switzerland."

"I went there, you know."

"When?"

"The day after you left. Allison was still there."

As they knit together their stories and their feelings, they were unaware of the door swinging open beside them and they were still in each other's arms when Frank saw him.

"Blake," he said lamely, "I'm sorry."

Blake said nothing as Brooke swung around to face him. He took out his cigarette case, selected a cigarette and tapped it against the case slowly, and then lit it. He was in no hurry to acknowledge or lessen their discomfiture.

"What can I say, buddy?" Frank floundered.

Brooke tried to absorb some of the onus of blame. "Blake, I've always loved Frank. I'm sorry. I didn't mean to lead you on."

"But it seems you have." He exhaled and put a screen of smoke between them. "Apparently I've been flying in formation with two Fokkers instead of Nieuports, as I'd thought. If you'll excuse me, I think I'll execute whatever maneuver will get me back to base as quickly as possible." His eyes were as cold as his voice.

Frank touched his friend's shoulder. "Blake, don't take it this way."

He shook loose. "Knock it off, you bastard, and watch your tail next time you fly with me. You've got more than Jerries to worry about now."

He stalked away, his swagger stick tucked up under his arm.

"Blake!" Brooke would have followed him had Frank not stopped her.

"Not now," he said.

"But that was awful, threatening you."

"He didn't mean it."

"Don't be so sure. He's always—"

"We're friends."

"More like enemies in some ways."

"He saved my life. Probably Teeter's, too. Almost got himself killed doing it. Can you call that an enemy?"

"But he's always competed with you. Seems obsessed with being the best, the bravest, the brashest—"

"Is that so bad?"

"It is when you're competing with your friend in a battle."

He had her by the arm, and they were walking slowly toward the cloakroom.

"Relationships get distorted in the war," he said. "You can hate a man and still die saving his life. You can have a friend and end up asking him to sacrifice himself for you."

"And in love," she said.

"What?"

"Relationships get complicated in love, too." He held her fur coat for her, exulting in her nearness as his hand touched the gleaming cluster of dark curls at the nape of her neck. The skin there was warm and so smooth. . . .

They stepped into the street where the taxicabs were beginning to line up in anticipation of the crowd that would soon be leaving the opera.

Suddenly there was a problem.

"We could go get something to eat," he said.

She said she wasn't hungry.

He suggested a bar where the pilots hung out. "It's

rowdy, I understand, but maybe you'd enjoy the experience."

"All right, Franklin, if you want to." She sounded
dubious.

"I don't," he said. He opened the door for her and
went around to the other side of the cab. As he
climbed in, he gave the driver the name of his hotel.

They kissed nervously, until she pulled away.
"Franklin, I don't go to men's hotel rooms."

"I know."

"Then tell the driver."

"Tell him what? To take us to the embassy?"

"No. But . . ."

"Do you have a parlor where we can be alone?
A front porch with a swing in the shadows where
the street lamp doesn't reach? A river bank? A park
where we could picnic off away from people?"

"No."

"Look, Brooke. I'm not walking out this time. If
you don't want to be alone with me, it'll have to be
you who tells the driver."

"Oh, darling, I don't know what I want and don't
want. I get so mixed up, everything pulling in different directions. It's this crazy war!"

"Yes. The war destroys and it builds on the ruins.
I never would have met you if there had been no
war."

The cab pulled to the curb and he handed the
driver the fare. He walked her into the lobby and
felt her arm clutch his as they passed the desk and
climbed the stairs.

When they were in his room with the door closed
behind them, she walked to the window and stood

staring into the street below. He took off his coat and tunic and hung them in the closet before he went to her, helped her off with her coat and laid it over a chair. He was careful not to touch her, giving her time to adjust to being alone with him in a hotel room, with only the glow from the street for light.

Finally he stood behind her with his hands on her elbows. "There are all kinds of friendships," he said. "Blake's and mine. Part big brother, part competitor, part enemy. Yet he's still my friend. And Teeter. I'm beginning to think he's really done all those crazy things he says he has. I've seen him play hero and forget to mention it. Try as I may, I can't catch him in a lie."

"What are you getting at?"

"Us. If we went by the book, we'd have held hands. There'd have been a few stolen kisses. I'd have met your folks and carried your books home from school. We'd have grown up together, and then one day we'd have been alone in the dark and it would have been so natural. We did it differently; we fell in love from a distance."

"But that doesn't—"

"No, it doesn't solve the problem. It *is* the problem. But the point is there's no one pattern that everyone has to follow. I know you, Brooke. I know you as if we'd had a thousand dates. I watched you with Blake, I heard Allison talk about you, and I savored every word. I read newspaper articles about your parents; I found a book in which your mother was mentioned. I know you, Brooke. And I love you."

"It is that way with us, isn't it? I've read and reread all that you gave me of your book, and Franklin

DeWitt came through in its pages. Yes, I think we know each other, at least in many ways. I just hope you're not expecting more of me than I have to give."

He turned her gently in his arms, lifted her chin and kissed her. "You're already more than I ever expected from anyone, my beautiful, beautiful Brooke."

"I'm not the child you first met," she said.

"And I'm not the kid you saw sitting on a curb, typing a story about life when he hadn't even lived yet."

"Maybe that's for the best, our changing."

"Yes, maybe it is. Let's see, shall we?"

24

THEY KNEW NO ONE would ever believe them, but they did not make love the first night, nor the second, nor the third. She stayed with him, slept in his arms, but they let sex claim them slowly. Each step in their relationship, accelerated though it had to be, was joy to be prolonged, savored. The first night they were satisfied with kissing and talking and kissing some more. They shared stories of childhood, of family, of frustrations.

The second night, as the luxury of returned love became a reality, he gingerly taught her to French kiss the way Allison had taught him. The intimacy of his tongue pressing between her lips confused her. It took her hours before she responded to something she would have considered dirty or lewd if any other man had tried. Before they fell asleep, she attempted it herself, barely putting her own tongue into his mouth. She liked it better when he probed her. It must be like real sex, she thought, and she moved closer to wanting the real thing.

In the morning they French kissed constantly, and she stopped wavering when he finally moved his hand to the rise of her breasts. She felt compelled to push his hand away, although she liked each new intimacy. She was embarrassed, though, when her nipples hardened. He would notice, she thought. But then he had moved his hips closer to her than he ever had before, and she was bewildered, then startled by the hard rod that touched her.

She felt foolish and stupid. She knew about men and how the penis swelled when they grew excited, but it still came as a surprise. When he put his hand between her legs, she pulled away as if he were tickling her. Then she regretted the rebuff and she put his hand where he wanted it. Half an hour passed before she became comfortable with his touch, his invasion of her privacy.

But then she didn't want there to be any secret or secret places that he couldn't touch, couldn't fondle.

Another day and another night passed before he came to bed without any pajamas. She wondered what her mother would think, her daughter in bed with a naked man. She wished he had worn something until she felt his hard, muscular body. Once she had touched him, she wanted to run her hands over every inch of his torso, but she could not bring herself to move her hand below his waist.

"Take off your nightgown, darling," he said unexpectedly.

He had startled her and she stalled until his hands

started sliding it up her legs. For the first few nights there had always been layers of cloth between them, but then he was helping her to sit up so he could pull the nightgown over her head.

She chilled, all over goose bumps.

He laughed and brought her close.

"You'll freeze," he said.

She was rigid when their bare flesh touched, but then he kissed her, French kissed her, returning to the familiar as he made the big step. She liked the kissing so much that she could accept their nakedness.

When he reached down and slid his huge organ between her legs, she panicked. She was too small. He would never be able to get it in her, she was certain. But again he proceeded with patience and control. They spent a night with his penis massaging her sensitive parts until they both came, the rush of orgasm frightening to her. It was as if she were about to die from the ecstacy. Nothing could feel that good without being dangerous.

Then he had rolled between her legs, pressing the very tip no more than half an inch into her waiting crevice. He withdrew and probed and withdrew and probed, ever deeper until she cried out in pain. He withdrew and rolled aside.

"Don't, please," she said.

"I'm not," he replied.

"I mean, don't stop."

"It hurts you."

She urged him back. She could endure pain if it meant not disappointing him. She stifled her cries as he slowly penetrated the narrow passage. He was gentle and tried to withdraw when he found tears

on her cheeks. She held him in place. The longer she
accepted the pain, the sooner it would begin to feel
good, like his tongue exploring her mouth.

Then he moved and she felt new sensations. He
withdrew part way and she drew him back. The first
night they quit in disappointment, and she turned
away so he wouldn't hear her crying softly.

In the morning, she could only remember how
much she loved him and she found herself bringing
him back on top of her again. There was pain again,
that day and the next night and the next.

Then suddenly she found herself relaxing, her natural juices lubricating the tender spots that ceased
giving her pain and began giving her pleasure.

Once she climaxed, she became an addict. She
wanted it night and morning, occasionally in the afternoon. They were no longer two people; just one
mind sharing the same sensations.

And she welcomed experimentation, accepting him
without question when he slid down her body, kissing her everywhere and finally burying his face in
the fine hair between her legs.

She didn't know whether she was supposed to re-
ciprocate or not. No one had ever discussed such
things in front of her, but the next day she kissed his
chest, sucked on his tiny nipples the way he did hers,
and then began lowering her head until she was
brushing her cheek and then her lips against his man-
hood.

His pleasure was so obvious, she tried her tongue
on him, thinking she was doing something no woman
ever had. When she took him in her mouth, it seemed
so natural, and afterward he was wild and they cli-

maxed together like lava meeting water and erupting in powerful blasts of steam.

"I love you, I love you, I love you," she said over and over. And she realized she couldn't be without him and his body ever again.

They pretended the war did not exist. Frank took off his uniform and bought new civilian clothes. In the evening they went to the Café de Paris and danced the tango, the fox trot and the Castle walk in the very place Vernon and Irene Castle had changed the dance styles of the western world.

"When I'm Out With You" became "their" song, and anything Irving Berlin wrote set them to thinking of home and the family they had already agreed they would have when it was over.

"It" had taken on a special meaning. Not only for them, but for everybody in Paris.

"It" was the war.

And like everyone else, they couldn't avoid the topic for very long. They read every tidbit in the daily papers. Increasingly, it looked as if Wilson would commit their homeland to the conflict.

"Once Wilson lets America in, it'll soon be over," Frank said to be reassuring.

Living on that hope, they were like the native Parisians, excited about anything American. When Ziegfeld brought over his Follies, they had seats in the orchestra. They were there to hear Eddie Cantor do his take-offs on "The Osteopath," to hear Fanny Brice sing "Rose of Washington Square."

When Marion Davies, one of the Ziegfeld girls, came on stage, Brooke pointed her out and whispered to Franklin, "She's a special friend of William Ran-

dolph Hearst. Mommie was one, too, you know, during the Spanish American War. I wonder if . . ."

She never finished what she wondered about.

They mimicked what they heard was popular at
home and bundled up to go tobogganing. Inevitably
they wound up at the end of the hill in a tumbled
heap of snow, arms, legs and laughter when the
treacherous vehicle, like one of Bulldog's legendary
broncos, bucked them into the drifts.

Another day Brooke lined up some shotguns and
they went hunting. Modishly dressed in laced boots,
flared pants, a leather jacket and mannish hat, she
drove into the country and they laughed when she
outshot him. They ate a picnic lunch in the car,
freezing and embracing as passionately as if they
weren't spending every night together in the hotel.
The cold wind had heightened the rosy tones in her
skin, and Frank was sure he had never seen anyone
so beautiful. They drove back to the city with two
pheasants in the trunk and gave them to the man
at the desk in the hotel.

They window-shopped. They selected furniture
they didn't buy, and looked at toys for the children
that were becoming part of their dream.

But a model airplane was enough to send shivers
down Brooke's spine, and she hurried Frank along
because she had been counting the days. Only ten
were left, and Frank, as aware as she was of their
diminishing time together, did not mention it. Instead
he kissed her on the mouth, grabbed her hand, and
pulled her toward the streetcar that would take them
back to the hotel.

They took in a number of plays and films in the
ensuing days and evenings. With the American col-

ony growing and the British military contingent burgeoning, there was a variety of English dialogue plays and films, in addition to the French fare, which was no problem to them since both spoke the language fluently. They saw young Eugene O'Neill's *Bound East from Cardiff* on stage and all the installments of *The Perils of Pauline* that had come out thus far, but with the end of Frank's leave coming up they might never know whether she would survive the crash of a car the madman drove off a cliff.

"Promise you won't see it until I get back," he said, then wished he hadn't. There were only three days left. "We'll see it together even if I have to rent a theater myself."

They quarreled once—over the suffragettes' fight for the vote in America; then they pouted through lunch and had a marvelous afternoon in bed making up.

Finally there was only one night left, and neither slept. When she cried, he would remind her, "We still have all day tomorrow. I don't leave until after supper."

Their young bodies, accustomed to each other now, met and merged and throbbed together in oneness. The nipples of her breasts responded to his slightest touch, and she learned quickly what pleased him— and her—as she stroked him gently at first, then firmly, faster. She could not let him leave her until he was flaccid, utterly spent.

The French were lovers; they would never expect a man to go anywhere, much less back to war, when he was still "involved," they lied to themselves.

"Involved" was her euphemism for sex, a word she could not bring herself to say. "If we went back to the hotel we'd get involved again," she had said more than once, or "We can't get involved here; someone might come along."

By the time dawn came, she knew he was spent and they would not get involved again, although they might spend the day naked in each other's arms, loving and petting under the heavy comforters that were supposed to substitute for heat now that the hotel had stopped providing it.

When she tried to rouse him one more time, he kissed her and looked into her eyes. He seemed shy again. She waited and finally he said what he was thinking.

"Will you marry me?" he asked.

"Of course. As soon as it's over." She ran her lips along his jaw and nuzzled into his neck.

"No. Now."

"Now?"

"Today." He sat up in bed and the covers fell away from his hairy chest, and he spewed out the words before they died in anticipation of rebuff. "Look, I know I could get killed. You could find another man. A million things could happen between now and when you see me again, but you could always get a divorce, and we could keep it secret so nobody would know, and—"

As they had when they first expressed their love for each other, they were speaking together, only half aware of what the other was saying.

"Of course—oh, yes, I'll marry you," she was saying. "Today. I think we go to a magistrate or something. The *concierge* here will know . . . oh, no, we can't ask him." She giggled. "And you are coming back and I'm never going to marry anyone else, and we'll tell the whole world the minute I can get a cablegram to mother and father. I couldn't have them hear from strangers . . . Good heavens, I really know almost nothing about your family."

"I'll tell you on the way to the judge or whoever is going to marry us." He jumped out of bed and continued to talk about his family as they bathed and dressed. "It's an old American name, DeWitt. Goes back before the Revolutionary War. There was a Magnus DeWitt who fought with the British at Quebec in the French and Indian wars, and both he and his brother, Schuyler, fought in the Revolutionary War—though on different sides. They were always military men, the DeWitts, although this is it for me. Now it looks like my younger brother, Ernest, is next in line to fight. But let me tell you, after this is over, I never want to see a uniform again."

Hand-in-hand, they ran out of the room and spent the day searching out officials who could tell them where to start, others who took "tips" for bending the rules, and finally embassy personnel who sent them back to the hotel to get their passports.

Not surprisingly, there was a hitch at the last moment; Brooke was too young, or so the little Frenchman claimed, and when Blake reached into his pocket for another "tip," he found he was down to his last franc. He panicked; they had kept the wizened magistrate waiting long past dinner and the bribe would have to be sizable.

He tried to think where he could borrow money quickly. Teeter would be broke. Blake Hunter would hardly be amenable to lending to the man he had threatened to kill. There was no one . . .

His eyes widened at the sheaf of French money

Brooke was peeling off to feed the Frenchman's avarice.

For the first time he thought about her wealth. During the quick ceremony he stared at the full-length mink coat and the ostrich-plumed hat, at the modish pumps and the designer dress she wore. And he remembered how often she had just happened to have tickets for the plays, concerts and shows they attended. It was her car they used. Now that he thought of it, the hotel bill had seemed surprisingly cheap when he had sought out the manager to discuss keeping the room for a month. And the restaurants . . . at least twice she had disappeared into the ladies' room after they had dined in exquisite restaurants, and he had been flattered when the maître d' announced that dinner was his "small contribution to the Lafayette Escadrille."

My God, she must be rich! How would he ever manage to support her in the manner she was accustomed to?

But when they kissed, after he had slipped on "Grandmother's wedding ring," which she happened to have handy, he forgot everything except that the only girl he had ever loved was now his wife.

It seemed ironic: now that they were married there was no more time to become "involved." In fact there was no more time for anything, even dinner, and she drove him to headquarters where the trucks were waiting.

Teeter was there, delightfully drunk, with three beautiful if gaudy girls hanging on his arms.

"Hey there, DeWitt," he called. "I see you-all shot yourself a bird," he yelled, using the British slang for ".girl." He took Frank's bag and tossed it up into the back of the open lorry.

Over near the last truck, Allison Hunter was kissing her brother good-bye as Franklin crushed his bride's lips under his for the last time. He pulled away and hopped on the back of a truck before Brooke could see the brightness in his eyes. Then Allison was waving and calling to him and trying to break through the noisy crowd to reach him. He couldn't believe the way Allison acted.

"Frank! Frank, there's something I—" The driver gunned the engine, and her words were lost in the engine's response.

For a moment she ran along behind the vehicle; it was Brooke who stood in place, waving and crying.

He could not help but wonder what Allison wanted. He hadn't seen her since his first few days of leave. He had put her off then, and she must have known that Brooke was with him the nights she didn't return to the embassy. Allison must have known why he had not gone to bed with her as they had each time they had met before . . . before Brooke, he thought a little guiltily.

"DeWitt!" He looked up, surprised. Blake had somehow managed to climb aboard and was leaning against the opposite side of the truck. "You bastard, DeWitt," he snarled. "You goddamned fucking bastard."

25

THEY DROVE only an hour beyond the edge of Paris to a place called Ravenel, near St. Just-en-Chaussée. When they heard their destination, Teeter brought out a map and the men around him took turns holding matches until they found the place, just outside Paris along the road from St. Just to the Porte de La Chapelle.

"You've been moved," was all the cryptic *sous lieutenant* had been willing to tell them.

The French, though, were never good at keeping secrets, and it seemed all the men had heard the rumor in Paris. The big spring "push" would be directed by General Nivelle. Teeter, sobering rapidly now, could even predict the battle plan.

"The kaiser's boys is still out here," he said, "forty-two miles from Paris." He tapped the map with his finger. "They're ahead of their main defenses like a scoutin' party."

The main defense he spoke of was the supposedly impregnable Hindenburg line.

"Nivelle will throw everything he has against the bulge now that it comes so close to the capital," Frank said, indicating Lassigny. "And soon."

"Why soon?" somebody asked from above the flickering circle of matches and lighters.

"The Yanks are coming," Frank said.

"Wilson is still making noises about peace," another flyer pointed out.

"It's just a matter of when. A month from now, two at the most, and the Americans will be in it."

"By April? What's that got to do with Nivelle?"

"French pride," Frank theorized. "The French have got to have the huns on the run so we won't be able to take credit for pulling their chestnuts out of the fire."

The *sous lieutenant* muttered something about the *Américains* always taking too much credit for what they did.

When the truck stopped, the men jumped out, eager to see the new base which they expected would surpass the poor facilities they had endured at Cachy. They were looking forward to weekends in Paris and a quick end to the war when the Americans stepped in officially.

They looked around, unwilling to comprehend what they saw . . . or didn't see. No lighted barracks awaited them. Not even the usual sheds. As they slogged through the mush of a late March thaw, all they saw was hangars.

For a few minutes they put aside their disappointment as they entered the hangars and discovered the Nieuports and the new Spads that their comrades had flown over from their last base.

Captain Thénault was there, and his three old-timers back from leave surrounded him, protesting that Spads and Nieuport 17s with guns that fired through the propeller could not possibly be given to the less experienced.

The French leader of the escadrille sniffed. "Synchronized machine guns, hah! The first we try, she chews up the propeller like a puppy shreds a slipper."

But he relented as they knew he would, and the trio who had been so close for so long shared a common pleasure again while each was shown to his own Spad by his mechanic.

All three had flown the Spad VIIs, borrowing them from the French, and they knew the advantages and disadvantages of the new aircraft. It was a brute in comparison to the graceful Nieuport. The wings were short, twenty-six feet from square tip to square tip, and were rigidly bound to each other with tough-looking struts. After the fabric in the parallel wings had been doped, it shrank to give a scalloped look on top. Set well forward under the cockpit was the landing gear, its location designed for greater safety than that of its predecessors.

Most important was the Vickers belt-fed machine gun, placed directly in front of the pilot for ease of aiming. The belt held five hundred .303 caliber rounds.

"No more reloading in the middle of a battle," Frank remarked, running his hand over the solidly built gun.

He liked that, not because of the killing it would accomplish but because it added to his chances of surviving until he could get back to Brooke.

The water-cooled engines would "high tail after them Jerry sons-a-bitches a hundred and twenty per, flat out," Teeter exulted over his new craft. "And I can dive this here honey better'n a eagle huntin' cottontail in the sage."

The weight and the airfoil section meant the Spads didn't glide once the engine conked out, and they were not as maneuverable as the old Nieuports. Like the other two men, though, Franklin was willing to accept the minor sacrifices for the extra speed, the better armament, and the stocky look of the new plane.

Climbing into the cockpit, he sat there until he noticed only he and Hunter were still in the hangar, where shadows hung long and gloomy in the dim light. A cold wind howled outside and coursed through the flimsy enclosure. Frank shivered. It was time he settled the rift between them. Now, before they joined the others in whatever their quarters were to be.

"Blake," he called.

"Go to hell." Contempt dripped from the words. Frank had not expected him to be such a poor sport.

"Blake, about Brooke . . ."

"I don't want to talk about it."

Frank climbed out of his plane and walked toward his erstwhile roommate, the man who had saved his life.

"We have to, Blake. We'll be flying together whether we want to or not."

"I treated you like a kid brother from the start,"

Blake said bitterly. "When we shared an apartment I paid most of the rent. I went into the legion to look after you."

"Since you put it that way, Blake, I'll admit you did treat me like a kid." Hunter had climbed down and would have stalked toward the exit if Frank had not clutched his arm and swung him around. "Why did you look after me, Blake? Because it made you important in front of Brooke?"

"Go to hell." Hunter wrenched his arm free.

"I thought we were friends, but it was never that, was it? I was someone you could compete with, somebody you could bounce your victories off. You're always competing—about everything, Blake. Why, I don't know. You've always been good at everything you do."

"You're damned right."

"Always the most daring, the best looking, the hottest pilot. And you needed me—Bulldog, too, I suppose—for contrast."

"I never gave a shit what anybody else thought about me."

"Oh, the hell you didn't!" Frank scoffed, laughing a little. "You can't stand to take second to anybody over anything, but it's not other people's opinion you care so much about now as your own. So what's your beef with me? Are you bitter because I shot down Richthofen?"

"I saved your life."

"Yep, that you did. You're no coward, Blake."

"I'll never do it again. You can bet on that, bastard."

"Why? Because of Brooke? Face it, Blake, she was never yours. There was no contest. I was just a damned fool who took two years seeing what you would have known in a single night. Brooke was in love with me. I was in love with her from the start."

"A piss ant writer with no balls—how could she love you?"

"I don't know. But she does."

Hunter doubled his fist and swung, but Frank stepped aside. Blake threw another blow, and this time Frank let him slip past so that he could catch both Blake's arms from behind and hold him until he cooled off.

"Blake, come on. I don't want to fight you."

"You will, though. In the air. When you're least expecting it."

"We can't be shooting at each other. We've got Germans to fight."

"The hell with the Germans. You're the one that screwed my sister."

Stunned, Frank slowly released his grip.

He had not expected Allison to tell her brother what went on between them. And maybe she hadn't; Blake could have guessed.

"Look," Frank began, "I don't know what Allison told you—"

"She told me she's pregnant!" Hunter said, his eyes drilling into Frank like bits of cold steel.

Frank cocked his head as if his ears had played some trick on him.

"By you, you cocksucker. My sister is pregnant by you."

Blake's lips were parted over his teeth and pulled down at the corners. Frank had seen the same look on his face one time in the trenches when a cock-

·roach showed up in his field rations, a look of utter
disgust and abhorrence.

"Aw, no!"

"Yes," Blake shrieked, his voice echoing through
the gloomy hangar. "She's pregnant, with child,
knocked up, and she can't get an abortion; not even
a quack will do it. She waited too long, waited for
you to come so she could tell you the good news."
Franklin winced and turned away as if to shut out
the words, but Blake grabbed his shoulder and swung
him around again. "Listen, you son-of-a-bitch. The
least you can do is listen. She was in love with you.
She said you're the first man who ever really meant
anything to her, and she thought you felt the same
way. She waited too long."

"Aw, no!" Frank said again.

"Aw, yes, and you're going to marry her, damn
you. The first weekend leave you get, you're going
to Paris and marry her."

"But . . ." Frank stammered. My God, what if she
told Brooke. And she would; they were friends. "I
can't. There's Brooke."

"Brooke probably already knows."

Frank felt the blood drain out of his face. "Brooke
knows I'm the father?"

"Hell, no. But Allison will have to tell Brooke she's
pregnant damned soon. It's getting obvious." He
paused, then continued with more control. "You
know what you've done? You know what it's been
like for Allison all the time you were in Paris, all
the time she waited for you to get over your little
fling with Brooke and come back to her? Do you have
any idea what she went through?"

"It wasn't just a little fling."

"Well, it doesn't matter now, shit head. You're going to be my brother-in-law whether you like it or not. If Allison doesn't tell Brooke, I will." Hunter shoved aside the man who had been his friend and went through the exit.

Frank slumped against the wall of the hangar. Outside, the last of the winter winds was howling across the field. It would be spring soon, but the warmth would not bring the pleasure it had in all the other years he could remember.

Usually he wrote a lot in the spring. It was as if his creative juices melted with the spring thaw and words burst forth and proliferated like early blades of grass. Sometimes he wrote poetry that he threw away as soon as the emotion had been vented onto the sheet of paper. He had always felt he was too stable, too realistic to be a poet, but he could capture life in the book he was writing, in the frayed pages stuffed at the bottom of his battered luggage and in the earlier chapters that Brooke still had.

During these last perfect weeks with Brooke he had felt the urge to write swirling in his brain. He had intended to drag out paper and pen and write tonight by a candle. The small, portable typewriter he had carried with him throughout most of the war would be too noisy in a barracks where men would rise at dawn to go on patrol.

Now, his tormented mind could not conceive a single coherent sentence.

Brooke. His wife.

Allison. Pregnant.

Good God, what had he done?

Maybe, though—his mind probed for hope—maybe

Allison wouldn't tell her friend who the father was. She hadn't so far, and there had been plenty of opportunity to tell her even after he and Brooke had begun spending day after day of his leave together.

Now he knew why Allison had tried to call to him as he'd left Paris; or maybe she had been trying to warn him about Blake. Either way, though, he just couldn't believe that she was in love with him. Perhaps Allison would never tell, especially when Brooke broke the news that they were married.

He could send money to Allison. She could say that there was a soldier she had married—one who had died in combat. He'd swear he had witnessed the secret marriage.

The soldier could be a Frenchman. Too low in rank to get permission from his superior to get married. They had to be married in secret.

Her honor would be guaranteed. He would not let her down in that regard. Allison was wild and crazy; she drank the last drops of life's wine, but she was a decent, loving person.

When had it happened? he wondered. When had he been so careless?

Hell, he could think of half a dozen times. When he was drinking. More than once he would have sworn he had sheaths in his pocket, and at the last, when she could stop neither him nor herself, he had told her he had forgotten. He'd be careful. How many times had he promised to be careful?

Somehow he would make it up to her.

After the war he would see to it that she remained a close friend of Brooke's so he would have excuses to see the child, their child. He could be sort of a substitute uncle to the nephew of his good friend

Blake Hunter. It would give him a reason to see the child, to help Allison until she married someone else.

Brooke would never know.

Allison would never tell her.

But Blake would tell.

DeWitt felt that cold, calm, relaxed sensation that he experienced when he survived a patrol and his wheels touched the ground. It was not a feeling of safety, because there were always more patrols. Tomorrow and tomorrow and tomorrow.

But at least now he had faced the cold truth. Blake would tell Brooke.

If he lived . . .

26

FOR WEEKS the grounded escadrille had lived underground where smoking stoves drove them into the early April rain to breathe. Eventually the French engineers had moved in and built barracks which the Americans had decorated before the big news came.

April 6, 1917, and the flyers lay on their bunks listening to a gramophone play "Poor Butterfly" for the twentieth time that day.

When the door to the barracks opened and the captain looked in, none of his subordinates stirred. Rank had few privileges and little respect in the escadrille.

"Your President Wilson has declared war on Germany, gentlemen," the officer said solemnly.

There was a pause while the impact registered and then the Yanks started cheering. They swarmed out of the barracks and danced around like kids on the last day of school.

Flare guns exploded into the sky. The drinking started and bets were taken on how long it would be before they were transferred into the American army. The guesses thrown into the pool ranged from days to weeks to months.

"A year," Bulldog said when there was a moment of silence.

"You're crazy," a chorus of voices answered, but his money was welcome in the pool.

There were more cheers when somebody came up with an American flag and affixed it above the door.

"Not until the spring push is over," a cynical voice said with surety. Gloom fell over the group for a time; his guess made sense. No one was going any-where until the big spring offensive was completed.

Those who survived would be able to apply for immediate transfer.

Those who survived.

But first came the push. Accepting that, the men continued celebrating—all except Blake Hunter, who sat across the room from the two men he had spent so many months with.

DeWitt sat on the edge of his bed, staring at the white sheet of paper in his typewriter.

"Well, DeWitt?" Hunter growled. "You going to ask for a leave before the push? A weekend in Paris is all it would take."

Teeter watched the writer look up from the typewriter, stare straight ahead, ignoring the question.

Then he punched several keys on the machine.

From where he sat Teeter saw the single word on the page.

"Kill!"

Teeter, unusually depressed, looked at the word without interest. Unlike the others, he was not happy about the coming American incursion; there would be no more Lafayette Escadrille. And where would the robin go then, poor thing?

He would be the robin in the childish rhyme, out in the cold without a home. He couldn't go into the American army. They would want his right name. Bulldog was good enough for the legion, but it would never satisfy an American paper-pusher.

They might check on him. The legion never did; that's why he had joined.

Strange, he thought. For nearly three years he had done just what he was told. He had killed.

Legally.

And that's what the American government would want and need most when they finally started arriving en masse.

Killers.

The more skilled, the more professional the killer, the better.

That was the way of war. But what would American authorities do if they checked their records and found they had a man who was more eminently qualified than they expected?

Did they take fugitives from murder charges into the gang of amateurs they would bring over as an army?

"They're coming!" he heard a voice exult between

drinks. And somebody echoed, "They're coming over!"

Yes, Teeter thought. And then he would have to start running again. The war had been the most peace he had found in years.

27

T HE HOUR HAS COME!"
    General Nivelle sent the message to his troops,
    and a quarter of a million men in French blue
rose cheering from the trenches along the thirty-mile
front. They aimed their bodies at the slopes of the
Chemin-des-Dames in a drive which was meant to
strike a stunning blow to the Germans before the
American troops arrived in force to claim the victory.

From their new base at Ham, the Lafayette Escadrille rose above the ground like a flock of black-
birds startled out of a field of grain. They were not
alone; hundreds of other French and British aviators
accompanied them.

A puff of blue smoke exhaled from Franklin De-
Witt's Spad VII when the Hispano-Suiza engines
kicked over, and as it raced down the runway, car-

bonized castor oil used for lubrication sprayed from
the cowling. He made a steep climb toward Bill Thaw.
Unofficially, the American Thaw had taken command
from Captain Thénault; with the entry of their government into the war, the Americans banded together
to exert their nationalism.

Still tormented by personal troubles, DeWitt
climbed above the designated ten-thousand-foot altitude, did a half roll and came down to Thaw's right.
Behind in a second Spad with the Indian head desig-
nation and the black cross for his confirmed kill would
be Blake Hunter. In the vee formation Hunter might
be able to enact his threat as they winged through
the cotton wad clouds ahead.

It was not his one-time roommate who flew behind
Frank, however. Glancing over his shoulder, he saw
the distinctive red and black checkerboard cowling
of Bulldog Teeter's plane. From his unassigned position the Cowboy grinned and gave a reassuring
thumbs-up signal.

Where was Blake Hunter? Frank swiveled his head
uneasily. There . . . to the left. The red cowling, a
glowering face at the controls, a white scarf stream-
ing in the wind . . . Then the plane sliced toward
the right, bearing down on Frank like a hawk teasing
a moth.

Frank had no stomach for the aerial game of Russian roulette, but neither would he play fox to Blake's
hound. He would defend himself aggressively against
Hunter's bluff. And that's what it was, he thought,
a bluff—ridiculous and dangerous as it was—designed
to punish him, to break his will and make him "do the
honorable thing," the impossible thing: marry Allison
Hunter.

By God, it was the old irate-father-with-a-shotgun technique, this time applied in the air. And now that he thought about it, it wasn't even surprising; it was typical of the horse's ass show-off coming at him.

In that split-second—while Frank hesitated and the plane-weapon knifed toward him like a falling star plummeting sideways in a night sky—he understood the enigmatic Hunter as he never had before. Here was a man so insecure that self-image dominated his life: he would pick up any gauntlet, fight for any cause—even one that threatened an entire mission—if it satisfied the hungry need that fed itself at the expense of others. Any others, friend or foe.

Frank kicked the pedals and banked hard to the left, watching Hunter's dour expression dissolve in startled fear. Instinctively, Blake veered down and away, his wings clearing Frank's wheels by inches. Jinking his craft up, then down, Frank pushed his stalker down another thousand feet.

Teeter, watching the dangerous high jinks, veered in to drive the jousting stags apart.

From his cockpit Bulldog jerked his hand toward the scraggly formation above them. Frank responded, regaining altitude to his designated position while he kept a wary eye on Hunter.

Bill Thaw was making violent motions with his arms; he wanted the shenanigans stopped at once. Then he was pointing downward, and Frank saw why. They were flying obliquely across the French trenches. Thaw led the escadrille lower to view the stupefying magnitude of the great French offensive.

Below were millions of humanoid lemmings rushing toward the sea in a mass migration from which

few would return. The blue dots were moving at a
walk across no-man's-land, like a strong wave coursing up onto a beach.

Ahead of the human surf, the artillery laid down
a ground fog of gray and black clouds that settled
in over the German entrenchments, and as the black
puffs thickened the wave of men swept in faster.

Looking down, Frank was a foot soldier again. He
could hear them cheering to build their own courage,
see them ducking their heads and plunging ahead,
feel their excited hearts thundering against their ribs.

With the observer's tactics learned in his early
days of flying, Frank pulled alongside and motioned
to Thaw that he was heading down for a closer look.
Thaw nodded approval and the Spad winged over
and dived full tilt until it leveled off two hundred
feet up.

From there he could see the *poilus* waving triumph-
antly at him, signaling their elation at the Germans'
lack of resistance. They were near the enemy's trenches, surprised and relieved that no deadly barrage had
met them.

Then Frank saw what awaited them.

"Oh my God!" The words came out like a grunt
as the flyer looked into the empty German trenches.
The communications ditches no longer even existed;
they had been filled to prevent their use by attackers.

The French had just spent the bulk of their artillery on a ghost. The foot soldiers had exposed and
exhausted themselves in an attack on a decoy. They
had taken the bait.

Obviously the Germans, anticipating the attack,
had left a few troops behind to fool probing patrols,

and then at the last minute had withdrawn even those. Now the triumphant French infantry was overrunning the old line, beginning the search for the enemy and scrambling up the long slope of Chemindes-Dames, unaware of what lay ahead.

Frank saw the first smoke of German artillery near the crest, saw the entire horizon bloom with the carbon of countless field pieces.

"Hit the dirt!" he shouted—he prayed. His words dissolved in the wind, as futile, as evanescent as the lives vanishing in the smothering fire below. Over the sputtering of his engine, he could hear the roar of a thousand freight trains slicing into the helpless blue ants coursing up the hill.

Simultaneously, a garden of lethal death-colored blossoms burst open amid the French uniforms and sent them flying like shattered pebbles. Two hundred feet away Frank's plane trembled in the concussion. One salvo followed another in devastating overkill. Surely nothing would survive below: not rocks, not trees, not humans. They flew—whole or in bits and pieces—in a maelstrom of debris.

Thinner, broken lines of blue emerged from the explosions that left ugly, open wounds gaping on the incline. From farther back, behind the explosions, men—thousands of them—dashed forward toward certain death. It was as if the French had an endless supply of bodies and could afford to spend twenty for every ten that emerged.

The survivors jogged forward in search of the new enemy emplacements. They were too successful. On signal, thousands of machine guns opened up from the east, laying a crisscrossing field of lead in a pat-

tern prearranged to pierce every sanctuary where a
man might hole up. The few protected indentations
took heavy mortar fire.

The forward French line seemed to drop as one.
When a few managed to charge twenty or thirty
yards farther than their comrades, they too were
felled. Those not mowed down by the scythe of machine gun strafing fell victim to the more selective
fire of the riflemen in the newly dug German trenches.

Still the French kept coming, in such numbers that
the machine gunners could not kill them all until the
barbed wire snagged and held them like targets hung
on a wall. Whole companies died in place.

Awed at the waste of human resources, Frank flew
lower, ignoring the half-hearted anti-aircraft fire Jerry
heaved aloft. Swooping low enough to make the
blue dots recognizable as men, he saw some of them
come to their senses long enough to attempt retreat.
They too died, shot down by their own officers or
fellow enlisted men before they had gone twenty
paces.

"You fools. You goddamned fools!" Frank's invective was for the French command which continued
to throw thousands of bodies into the pointless slaughter. In desperation he aimed his Spad at a machine
gun emplacement and poised his fingers around the
trigger on his weapon. Close in, at the last moment,
he saw that the Germans were dug into reinforced
bunkers that even an artillery shell might not penetrate. Nothing would stop the Maxim guns from wearing their barrels thin as they spat death into the
legions of charging Frenchmen.

Saddened at his helplessness, Frank had begun to
climb before he realized Bill Thaw had brought the

entire formation down for a look. Reaching the same
conclusion as DeWitt, he motioned his flight to regain altitude.

As if the Frenchmen weren't climbing into the
meat grinder fast enough, swarms of German bombers and fighters were streaking in from the east, heading to the rear of the suicidal assault. Behind the
lines they would cut off supplies and discourage the
ambulance drivers.

Once again Frank scanned his group as it climbed
above the incoming Fokkers, Albatros, and Hanover-
anners. To his left was Hunter, engrossed now with
the enemy. For the moment they would provide fod-
der for his revenge, Frank hoped. They could deal
with each other later . . . if later ever came.

28

THE LAFAYETTE ESCADRILLE, welded in formation like geese flying south for the winter, aimed its point far behind the protective line of German fighters. In every cockpit, a man was becoming increasingly anxious about his limited fuel supply.

Finally, without direction or permission from a superior, one dropped away from the formation and flew directly at the fighters.

"Chapman, I'll bet," Frank told himself.

A rich snob who had bought his way into the group with enough money to buy his own plane, the muscular Harvard football captain had ridden into camp in a Stutz Bearcat only days before. Swinging a walnut cane, he strutted into the barracks and outfitted himself in a uniform with the bellows pockets and long-skirted tunic of British officers. He wore a dapper

Sam Browne belt and smoked a sculptured pipe with a tiny Spad cut into each side. His plane was as distinctive as his attire, marked by a white stripe leading along the length of the fuselage from the Indian Head trademark in front of the cockpit.

Firing while he was still far out of range, he drove straight into the flight of Albatros. The orderly formation broke into a frenetic, swirling mass as Chapman found a mark. A German squirted flame, and the American swung away, content with his one quick victory. His intent was to hit and run, but he found himself driving headlong toward an all-red Albatros D II.

"Richthofen!" Frank said aloud.

It was true. The Red Baron, Manfred von Richthofen, had survived. Frank watched fascinated as the Baron gracefully rolled away from the oncoming Spad and came up on its tail. The twin fixed Spandau guns tore into the American craft. Bits of fabric and struts tore loose. Although Chapman climbed, dived and twisted in frantic aerobatics, his tail disintegrated; the right wings split away from the fuselage and plummeted into the airstream.

Richthofen pulled away. The hornet had delivered its killing sting; its paralyzed victim spiraled away toward oblivion.

Chapman had had less than a minute of glory before his moment of truth.

On signal the Germans rose to engage the escadrille.

Thaw, however, was intent on a more vital target, a flight of two dozen Gotha G V bombers lumbering along behind the fighter protection. They were twin-engine biplanes capable of carrying six hundred-pound bombs and two gunners, one located aft of the wings and the other mounted in an open cockpit in the nose. There was little open area for a fighter to strike.

Flyers who had previously encountered the Gothas advised attack from below, but in a formation of the bombers the German machine gunners could cover each other from low-angle intruders.

They were a prize worthy of contention, though. Knocking down a machine capable of carrying the air war to England was as good as burning an armed dirigible. To the hunters in the escadrille, bagging a German fighter was like shooting a deer; after the first elation you took snapshots and that was about it. But the Gotha was a moose, a proud trophy to be mounted and exclaimed over for years to come.

Thaw peeled off and one by one the others followed him.

Frank chose a target, one off to the left of the bomber formation. It had fallen behind the others, limping along on an engine that sputtered as if the fuel line might be partially blocked. Aware that the lagging bomber might be bait for foxes lurking above in the low-hanging clouds, Frank dropped below the other Spads, intending to come up from beneath.

The bomber pilot, spotting him, tried evasive action, veering the ponderous aircraft to one side. Frank squeezed the trigger and watched his bullets puncture the plane from one end of the exposed wing to the other. Then he zipped past it into the clouds. Blinded briefly, he peered first into fog and then at a Fokker emerging from the misty froth like a toy plucked from a bucket of white paint. He fired the Vickers machine gun again while the two aircraft executed a *pas de deux* in the clouds.

There was no telling whether or not he had hit the Fokker. Suddenly the filmy whiteness was swarming with fighters intent on sacking the Americans who had taken on the Gothas. They had misjudged the time it would take the escadrille to reach the bombers, and the single-seaters were dropping out of the clouds just as Thaw led his men into the formation of heavily armed aircraft.

Frank sensed crisis. The escadrille would be hit from above and below—by the fighters turning back from the lead and climbing to defend the bombers, while this second squadron pounced from the cloud bank. Despite the instinct of self-preservation, telling him he could stay in the misty cover and save himself, he rolled into a dive and burst into the midst of the Fokkers. Seeing the more numerous targets below and recognizing their responsibility to the bombers, the Germans took little notice of the single Spad among them.

While their attention was diverted, Frank pulled in behind one of the older Fokker Eindekker E IIIs and raked the circular curved tail fin with a burst, then dropped to fire into the single wing. After again adjusting his position, he ripped the body of the fuselage, his bullets driving straight into the cockpit from below.

When the E III lurched as if the pilot had jerked on the stick, Frank full-throttled his Spad and heeled over to nail another Eindekker. Although only a few of his bullets stung the black cross on the outer side of the ship's starboard wings, the hits created the desired effect.

Havoc.

When the E III pilots—well aware that their older, ninety-five-hour ships were pitted against speedier, newer Spads—saw two of their number floundering, the squadron came apart. In the interests of survival, the ultimate measure of success for even the best equipment, they splayed off in different directions to avoid the plane that dipped and hit and veered away like a vicious hummingbird.

Seconds later, recognizing that a solitary flyer had routed them, they came back to get him. Intent upon knocking him out of the sky, they fired from all angles, their bullets creating a mesh of tracers which endangered their comrades as much as him.

Holes opened along his wings and a slug twanged off his metal cowling, which was painted gray like the rest of his plane. His goggles fell off; a bullet had grazed the side of his head and sliced the band that held them in place.

"Shit!" That was too close!

Executing a *renversement,* a sudden change of direction using a hard rudder and no aileron, he glanced down, hoping to see help on the way. He was disappointed, however; Thaw's entire group was chipping away at the bombers. Two were already in flames. A third lit up in a fireball when a slug hit one of its shells.

"Fuck you guys!" Abandoned by the men he protected while they chalked up confirmed kills, he looked up into the clouds that offered safe haven. He could go upstairs and wait. But for how long? And for what? As if turned on by an automatic switch, the mess that awaited him on the ground returned. Brooke . . . Allison . . . the child that would be his. What the hell did he have to live for? A wrecked marriage, a bastard offspring, and the hatred of the man who had been his closest friend.

"The hell with it!" he said, his fear dissolving in futility. With a vicious jerk on the stick, he headed straight into the scattered enemy, caught one in his sights and fired. He was riding the E III's tail when the young pilot twisted and looked over his shoulder, his face contorted with fear, his mouth open, screaming. Frank could not hear the words but the message was eloquent: Don't! I don't want to die! Let me live! And Frank would have . . . he wanted to . . . but he could not release the trigger soon enough.

Blood bathed the boyish face in red and blotted out the pleading eyes. The plane nosed down into a long, leisurely descent, its mechanical body still in fighting trim but her brain dead at the controls.

Remorse washed over the American. Here was another of the ironies of life and war. The youth who lusted for life died at the hands of another who wanted to die.

The Germans, angered by their lone tormenter, seemed intent upon granting Frank's wish, at once. A Fokker hovered over his tail like a bird about to mate. Determined to mete out maximum punishment before they shot him out of the sky, DeWitt flew level at full speed, then turned suddenly by jamming the control stick to one side as far and as fast as it would go and then jerking it back toward himself. At the same time he applied a delicate pressure with his opposite foot, only enough to hold the tail level.

He felt as if he would be forced through his seat, but he had lost the German.

Once again, to lure the Fokkers away from his unit, he dropped into the hive where the krauts swarmed. In a sky where planes tumbled, arching and dipping as if churned in the funnel of a tornado, where bullets crossed and recrossed like wires in a switchboard, Frank took on one opponent at a time, unconcerned with peripheral dangers. On collision course with one, he fired, watched his bullets chew up the enemy's prop, and saw the unbalanced engine wrenched from its moorings. As he dropped under the plane, fire flared from the ruined engine, the heat forcing the pilot to unfasten his seat belt. He hoisted himself out of the doomed plane. Then he sailed away, arms whipping the air, feet flailing in the flutter kick of a swimmer.

Poor devil. It was the fate most airmen dreaded. To fall naked, without the protective wrapper of his plane, his second skin, was the penultimate nightmare, second only to the fear of death by fire. With slow-flying aircraft, miraculous escapes from crashes were almost the rule, but the free-falling pilot could not survive. He was doomed, and he had the rest of his life to wait for the impact.

Coming around again, Frank found the Oberursel rotary engines pushing the E IIIs back toward their base. He had singlehandedly scattered the flock that would have swooped down onto Thaw's squadron from above. Only now, at the lower altitude, were the Spads being tested by some of the newer fighters that had turned around to engage them.

"I ought to leave all you bastards," Frank said,

blocking the wind from his eyes with one hand. None of them had come to his rescue.

Still, he understood. The mission—stopping the bombers—had to come first. His mood, he recognized, was more depression than bitterness.

Then a flash of red caught his eye, and his heart leaped in his chest. He nosed down.

The Red Baron was directly below him, latching onto the tail of a Spad.

"Hot damn!" he exulted, although most men would have given the top ace of the war a wide berth. Throttling back as he dropped, he waited while the Spad flew past with the red dragon spitting on his tail. Frank, at the precise moment he leveled off, gave his machine more throttle and began pumping slugs toward von Richthofen's Albatros. The ace was caught off guard, apparently having accounted for every aircraft in the sky except the one that had climbed into the clouds to do battle with the fighters.

With the reaction time that had made him a champion of death, he dropped away from the Spad he had been attacking and went into a *vrille,* or tailspin. He closed the throttle, pulled back on the stick, used a little aileron and full opposite rudder. Frank might have matched the action except that he was distracted by the plane he had just saved.

A Spad with a red cowling.

Blake Langley Hunter.

A morass of thoughts tumbled in Frank's mind as he executed a delayed turn to pursue the Red Baron. Why hadn't he let the German ace finish off Hunter? Another half minute at the most and Blake would have been no more than another score on the champion's long list of forgotten victims. If he had only known. If he had held his fire, let Richthofen perform his aerial surgery, there would have been no one holding a threat over his head. Allison might never have publicly acknowledged the father of her unborn child. Frank might have returned to a life with the woman he loved.

The most tantalizing question of all was still unanswered. If he had recognized Blake's plane before he dipped to pursue the German, would he have fired that one burst which could have finished Hunter?

He could have gotten by with it. Even if any of his flying mates had witnessed the kill, they would have testified that it was an accident, some of them out of loyalty, others out of pride in their outfit. A personal duel between two members of the squadron could stain a record they had all risked their lives to build.

By now the Red Baron, having exited the tailspin, using control stick and rudders, was leveling. As he swept back toward the Spads, Frank tensed himself again and squeezed the trigger.

Two pops and then . . . nothing.

"Jeezus!" He checked the belt feed.

He was out of ammunition. And that smart German son-of-a-bitch knew it. He rolled and came charging in at the Spad's tail as Frank dived, gathering all available speed for the only maneuver left to him: retreat.

Retreat while the German ace took his time, drifting from side to side lining up his sights for what would be an easy kill. Retreat with the bullets already chipping away at the Spad's thin skin. Retreat and wait for the end and hope it was quick.

His back, so tense it ached, stiffened in expectation

of piercing lead, but it didn't come. The shooting
stopped. Why? Startled, Frank jerked his head around
in time to see Blake Hunter diving on von Richthofen.

And the capricious red bird, tired of deviling sparrows, flew away as if disinterested in the whole affair. His comrades followed his lead, and the sky
emptied. The bombers, what remained of them, made
slow banks toward home, their escorts snuggled in
close to protect them.

Minus only one plane—Chapman's—the escadrille
also turned homeward, low on both fuel and ammunition.

Frank eased off on the engine; it was overheating,
protesting the prolonged abuse by its pilot. He flew
that way momentarily, coasting and cooling, and then,
just when he had begun to feel safe, a shadow passed
over him. Flipping his head back, he saw Blake drifting down on him, drifting down until less than a foot
separated his undercarriage from Frank's propeller.

The goddamned show-off is trying to set his wheels
on my wing, Frank thought, trying to push me out
of the sky!

He couldn't see Blake's face but it was easy to
imagine his grim enjoyment. Frank's fingers tightened
on the stick. It was so tempting. All he'd have to
do was haul back on it and that would write the
end to his story. Their two machines would lock together like jealous stags and then scatter their skele-
tons where they fell.

He could do that . . . but not yet. It was too soon,
the contrived *deus ex machina* solution a writer had
to avoid. Your main character had to at least try
to resolve the conflict first. He couldn't rely on some

god or unrelated phenomenon to do it for him. To pull back on that stick now would be the course of least resistance, a course he could resort to later if all else failed.

He gave way, and the two planes sank to within a hundred feet of the earth. Amorphous blobs of blue that had been men littered the ground like garments blown from a clothesline. Everywhere, black craters pocked the surface.

They were flying recklessly low, almost eye-level with the gnarled grove the battle had denuded. One mistake, the slightest malfunction, any change in air pressure—and one or both of the planes would crumple into the snaggy trees which springtime had forgotten.

Death was close. It surrounded him, absorbed him there in the cockpit, so much a part of him that when it came, it would be more a continuation than a cessation. It was as if he were flying halfway into a narrowing tunnel. Death would take him farther in . . . or perhaps out the other side. A kind of peace, almost a euphoria, settled over him. If it came . . .

A new presence jerked him alert. Frank looked out to the right and saw the checkerboard cowling of Bulldog Teeter's plane bearing down at Hunter's altitude. The Cowboy was probably intent upon ending the madness between his two friends, but with another line of timber looming a half mile distant, he might become the victim.

"Get back, Bulldog!" Frank shouted and flailed one arm, knowing it was useless. This was not Bulldog's fight, though; he shouldn't die in it.

In desperation Frank scanned the gouged landscape. Bodies were stirring; litterbearers were picking

their way among the fallen. Even to save his buddy
he could not crash-land there, could not add to that
mayhem.

In the periphery of his vision he could see Bulldog
sliding in closer . . . closer . . . his wing tip between
the edges of Hunter's airfoil surfaces. Teeter dipped
and rose, brushing the top wing, then the lower.
Frank read Bulldog's message clearly: cut out the
games, Hunter, or I'll dig in with you.

Trees ahead! Eye-level, coming on fast. Frank
clamped his teeth together, his lips set in a thin,
hard line. It was climb or crash . . .

He hauled back on the stick.

The engine groaned in the effort to push its burden against gravity; then it swooned, hesitated, sputtered as Blake's wheels thrust downward against it,
hard . . . then harder still.

Frank lay back against the seat, braced for the
crash.

Suddenly the plane above him peeled off to the
right. Bulldog climbed left and DeWitt's wheels
skimmed the scraggly, reaching branches. He breathed
for the first time in thirty or forty seconds.

Why had Blake allowed him to clear the trees? Had
Bulldog scared him off or had it been his own decision?

Frank did not know. He only knew he had survived another day of battle, as he had so often before. But this time was different.

There was no joy.

29

HE SAT in the cockpit for a long time after he landed, covering his wind-burned eyes with his hands. Fatigued, depressed, so limp he felt his body might cave in on itself, he did not answer when his mechanic questioned him. Nor did he stir when the other escadrille combatants converged on his plane.

In the lead was Blake Hunter, who marched straight to the cockpit. Still enraged, he might have dragged DeWitt from his craft if Teeter had not stopped him. When Hunter tried to shake him off, the former boxer pulled his arm back and looped a long, hard upper-cut into the younger man's jaw. Blake skidded across the grass on his rump, and before he could rise Bill Thaw and Captain Thénault were there, shouting and demanding explanations.

"Hunter! You maniac!" Thaw roared. "What the hell kind of stupid-ass horseplay was that on the way home? I'd have you court-martialed if I could. As it is, you're through. Finished."

Hunter stood, still belligerent. "You haven't got the authority," he told Thaw.

"What kinda rodeo did you think you was ridin' in up there?" Teeter said. "Why were you trying to kill Frank?"

Blake snorted and brushed off the dirt. "He knows. He goddamn well knows. And I'll do it again. He knows what he has to do."

DeWitt climbed from the plane, still rubbing his painful eyes.

"He saved your life," Thaw said incredulously. "That was the Red Baron ready to give you a hot lead enema until DeWitt came along."

"Fuck the Red Baron. I didn't ask for any help."

"Neither did any of the rest of us," Bulldog said. "But did you see Frank alone with those Eindekkers? If it hadn't been for two-gun DeWitt, we'd have all been hit from above and below while we were trying to knock out the bombers."

"I don't give a shit."

Thaw growled. "Well, I do. Frank got two confirmed kills and saved God knows how many of us. I'm putting him in for the *Médaille Militaire* and the *Croix de Guerre*."

There was a chorus of approval from the men. "Yeah! Great! Deserves it and more!"

Frank swung around, made a pretense of being disinterested, and studied the damage to his aircraft.

"Yeah," a pilot challenged Blake. "What did you get today? Two sparrows for all your shooting?"

Blake turned away and spoke to his mechanic, who had been standing silently nearby. "Load her up. I'm going back again."

"Big hero," Thaw said. "Every one of us who has a fit plane is going back up again."

Frank and his mechanic examined their plane and decided it would take until late afternoon to ready it for further flying. Satisfied, the pilot walked toward the bar while the others, with the exception of Hunter, headed for the mess.

Props from wrecked aircraft, photographs of the living and the dead and pictures from the racier French magazines decorated the walls inside the hut that contained the squadron's open bar.

DeWitt was pouring himself a drink when his one-time friend came in. Without asking, he put another shot glass on the counter and poured it full of gin.

"You're going to tell Brooke about you and Allison," Blake demanded. "Tonight. You're going to write her. Got that?"

"And marry Allison?"

"Yes."

"There's only one problem, Blake. I'm already married."

Hunter's eyes lifted and drilled into Frank's. "To Brooke?"

"Yes."

"You're lying."

Frank shook his head. "No. We've been friends too long for me to lie about this."

Anger replaced Blake's shock. "Don't give me that friendship crap. I don't give a damn if you're married. Divorce her. My sister's kid deserves a name, even if it belongs to a weakling like you."

"And if I don't?"

"And if you don't, smart-ass, today was only the beginning."

Frank chose not to respond and for a time the two sat in silence.

Finally Frank broached the idea that had occurred to him hours ago in the air. "I could have let the Red Baron finish you today," he started.

"You didn't know it was me he was after," Blake argued.

"True. But there was a second there when he veered away that I was on your tail instead of his. I recognized you. I came within an eyelash of shooting you down."

"But you didn't. So what's the point?"

"If I kill you, I'm off the hook. I don't think Allison would ever try to force me into a marriage."

"But I will. Or I'll see you dead."

Frank tossed down the drink and poured another. "You'd prefer that to a marriage, Blake."

"The hell I would. I'm thinking about my sister. You know how damn narrow-minded they are back in the States—especially about a family like ours."

"Come on now. You're not that concerned about appearances."

"What do you know about it?"

"You're screwed up inside, Hunter. You're the world's sorest loser. You can't stand to see anybody else beat you, especially me. I'm the guy who knocked down the Red Baron, the one with the medals."

"Two kills and you think you're an ace. I got a confirmed kill and two others when nobody else was watching."

"I was your kid brother."

"My what?" Blake's laugh was a short bark.

"The friend you had to look after. The glass that made the diamond brighter. My guess is you've always used somebody as a foil. Allison isn't the reason for your hating me all of a sudden. You know damned well she wouldn't want to marry me just to give our child my name. She's not that conventional."

"You saw her screaming after you when we left Paris."

"Not to beg me to marry her. She wanted to tell me. She and I are going to have a child. I'd want to know. She knew that and she was right. I'll spend the rest of my life trying to take care of her and our kid. But Allison wouldn't want me to hurt the only innocent one involved—Brooke."

"You just haven't got the guts to tell your bride you've sired a bastard."

Frank grabbed Blake by the front of the jacket and drew him up against the edge of the bar. With his free hand he sloshed his drink into his captive's face.

"Don't call my kid—your niece or nephew—rotten names, Hunter." He spat the words out so quickly that the larger man did not move, not even to wipe the liquor from his face. "Save those for Allison and me. And as for Brooke, if I live long enough to get a few days off, I'm going to Paris and tell her the truth. In the meantime, I'm going to concentrate on fighting a war and making you look like the flop you are—at flying, at love, at being a man."

He shoved his nemesis away and reached for the bottle again.

He expected Blake to punch him. Instead Hunter straightened his jacket and nodded at the gin bottle.

"All right, you damn drunk," he sneered. "Get your courage out of the bottle. And when you get enough, join me in the sky. We'll see who comes back alive."

"Today?"

"Today and every day until there's only one of us left."

Frank looked down at the bottle in his hand. Then he flung it aside, and it rolled and spilled across the floor. With his other hand he swept the two shot glasses from the bar.

"You're on," he said.

The opening door ended the conversation, but the animosity hung in the air like smoke.

"You two dudes goin' up again?" Bulldog asked.

"Hell, yes," Blake answered.

Frank nodded. "Soon as my plane's patched, refueled and the gun reloaded."

"I'm goin' with you," Teeter said.

"Stay out of it, Bulldog," DeWitt warned.

Hunter agreed. "Two-man patrols, that's what we send up in the afternoon."

"They're short one man, seein' as how Chapman tried to attack a wolf pack before he'd learned to kill a deer."

"Stay out of this, damnit."

"Go to hell," Teeter said. "I'm goin' up with you." He swung around and slammed the door.

Blake followed him to the exit. "I'll be waiting for you on the field. The usual time," he said over his shoulder.

"I'll be there."

The door closed, and Franklin DeWitt stared at the shelf laden with bottles of liquor. There was plenty. A man could drown a lot of thoughts in the contents of those bottles. He reached out a hand, then pulled it back.

Being drunk in the air didn't bother him, but he had to stay sober for a while yet. He had to write Brooke.

Wearily, he crossed to the barracks, went to the cubicle he had walled off with wood from discarded aircraft crates, and pulled out his typewriter. He placed it on the stand made of ammunition boxes, and rolled in a sheet of paper.

"Darling Brooke," he typed. "Although I love you dearly and would never deliberately do anything to hurt you, I feel compelled to tell you . . ."

He tore the sheet from the platen and crushed it into a ball before pitching it across the room.

He tried again.

"Dear Brooke . . ."

Hours later the same two words were the only ones on the paper.

30

THE BOY laid the telegram in Brooke's shaking hand. He turned away quickly, as loath to observe her reaction as she was to open the fearsome missive. Lately, whenever he knocked doors to make deliveries, the response was always the same. Surprise. Withdrawal. Misgivings. Fear . . . He had learned to leave as soon as the trembling fingers closed on the paper. Too often now he was the herald of tragedy.

Brooks closed the door behind his departing back and looked down at the thing in her hand. No, not Frank. Please, God, she whispered to herself. Not Frank.

How her life had changed since that child of seventeen had snatched the telegrams from the messenger's hand and ripped them open in high anticipation.

In those innocent days the telegrams had been from her parents or beaus. Dear Brooke, they would say, arriving *Queen Mary* . . .; or, Money wired to bank . . .; or, Must see you . . . will wither away unless you marry me. . . . Had she ever been that young? Was life ever really like that? A vital world, a world of music and dancing, had aged quickly, like a body wracked with disease. War had leeched away its youth and its vitality.

"Something wrong?" Allison asked from the top of the stairs.

It was early morning, and she stood wrapped in a heavy robe. Since their country had finally declared war, Allison had spent more time in her room. With the embassy overflowing during office hours, she had become a recluse, remote even from Brooke. That she had appeared now suggested she had guessed the significance of the early morning chimes.

"A telegram," Brooke said. "For me."

"Not through the embassy communications room?"

"No. A regular telegram." She crossed to the foot of the stairs. "Do the French send telegrams to the next-of-kin?" Her voice faltered.

Allison came slowly down the steps. "I don't think so. No, don't open it. Let me read it first." She took the envelope and tore it open, holding it so her friend would not get the word in cold, stark print if it should be about Frank. She read the source and laughed. "It's from your parents, silly."

"Oh, thank God!" Brooke sank to the lowest step and leaned against the wall. "Read it to me," she said. "My hands are shaking so, I don't think I could hold the paper. I was so sure it was Frank."

"It says, 'Congratulations on your—'" Allison stopped.

The younger woman's face brightened. "Then they approve. I couldn't get up the courage to tell them at first . . ." She saw her friend blanch. "Allison," she said quickly, "I'm sorry. I should have told you Frank and I were married. But I thought I owed it to my parents to tell them first, and I was so afraid they wouldn't approve. I should have known. But they—and you now—are the only ones who know. I didn't mean to keep secrets from you . . ."

"I'm so happy for you." Her voice was choked and she cleared her throat. "He's a wonderful guy."

They hugged briefly. Then Allison stepped away, lifted her chin, and spoke with a little smile. "Well, as long as we're revealing secrets, you're not the only one with good news."

"Tell me!"

"No, on second thought, maybe I shan't," she teased. "You didn't tell me about Frank until your parents knew. Why should I tell all?"

"Oh, come on, Allison. Don't tease. Tell me!"

"I'm going to have a child in . . . let's see, how many months? I'm always poor with dates."

"Allison! You're not—"

"Married?" She brushed her fingers across her lips and touched them to Brooke's forehead. "Don't fret, little friend. I will be."

"But who?"

"Who's the father?"

"Of course. Tell me. I'm dying of curiosity."

"I don't know that I should." She rose and started up the steps, not ready to answer while she was face-to-face with Brooke. Then she turned and thought for a moment before she spoke. "Just the handsomest, most adorable . . . French officer you've ever seen!"

"What's his name? Do I know him? Ooh! This is such good news, Allison. I can't wait to meet him!" Her words ran together in her excitement.

"You will. You'll be invited to the wedding. Ours won't be a secret like yours."

"But tell me his name."

"I can't yet," Allison lied. "He has to get his superior's approval first. An old army custom."

"I know. Frank would have been required to get permission, too, except he's not in the American army yet. But tell me about him. What's he like?"

"Well," she began as they started up the stairs together, "he's not as young as Frank. Not your prototype 'callow youth,' so to speak. And I wasn't going to tell him I was pregnant, but then he asked me to marry him before he even knew. When I told him, he was so excited he left early to get back to his unit for the papers. He's hoping to get leave any day now so that he can come to Paris."

"Oh, Allison, isn't it wonderful? A few short weeks ago neither of us had anybody, and now we both . . ."

Allison looked down at the knotted belt of her robe. "And now we both," she repeated with a wry smile.

She squeezed Brooke's hand and disappeared into her room, closing the door behind her.

31

T HE PRIEST from the village appeared at the aviators' mess and spoke humbly of the church that the war had destroyed. "We haven't rebuilt it because we feared the Germans would return and destroy it again. But with you Americans here, we feel safe."

"You may be premature, father," Thénault said. "It may take months, perhaps a year, before the Americans arrive in great enough numbers to divert the Germans, if they choose to attack again."

"Bullshit!" It was Blake Hunter, always the insouciant and recently a bitter one, whose profanity disregarded the presence of clergy. He sat a chair apart —the chair that Chambers had occupied only that morning. "We're here—I'm here. That's enough."

Digging into his pockets, he brought out a fistful of change and dropped it on his plate. Then he pulled out his wallet, removed half of the paper francs from it, and added them to the coins. "Here," he said, passing the plate to the man on his left. "My money is bet on the escadrille. I say the father can go ahead and start rebuilding."

"First thing you ever said that made sense, Hunter," the man nearest him said, adding his contribution to the plate.

Rounding the table, the plate was heaped and overflowing when it reached the last of the escadrille, Bulldog Teeter. He passed it on to the priest without a word and without a contribution.

"Hey," Thaw called from several seats away. "Make it unanimous, Teeter. The way you fly you won't live to spend it anyway."

The westerner shook his head. "After I'm dead, I'll figure how much I should drop in the plate."

"After you're dead?"

"Never pay for a horse you ain't seen. That's what my daddy taught me."

The men laughed and somebody joked that Teeter probably didn't even know who his father was. Frank pulled a few more bills from his pocket.

"Buy some insurance for this atheistic sage, will you, father?" he asked, tossing the paper on the pile.

"Bless you. Bless you all."

The young priest took the money, turned, and started for the door. He stopped, facing the flyers again while he made the Sign of the Cross.

"You all seem so confident," he said.

Bill Thaw laughed. "They're all such rotters they

figure God won't have them and the devil is afraid they'd take his place. So what's to kill 'em?"

"That's not what I mean." He fingered a fold in his black soutane. "You seem so sure that you're doing the right thing, fighting the *boches*. And I . . . I wonder sometimes if I shouldn't be wearing a uniform instead of this." He touched the cross again. "Perhaps I could save lives instead of blessing the dead."

The room was silent. Each man expected another to reply, but the priest was gone before an answer came.

Thénault looked guilty. "We should have reassured him. He may have real doubts."

"Do we know the answer?" Frank asked.

Thaw was appalled. "Do we know whether it's better to be a priest than a killer? You must be crazy if you can't answer that one, DeWitt!"

"Even the priest had doubts."

"No, not really," Thénault insisted. "Not that kind."

"This morning when I flew over all those dead bodies, I wondered."

"Shut up, DeWitt," Blake barked. "Keep your shit to yourself."

Frank tightened his lips and looked down at the horsemeat steak the orderly had laid on his plate. Like the others, he had grown to like the taste despite its origin. At first he had demurred when he learned that most of it came from animals which had died pulling artillery or carting loads of dead back from the front lines.

Strange, he mused. This was the first time he had thought about religion since the war began.

There was a quotation from the Bible that might

absolve him: "*Thou art my battle axe and weapons of war . . .*"

He hoped that was the case, that he was in the right. If not, the few francs he had tossed into the offering plate would not protect him through the day. Pushing back his chair, he took his flying gear from the hook on the wall and went out.

He crossed to the pilot's bar and stood leaning with his elbows on the counter, a bottle of cognac in front of him. He poured a drink but did not lift the glass.

His mind had leaped ahead, into the coming duel with Blake Hunter.

How long could he fight his old friend?

But could he allow Blake to destroy Brooke's life?

Which was the greater sin? Destroying the love between two people—God knows there was little enough love on this war-ravaged continent—or killing one man? What was one more death? Who would notice? What reason was there to believe Blake would survive the war anyway? "Shit," he said aloud. "Kill the damn fool before he screws up four lives: mine, Brooke's, Allison's, my kid's."

Face it. Blake didn't give a damn for his sister; if he did he wouldn't pressure for a marriage that would never last. He wanted one thing: revenge for his loss of Brooke and revenge from the man who had bested him as a flyer.

Blake . . .

Why worry the question any longer? The mind could twist and reason through a complex maze and still come up with the conclusion it wanted. And there were plenty of reasons for killing Hunter, not the least of which was self-defense. Take a drink and then go up and finish him off.

He lifted the glass and swallowed the cognac in one burning gulp.

Then he left the bar and walked to his barracks.

Hunter had just come out. He was handing a letter to the mail clerk, who was heading toward his lorry.

Frank grabbed Hunter by the arm. "That letter isn't to Brooke, is it?"

"So?" A sardonic smirk accompanied the implied acquiescence.

"You scum!" He looked after the lorry. Maybe he could catch it. Maybe . . .

His feet seemed rooted in the mud that had mired so much of his life these past years.

"How can you do that to Brooke, let her find out that way? She's the innocent one in all this."

"How can *you* do this to Brooke?" Blake countered. "You're the one who's played the weakling. You don't like my way of doing it? So do it yourself. Call her. Tell her not to read my letter. Come on, you're the writer. Think of a plot. Get in a plane and strafe the postal lorry—yeah, that's a great idea. Hero kills the postman to save his wife from discovering what a rounder he is. Make your call. I'm going flying."

He strode toward the field, Frank on his heels.

"You wanted a duel? Okay, you're on!" He veered off in the direction of his plane.

Teeter appeared on the run. "You guys going up?" he asked.

"If my plane is ready," Hunter replied. "And find somebody else to fly with, Teeter. This is between me and Lothario here."

"Aw, now. You two cowchips ain't hatchin' another shoot-out, are you? I don't know what's been eatin' at your brains lately, but you can't get caught shootin' at each other, no matter how big the burrs you got under your saddles."

"Nobody's going to see us except krauts," Frank answered.

"And me. If y'all're plannin' to cross into kaiser country, I'll just toddle along with you."

Both Hunter and the Cowboy stopped. DeWitt walked away from them.

"You ain't goin' through with this, are you, Hunter?" Teeter asked. "You try to wreck him again and sure as foot soldiers got lice, I'll knock you outta the skies myself. That goes for you too, DeWitt. DeWitt!" He shouted the last. "You hear, DeWitt? Ain't neither of you comin' back if you start playin' Wyatt Earp and Billy the Kid up there today!"

DeWitt continued on to his Spad where his mechanic was using a smeared rag to wipe the castor oil from his hands.

"Is she ready?"

The mechanic nodded. *"Oui, monsieur."* He moved around to the front of the aircraft, made last-minute checks, then began the starting procedure. When the engine popped into life, he hurried away from the whirling blades.

Franklin DeWitt, inside the cockpit, felt at peace. For as long as his fuel and ammo held out he would be in control, making the decisions. Life wouldn't just happen to him; he would be the player, not the pawn. Until he had to, he would not concern himself with the two aircraft he could hear across the field. They were taxiing down parallel runways that were little more than paths planes like his own had worn in the grass.

He did not look back. He did not want to know whether Hunter was on his right or his left. They would begin the contest back to back, stepping the first paces apart, but until the final count he could not turn and take aim.

He climbed to fifteen thousand feet. Best for the hawk to fly high and use his powerful eye to sight his quarry. It was unlikely the enemy would be up here. The atmosphere was thin enough that a man found himself breathing deeply of the frigid air.

Besides, he had no desire to fly low over the surface graveyard that the ego of the high command had created. It was bad enough from this distance. He could still see the dark mushrooms of the German artillery, and he could visualize the thousands of men the French were throwing like fertilizer into the barbed wire and the chattering machine guns.

Surely by now the enemy weapons must be wearing away the distinction between the lands and grooves of the barrels that had been spinning out bullets since early morning. Surely the Germans must be growing bored with the slaughter.

Why did the French generals continue the carnage?

Don't look down, he told himself. Don't ponder the imponderables.

He must deal only with his small war, the one with Blake Hunter.

When they had passed over the front line, he climbed higher, executed the wing slide—dipping left, then leveling again—and went directly into a right-hand dip. Looking back, he could see that Blake

Hunter had executed a reverse maneuver, separating them by half a mile.

They had stepped off their paces.

The duel had begun.

They circled like vicious dogs waiting for the best moment to attack. When Teeter tried to come between them, they used his presence as a signal to attack. The two Spads drove at each other head-on, playing a game of chicken with their lives as the betting money.

"Do it!" Frank gritted aloud as he rushed at the other plane. "Shoot him down!"

With Blake dead he might be able to beat the letter to Paris, even intercept it and never allow her to see it. Or maybe they would read it together, after he had told her about Allison.

Hell, he didn't know what he would do. He only knew the letter must not reach her before he talked to her.

Hunter's plane loomed ahead, startling Frank from his thoughts, and he veered off, the first to give ground. Bullets from Blake's gun sliced the air where he had been.

The dogfight had begun in earnest. Frank climbed and rolled over, shaking Hunter off his tail. A moment later the roles reversed, with Hunter on the defense, executing one twist after another to elude the other Spad.

In the instant when they were both recovering from a loop, Frank depressed his trigger, firing a short burst and missing. Now both had used their guns.

The duel had taken on a deadly tone. They had called each other's bluff, and they tightened the ring of air that penned them together. Their planes danced in the sky in a ballet of upward spirals, somersaults, and vertical corkscrews. Seldom more than a hundred yards apart, they shot at each other sporadically.

Teeter tried again to intervene, but they swung around him and charged each other again, guns spitting before them.

Frank's tracers revealed that he was aiming too low; Blake's bullets streaked just over his head. Both tried to correct and then banked away, recognizing the fatal course they followed.

They tangled again and put holes in the tips of each other's wing before they barrel-rolled apart. Then Frank was above his opponent, on his tail. No more than fifty yards separated him from the red cowling. A touch of the trigger and it could be over. He took a deep breath and . . . hesitated. Looking back at him, Blake tried to shake free while Frank hung onto his position, anticipating the other's every movement, toying with him like a cat enjoys a mouse before he crushes the soft little body in his teeth.

He was humiliating Blake, proving he was the better flyer. No matter what the lead Spad attempted, it was helpless, at the mercy of its captor.

Frank fired: too low, then too high; a burst to the left, then to the right. And finally, when he had maneuvered into the optimum position, he narrowed the distance between him and his target.

He couldn't miss.

His finger lay against the trigger.

Do it, he told himself. *Do it*!

From where he sat, he saw Blake twist around and recognize the moment of truth.

The next move was Bulldog's. He appeared from nowhere, dead ahead of Blake. The three Spads were in a direct line, so close that Teeter was flying with his neck twisted around so he could look back rather than ahead. The options of the two behind him were minimal. Blake could not so much as chance touching his throttle. Frank could drop back or fire; the latter was unacceptable because he might hit the Cowboy.

Damn you, Teeter, he cursed to himself.

Then he saw the Cowboy waving an arm out of the plane, jabbing his forefinger toward the earth.

Frank took a look, and there they were. The Fokker Eindekkers, as he had thought they would, had returned to the scene of their earlier rout, ready to avenge themselves. The two-man war would have to wait. Outnumbered, they might well need each other if they were to survive.

Banking left, DeWitt went into a lazy circle, observing the young and perhaps inexperienced pilots of the old monoplanes as he passed over them. The Model E I of the Fokker-designed plane had once been the scourge of the air, the first plane to have a fixed machine gun synchronized to fire between the propeller blades so that the pilot could aim his weapon by aiming his aircraft.

For nearly two years, the Allies, unable to master the synchronization, were forced to fit the guns above the pilot's head where the bullets could clear the propeller. It was like holding a rifle over your head and trying to look parallel to the trajectory when you took aim. But for accuracy you hold the barrel at eye-level.

Their earlier superiority notwithstanding, the planes below were obsolete, probably sent up a second time in the same day more to season the luckless pilots than to accomplish any real objective. At the moment they were swooping low over the battlefield, strafing the wounded and the already dead.

"Bait!" Frank muttered the word into the wind. A combination of reason and intuition pushed the thought into his mind. The chances were these novices were bait for a trap.

The German flyers had taken a humiliating beating from the Americans earlier in the day. While they had not lost an exorbitant number of aircraft, their tactics had failed and their bombers had been forced to retreat. The air commander would be livid. During a day when the German ground forces were inflicting casualties in numbers that strained comprehension, his fleet and his greatest ace had given way to a few reckless flyboys who painted Indian heads on their ships.

And there was a matter of morale at stake.

The Lafayette Escadrille had been a troublesome but insignificant gnat in the busy wartime skies. But these Americans were a special breed; today the gnats had chased off wasps and killer bees. More important, they were only the forerunner of what was to come. More, thousands more of them, were on the way, and if a few were allowed to claim a stunning victory, what would swarms of them do?

The Germans needed to know they could handle the threat.

Somewhere not far away the Germans were waiting—not the inexperienced pilots in the Eindekkers below, but the professional killers in the most modern Albatros.

Out there, over the horizon or amid the high-piled cumulonimbus clouds, the pros were lurking. On signal, when their victims had exposed themselves to snatch the bait, the Albatros would sweep from their hidden lairs and dive in for the kill.

It was this thinking that kept Frank circling even when Teeter drew alongside and again pointed to the planes just waiting to be hit.

Frank shook his head.

He wanted aces today, not kids. Kids could consume fuel and ammunition. Aces were the real assets of the air corps; they racked up the kills and by method or myth became the zenith which novices would risk their lives to attain.

Then Blake's Spad was next to him, and Hunter was repeating Bulldog's signal. They both seemed to think Frank was blind, stupid, or chicken. He should have told them before they took off about what he had foreseen this morning. Ordinarily, had there been no animosity between them, they would have discussed the patrol in detail. In the past the three had always agreed on various game plans before they flew together.

The mistake was his.

Using both arms to gesture at the sky around them, he tried to communicate his meaning. With a look of disgust and a lifted finger, Blake peeled off and began the long dive at the lures. Teeter followed.

Frank, his heart sinking, leveled off at eleven thousand feet.

Maybe I'm wrong, he thought. God, I hope I am. Watching his two flight mates plummeting downward, he considered joining them. The three of them together might be safer.

Wrong, he concluded.

If his calculations were right, the duo's only chance was the slim back-up he could provide them.

32

BLAKE HUNTER dived at the old Fokkers like a miser counting his shekels. He had a twenty-five-mile-per-hour advantage over the enemy. He was coming in out of the sun, a cliché of aerial warfare that had made aces of many a man who might have died on his first attack. Like DeWitt, he guessed the outdated models had been relegated to beginners.

And he had Bulldog for his wing man.

To hell with Frank DeWitt, he thought. He wouldn't break off the attack until he had two hits, even if he had to cut the tail off one of the old crates with his prop. He'd have three to DeWitt's two confirmed kills before the day was out. And he had Bulldog with him to prove that Frank was a coward, that his success earlier in the day had been more accident than skill.

Within the hour he would have humiliated the man who had mocked him. The rest could wait until later.

Involved in his thoughts, he was less than a thousand feet from the enemy when he pulled up, and it took every foot of it to level off. He shot past the first aircraft he might have taken on and chose the one beyond it, although the choice left the first Eindekker behind him. Ignoring the scattered bullets that twanged past him, he brought his plane directly onto the curved tail of the monoplane. He slowed to the ninety-five-mile-per-hour maximum speed of his target and fired before the boy at the controls realized he was there.

His bullets tore into the thirteen hundred pounds of fabric, wire, and metal. They snapped one of the two dozen cables that held the single wing to the fuselage. The broken cable lashed like a whip near the pilot's head. His reaction—and Blake was sure he was fighting a beginner—was quicker than the American expected. The old plane jabbed one black-crossed wing toward the ground and went into a tight turn. Tracers from the Spad streaked off into the vacant air where the German had been. Blake kicked the rudder pedal and shoved the stick sharply to the right. The less maneuverable Spad made a clumsy, wide turn, sweeping away from the formation.

"Goddamn," Blake cursed himself, knowing he should have taken into account the weak and strong points of the respective craft.

To come full around he used what his aircraft had most of: speed. He roared into the pack of Germans, seeing Bulldog rake the craft he had just overshot.

The Cowboy hung onto the slower craft like a stubborn dog with a cow's tail in his teeth. Meanwhile, Blake shot through the formation at full speed, sending bullets into every plane he passed.

As he banked and came back around, the old monoplane in front of Teeter jerked as if it had hit a stone wall. A ball of flame exploded in the front of the Fokker, and the rest of the plane seemed to fly into the destructive force.

"Shit!" Bulldog already had his first kill. It would be confirmed, too, Blake thought bitterly. They were over French territory. And he had wasted the all-important first pass. As he came around for the second try, the Eindekkers were splitting apart like fragments of a hand grenade. Hunter strafed one plane, found another, pumped bullets in its direction, and then encountered the irresistible temptation. A crippled plane, its engine sputtering loud enough to be heard above the roar and whine of battle, wobbled ahead of him like a wounded bird.

"This one's mine. Number two confirmed," he said. "Number four, actually." He worked the throttle, settled in, and unleashed a long, steady burst that allowed him to correct his aim until he could see the bullets chewing away at the German's tail. He followed, even when he saw the pilot fall forward in the cockpit and the plane started to dive for the earth.

This was his.

Proof that he was as good as Frank DeWitt. Better. He would prove that the instant he had this kill on the ground.

With a triumphant chuckle, he tilted his head to see if Teeter had observed his catch.

The laughter caught in his throat and his heart stopped.

Six Albatros, led by one that was painted brilliant red, were hurtling toward him and Teeter from the cotton cloud at his upper right.

They opened fire, all six of them, even before he was in range. Bullets sang past him or poked into his aircraft. A slug passed through the cockpit inches from his groin.

"Hey!" he yelped, a ridiculous cry nobody could hear. But he continued to yell as he worked his controls; a man shouldn't die in silent acceptance.

The next words were for himself. "You goddamn horse's ass," he stormed aloud. The realization of his stupidity was almost as much a shock as the unexpected presence of the Albatros.

He had pulled beginner stunts, let the Germans surprise him, and allowed himself to be trapped. He was a fool.

Expecting somebody to latch onto his tail for a fatal game of crack the whip, he rolled away, but when he looked back in terror, the six skilled Germans had broken their converging formation. They were scattering, another Spad directly behind them.

Farther back, Teeter was trying to escape a mess of his own.

That left one man—DeWitt.

Where had he come from? How could he have gotten behind the six Albatros unless he had been waiting for them?

Now he knew why his former friend had tried to keep him and Teeter from the easy pickings offered by the two-year-old Fokkers. The lucky shit had called it again. Bursting with anger, he turned on his attackers and aimed his plane between two of them.

Now, however, escape was not as easy as it would have been moments before. The Albatros could just about match the level speed of his Spad, and they were between him and his base. Besides, Teeter and DeWitt were rolling and spiraling through the busy sky. He ought to pull out, he thought. One man might get away while the Germans were concentrating on the other two in their midst.

Go, he told himself. You wanted DeWitt dead. Let the huns finish him.

But there's Teeter. You can't run out on him. That decided, he swept into the patch of sky filled with rolling, pitching airplanes. With one burst he scared the Albatros off the Cowboy's tail and coursed ahead to overtake an old Fokker. Ordinarily he would have throttled down and positioned himself for the kill. Today, though, every second of level flight gave his enemy a better chance to nail him. So he fired into the engine just behind the cockpit. Almost sure that he had struck a lethal blow, he climbed into a loop for another look and came out behind his target.

There was a moment in which he realized the propeller of the old Fokker had stopped, a moment in which he had to judge whether the design would allow the pilot to glide in for a crash landing behind the German lines or whether he would crash in French territory.

The German was going down, he decided, but he stood a chance of surviving to fight again.

Sorry, he thought. He fired into the wounded bird,

releasing the trigger only when flames poured from the cowling.

His next problem was an awesome one: the Red Baron himself. The German ace was tenacious, skilled with his plane, frugal with his ammunition, and cautious. Now he was trying to single Hunter from the pack.

The American did not fall for the tactic. Although vulnerable and exposed, he made one of the Spad's wide turns and deliberately scooted into the heart of the milling fighters. The Baron, obviously disliking confusion, let his prey escape.

It was Bulldog's turn now. His engine sputtering and spraying gasoline and castor oil, he had little choice. The Spad's heavy design precluded a long glide, so he nosed down into a spin, leaving his attacker disoriented and easily driven off by a few shots from Hunter's gun.

The wounded Spad fell thousands of feet, and Hunter went after him. So did DeWitt and most of the Germans, with the exception of the Red Baron. He stayed aloof from the falling rabble.

"Pull out!" Blake willed aloud. "Pull out. Now, Bulldog. Now!"

Finally the cripple emerged from its candy-stripe trajectory, leveled off, slowed, and sank to the pock-marked earth. It rolled a few dozen yards before its wheels caught on a fallen tree. The Spad's nose poked into the earth.

Still streaking toward the ground, Blake watched Teeter leap from the aircraft and stumble away from the potential fire. Hunter exhaled with relief. Teeter was alive.

Then sprays of dirt geysered along the ground like

water from a punctured hose, closing in on the fallen pilot.

Ground fire, Blake thought, until he saw an Eindekker diving parallel with him off his left wing. The German's guns were rat-tat-tatting without let-up. A second Fokker was blazing away at Teeter from another direction.

"No!" The single word escaped Blake's throat of its own volition.

Teeter stumbled, fell, rose, ran, and was hit again. He pitched face-first into a crater and did not rise.

Teeter was dead.

It had been an execution. There was rage in Blake Hunter's eyes and in the set of his jaw and in the way he hauled back on the stick. The tail came down and he straightened out with the sturdy craft howling from demands that exceeded its design limits. A split in the doped fabric of one wing forced him to ease off some, but he was up instantly, straining the wings again as he banked hard to come around with his guns on one of the Cowboy's killers.

If the German pilot savored the elation of his shared victory, it was brief glory. Blake sidled up so close his propeller fanned the rear fin. His gun was sucking in shells and spitting out lead like a hose spewing water.

In front of him the young pilot rose in his seat, one arm almost severed. A second shell hit him and threw him forward against the windscreen. He disappeared in the cockpit.

Another confirmed kill, Blake thought, but he probably wouldn't live to see it acknowledged.

Almost simultaneously DeWitt registered another sack. Enraged at seeing his friend gunned down on the grounnd, Frank might easily have rammed the other Fokker Eindekker. He was so close his first burst exploded the fuel tanks of the old plane.

But DeWitt was a man possessed. While the Germans showed signs of disengaging, Frank streaked after them. Outnumbered as he was, he pounced on a stray Albatros and blew it out of the sky.

Break off. Break off, Blake wanted to tell his former roommate. To continue was suicide. .

But wasn't that what he wanted? Franklin DeWitt dead?

Blake's mind was a maelstrom of ambivalence. In one sense he still wanted to force DeWitt to marry his sister—whether for her sake or to punish Frank, even to Blake the reasons were obscure. Conversely, he wanted Frank dead. Being bested, humiliated by him, was insufferable.

Most confusing of all was his nostalgic desire to return to life as it was, to resurrect the good times when Frank had been a younger and lesser brother to him, a foil instead of the threat he was today.

Frustrated at his own indecision, he chose the one decisive path he knew. He pointed his airplane into the mess, firing first at a Fokker and then an Albatros.

DeWitt's disdain for life, even his own, had narrowed otherwise impossible odds. A madman, one unconcerned with survival, is the most difficult to fight. Obviously, the too-sensitive writer had been pushed over the edge by the death of his friend. That, coupled with guilt and a marriage that would dissolve, was more than he could handle, Blake decided.

Frank spun and rolled, dived and climbed, slowed and jerked up sharply. He seemed to be all over the sky, using his ammunition recklessly, weakening the vital organs of his machine. Startled by his irrational jousts, the Germans kept their guard up. A man intent on death would ram or clip or hit from any direction. His madness was a secret weapon, one they could not deal with.

Blake was in it with him now, darting forward to attack, withdrawing, and then driving in to strike again. In the melee he thought he scored a hit; he was sure that at least one additional Albatros was crippled.

Unwilling to fight a lunatic, one devoid of respect for man or machine, the Germans climbed toward the protection of the Red Baron, who was returning to save his tattered corps.

Enough, Blake thought.

His gun underscored his decision. His ammunition was gone. Convinced Frank would follow, he flew in front of the other Spad and motioned wildly with his arm, signaling that it was time to head for home.

He was a quarter of a mile from the fight with his engine running full out when he looked over his shoulder and spotted the last Spad.

Frank DeWitt was in a steep dive, on the tail of an Eindekker, firing a continuous blast. Either he did not see or did not care that the Red Baron was approaching from above.

Was he bent on suicide? Could that be what lay behind his fury? "But I didn't tell Brooke," Hunter groaned aloud. He turned back. Maybe he could mouth or gesture the message so that Frank would understand.

The diving Spad stopped firing and pulled out. DeWitt's ammunition was gone, too.

Their only choice was to head home; their personal differences would have to wait.

Orienting himself, Blake headed east. Frank was close to him at the same altitude. "The letter was not about the baby," Blake said with exaggerated motions of his mouth. He shaped an envelope with his fingers and tried to show that the letter was unimportant by making his thumb and finger in to a zero.

Frank seemed to understand. He nodded, then looked up, pointing his finger straight ahead.

The Red Baron, like a catcher waiting with ball-in-glove for the hapless runner to slide into home plate stood between the two Americans and their headquarters.

He was coming in fast, straight between the two remaining Spads, saving his decision until the last.

Von Richthofen would get one of them for sure. He might even get both, Blake thought. He banked away, hoping to force the ace to settle for a single kill. Make him choose. *Make him choose!*

Blake's motor sputtered. His air speed dropped. The overworked engine would push itself no longer.

He went into a long, shallow dive, gaining as much speed as he could with the least exertion on his power plant. He knew the danger in the situation: when the German saw one Spad faltering, he would go after the other first, finish him off, and then take the cripple. Two easy kills.

And Blake Hunter was helpless.

In the most desperate situation of his life his thoughts surprised him. Frank, he said inside his head, I can't help you. Frank, believe me. I can't help you. I want to but I can't . . .

He could try to go back but he doubted that his engine would stand a climbing turn.

His frustration now was that he could not help the man he had wanted to kill an hour before.

Ashamed of his inadequacy, he looked back. Frank DeWitt was climbing, heading straight at the ace of aces. Baron von Richthofen's guns were chattering steadily, but no tracers were streaking in the opposite direction.

"Oh, my God," Blake groaned, knowing there was no way he could affect the outcome.

DeWitt intended to ram the German.

Why? To save Blake? To kill himself and avoid the pain of facing his wife with the truth?

Or was it simpler than that? Was he applying his flying skill in a desperate situation? If his luck held and he did not take a fatal hit, perhaps he could force the baron to veer away from the impending collision. Von Richthofen would have to make a wide turn, one that might give Hunter and even himself time to outrun him or find a cloud to hide in.

In any case, the German was forced to throttle back, prolonging the seconds for his guns to do their killing.

Time waited. Stopped. The Spad and the red Albatros moved toward each other as if in a dream, slowly, on collision course, at half the speed required to stay aloft.

Turn away! Turn away! It was a prayer on Blake Hunter's lips. *Don't die, Frank. I don't want you to die!*

Then, inexplicably, he was quiet inside, as calm as he would have been at the escadrille bar talking over a glass of wine with the other pilots on a rainy, socked-in day.

Frank was making the ultimate contribution, the final sacrifice, trying to kill the ace of aces. There should be a roll of drums, bugles, a shouted "Charge!" The moment deserved more than the sputtering of engines and the whistle of the wind.

Then, when the sky blazed with a new sun, Blake Hunter closed his eyes against the ball of fire that bloomed with the startling suddenness of fireworks after dark.

Looking again, he could not at once tell what had happened. Not until the red bird separated itself from the smoke and flame. The sunburst had once been a Spad.

The Red Baron had survived another kill. Frank had failed. Von Richthofen would live to kill again.

Or would he? Blake wondered, as he followed the German with his eyes. The airplane was trailing red fabric, and the tip of one wing had folded in on itself when it passed through the exploding wreckage of DeWitt's Spad.

The Red Baron was crippled. He could no longer hope to overtake the remaining Spad, and he turned toward his own lines.

With the battle over, Blake searched the sky and found himself alone. Making a lazy turn that allowed the Germans to put plenty of distance between them and the battleline, he lost altitude slowly, his motor cooling and functioning properly again. He circled until he could see the remains of the aerial carnage.

Bulldog's airplane was the easiest to distinguish. Some of the checkerboard cowling was still visible.

The lump in the hole nearby would be the Cowboy's body.

Holding the stick between his knees while he unbuttoned his outer jacket, he fumbled through the layers of clothing until he could extract his cigarette case.

He popped the latch with his thumb and glided in low over the wreckage, holding the case outside the cockpit. The wind tore the ready-mades from the container and sprinkled them in a long, broken streak along the last path of the downed aircraft.

"Hope you got a match, Bulldog," Hunter said, and he touched his hand to his helmet in a final salute.

Finding the wreckage of Franklin DeWitt's plane was more difficult. It was scattered over a wider area and there was little to distinguish the burned debris from the rest of the litter left behind by the attacking French. But he could identify part of a propeller and some wheels; somewhere, nearby, Franklin DeWitt would have fallen.

He circled and came back in again, this time tossing his gold cigarette case over the rim of his cockpit. He did not look down or back.

Then he banked and headed west.

33

THE SPAD circled the field once before it came in for a short, smooth landing. When it had taxied to its position near the hangar, the sun was setting in the west, the thunder of the continuing offensive still rumbling in the east.

Stepping from his plane, Hunter stripped off his gloves and walked into the squadron bar. The men already there turned around to watch him hang up his hat and flight jacket. Thaw and Thénault were at the end of the counter, and he joined them.

They waited silently as he poured himself a drink.

"Is Teeter all right?" Thaw asked then.

They knew the time lapse involved. Unless Teeter had landed at some other field, he was nearing the end of his fuel supply.

Blake shook his head. "He's dead," he said, looking into his drink.

"You sure?"

"I saw him land, saw him get out of the plane."

"Where?"

"In the ground the French crossed this morning."

"Then?"

"The Germans strafed him. Killed him on the ground."

"Ah, shit," Thaw muttered. "Why can't it be enough to shoot down airplanes? Why do we have to kill?"

Blake shrugged. "That's our job, Thaw." He finished his shot.

"Yeah."

Thénault filled Blake's glass a second time. "And DeWitt?" he asked almost reluctantly.

Hunter studied the amber liquid in his hand.

"He took on the Red Baron."

"Richthofen? Again?"

"Yes. I don't think Frank had any ammunition left when he tried it."

"Took on Richthofen without ammo?" a newcomer echoed from a table. "He must have been a maniac."

Blake swung around, his face flushed with anger.

"He was going to ram von Richthofen," he snapped. "If he had succeeded, the Red Baron wouldn't get any more of us. As it is, you may be one of the Allied pilots that kraut ace will kill before this war is over. So that 'maniac' was trying to save our lives."

"Easy, Blake." Thaw placed a hand on Hunter's shoulders. "We're all sorry you lost your friends, both of them."

"Friends, hell," a runty flyer scoffed. "DeWitt and

Hunter had been at each other's throat's ever since
we came back from Paris. How do we know—"

"Don't say it," Thaw warned.

Blake made no comment.

The remark had come too close to the truth, and
he searched his mind, wondering if his animosity had
contributed to Frank's death.

He would never know.

It was a question that would skewer his conscience
for years to come.

"A shame," Thénault remarked. "Good men. And
so soon more Americans will be arriving. We'll blacken
the skies with so many planes the Germans won't
have enough sunlight to take off."

"Sure," Hunter mused. "And nobody gets killed."

He took the bottle from the counter and started for
the door. He needed some time alone.

"You want to skip tomorrow's patrols," Thaw said
after him, "it's okay. We're an odd number again.
Thénault and I like two-man patrols."

Hunter replied, "I'm going. Alone."

He kicked open the door, nipping at the bottle
while he crossed to the barracks.

Inside he paused for a moment, then walked to
Franklin DeWitt's cubicle instead of his own. It had
a better desk.

With the bottle in front of him, he found the manuscript before he located the paper he was looking
for. He held the unfinished work in his hands. An
unfinished life.

Frank was just starting to live. Teeter, too.

He was probably in the book, Blake thought, and
he thumbed through the pages. A few were cleanly

typed, but most were in rough form with words and phrases struck out, substitutes scrawled in longhand between the double-spaced lines.

What would Frank have written about him?

Scanning the pages, he found a reference he knew pertained to himself. The character had a different name, but it was easy to recognize Blake Hunter— the good, the bad, the anomaly.

Wearily, he replaced the manuscript and found paper and pen. He bent over the makeshift desk and began to write.

My dear Brooke:

It is with the deepest regret that I must inform you that my best friend—your husband—sacrificed his life today while scoring a victory over the enemy that I shall spend the rest of my days trying to equal.

Postscript

For I dipt into the future, far as human eye
    could see,
Saw the Vision of the world, and all the
    wonder that would be;

Saw the heavens fill with commerce, argo-
    sies of magic sails,
Pilots of the purple twilight, dropping
    down with costly bales;

Heard the heavens fill with shouting, and
    there rain'd a ghastly dew
From the nations' airy navies grappling in
    the central blue.

From Locksley Hall
By ALFRED LORD TENNYSON

NINTH IN THE DRAMATIC
FREEDOM FIGHTERS
SERIES:

Shellfire on the Bay

by Jonathan Scofield

What the Cubans saw lying off their coast was the answer to a decade of prayers and deprivation. Most of them had been living like animals in the hills. They had seen their families die of starvation or fever and watched the ever-lengthening arm of Spanish authority tighten its grip on all their lives.

Among the Americans who had come to their rescue were the idealistic Charles Bell and the dashing, deceptive Lowell DeWitt. Locked in an intense rivalry for the love of a young nurse, they fought bravely side by side to defend their nation's honor in the explosive Spanish-American War.

ELEVENTH IN THE DRAMATIC
FREEDOM FIGHTERS
SERIES:

Bayonets in No-Man's Land

by Jonathan Scofield

The doughboys came from all walks of life and from all parts of the United States. Most of them were green rookies; the rest were grizzled old Army men who'd served with the cavalry on the Mexican front.

Sam Bell was the wiry young private who took his chances and became a hero. Duncan Hunter was the aristocratic officer who learned to sweat and swear alongside the rowdy men he led.

Often outnumbered in battle, the doughboys were as undisciplined and unruly as they were courageous. Could General Pershing mold and lead this army to victory against the most devastating war-machine the world had ever known?

BE SURE TO READ
BAYONETS IN NO-MAN'S LAND—
COMING IN JANUARY

TWELFTH IN THE DRAMATIC
FREEDOM FIGHTERS
SERIES:

Armageddon in the West

by Jonathan Scofield

In the cause of liberty, American Airborne
Division 101 joins the allied battle to crush the
seemingly unstoppable power of Nazi Germany.
For Lieutenant Logan Hunter, war draws a thin
line between friend and foe, lover and enemy, as
an American officer plots his countryman's
doom—and a beautiful Dutch lover is revealed as
an enemy spy. A war-hardened hero loses his
heart to a lovely young war correspondent whom
he may never see again, and an army of
greenhorns prepares for its final confrontation
with Hitler's awesome forces as the battle rages to
its bloody climax.

BE SURE TO READ
ARMAGEDDON IN THE WEST
COMING IN FEBRUARY FROM
DELL/BRYANS

SEVENTH IN THE SERIES
FREEDOM FIGHTERS:

The Turning of the Tide

by Jonathan Scofield

The Union forces under General U.S. Grant were reeling, their officer corps decimated by fire from the gray-clad Confederate ranks, when an unlikely hero came forward to lead them to a stunning victory. Fighting under the name of Lawrence DeWitt Dahlgren— a name that was not even his own—this mere corporal held the key to the turning of the tide against the Cause of the South.

Meantime, up north on the home-front Laura, lovely young heiress of the DeWitt clan, found herself caught up in the poisonous winds of deceit and treason—as the fanatical Fremont Hunter schemed at her betrayal and a monstrous assassination plot against the gaunt, hard-beset man in the White House.

LOOK FOR
*THE TURNING OF THE TIDE—
ON SALE NOW FROM DELL/BRYANS*